REBECCA LOUISE DOBSON

The Girl Beneath the Willow

First published by Smoky opal books 2021

First edition

ISBN: 978-1-9168836-0-4

This book was professionally typeset on Reedsy.
Find out more at reedsy.com

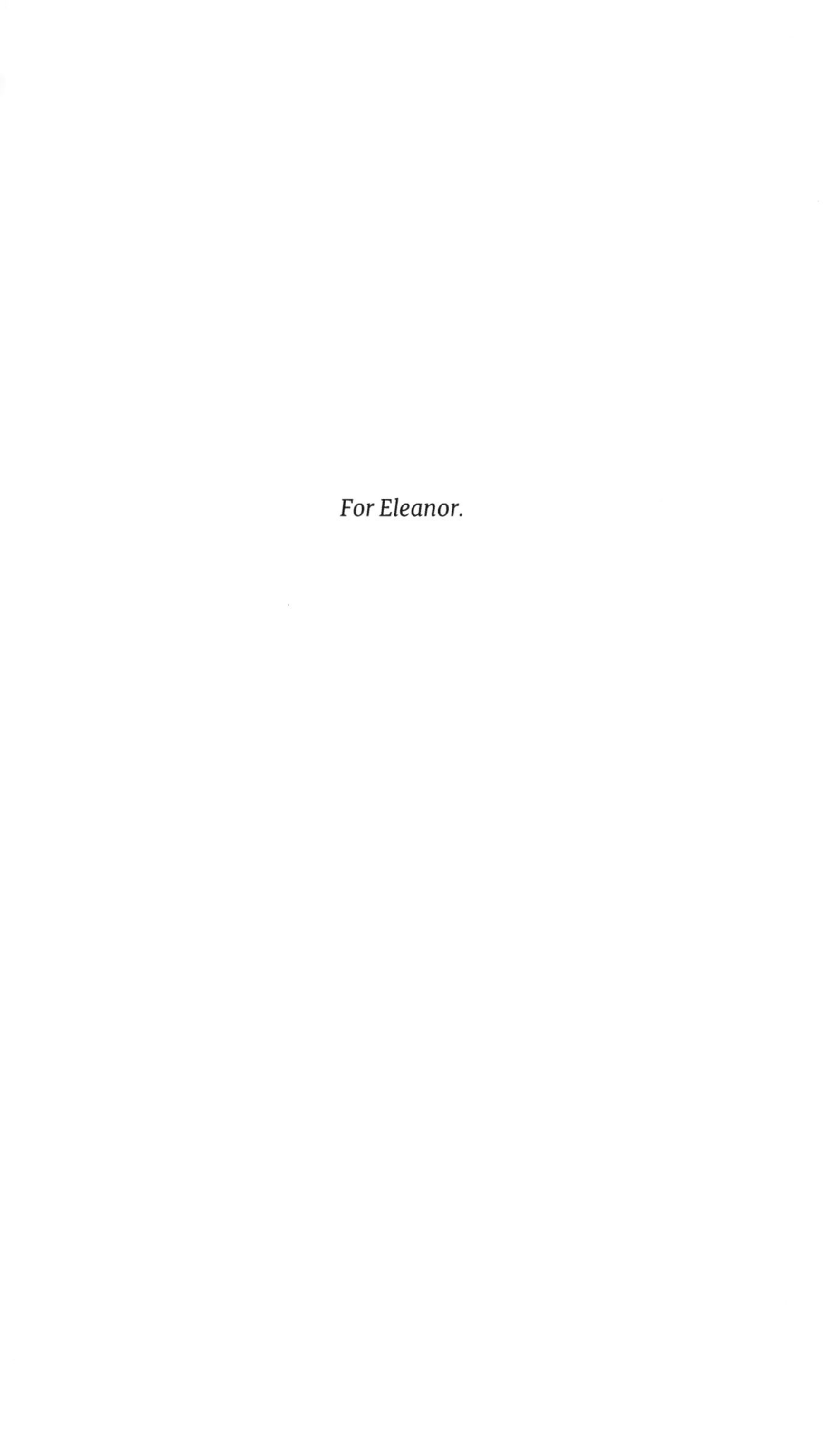

For Eleanor.

Contents

Preface

"I feel like I am on the verge of just falling apart – shattering in some explosive way so that there will be no pieces of me left big enough to recognise. No matter how I feel – no matter what has happened, the world carries on. It just carries on."

Emmy.

New starts and old selves

I always used to fall asleep on car journeys. It never mattered how far we were traveling or what time of day it was, there was just something about the rhythm, I think. How the seat beneath me and the plastic walls encasing me would purr; slowing my heart and mind despite cold glass pillows and scratching seatbelts. How, as I would sit in the back seat watching the grey road through my window blur and turn soft, I'd feel completely safe. At no matter what speed we'd travel, no matter the fog on the road: I would close my eyes and dare to dream without fear.

Tonight, I cannot sleep.

I lean my head against the cool glass, watching the raindrops race and fly past bravely on the wings of the wind. There is one raindrop in particular that has piqued my interest as it spirals clumsily down the window. It gathers up smaller ones as it travels likes a magnet, defying gravity and logic as it reaches out to them: swallowing them and getting bigger and bigger. As it reaches the tip of my nose it starts to lose control, others racing past it as it stutters. They aren't stealing other drops as they glide; they choose to find the smoothest and easiest of paths instead, and I feel a sudden panic rise in my chest for my little raindrop. I force myself to keep watching though; my raindrop now clinging desperately to the glass as others reach the safety of window's rim where they nestle out of reach along the rubber. It eventually loses its battle. Snatched by the dark wind to go crashing into the car behind us.

"Right, it's your turn Emmy." Dad smiles back at me from the rear view mirror. I can only see his eyes of course; dark brown and masked by his glasses that are too big for his face. I can tell that he is smiling though. His eyes go all crinkly when he smiles, and they crinkle at me now. My stomach flitters stubbornly.

"Nah, its Nathan's turn."

"No way!" Nathan protests from the front seat, turning around to scowl at me. "I won the last round, so I am immune! It's your turn, dipstick!"

His face is so annoying. I could easily punch it every time I lay eyes on it. He has mean, squinty eyes. Not crinkly and happy like Dad's, but squinty, as if he always has the sun shining in them, or as if he is always smelling something terrible. Probably his own breath. He has one of those voices that is too squeaky for his body too; it's as if some weird troll lives in his throat and squeezes on his vocal chords. I have no idea how he has a girlfriend. She used to come around to the house sometimes, but I hadn't spoken to her much. She has one of those faces too though; the kind that makes you want to throw something at them.

"Now, Nathan. Don't call your sister names."

Nathan sticks his tongue out at me before moving back into his seat. Dad gives me a little wink in that mirror.

"Come on, Ems, give it a go. Remember, pick a topic, say

how many you can name and we will say whose bluffing."

I roll my eyes. I cannot think of anything more boring.

"Fine. I can name a thousand songs."

"A thousand! Yeah right – and how are we going to test you on that? We will be here forever." Nathan scoffs. "Don't be stupid. Pick something else."

I prickle. The road looks wet tonight.

"Whatever. I don't want to play anymore."

I grab my earphones and attach them to my phone. The port is worn and cracked around the edges from the amount of times I have shoved the cable in a little too roughly. I don't care. I am due a new phone soon anyway.

"Now come on, Emmy. Don't be like that please. We aren't driving for long – nearly there! I just thought it would be a little bit of fun!"

I meet his eyes in the mirror with a cold stare, and watch their happy creases fall smooth.

"Okay. I'll go instead. Right...I can name three –"

His voice is cut off by screaming guitars as I shove in my earphones, flinching with the sound that shakes me. The goose bumps soon coat my arms though, and I settle my forehead back against the car window without touching the volume key. This is my favourite old rock song...no lyrics. Music like this can take you momentarily to a world where words don't exist or matter, if you let it. Let you lose yourself in swirling colour instead of pictures that take form. They're not a band my Dad approves of for a girl my age, but he had been the one who owned the CD I found.

"Nearly there", he had said. Nearly where? I have no idea what lies ahead of us now; I have no idea what it means when we get out of this car. All I know is that we can't go back. Can't get back.

I focus on the melody, set my teeth and close my eyes. Don't think. Well, easier said than done I guess, despite the promises I made myself. My chest tenses in a moment of weakness as I try and take charge of my breath, and I dare to turn the volume up until I can barely stand it.

I must have drifted off. I am met by silence when I open my eyes and it is properly dark now; seeing nothing but my own face as it reflects in the window like mirror. I can't quite believe it; how did I fall asleep? I wipe my mouth somewhat defensively with the back of my hand before anyone else sees, and give the Emmy in the window a dark and hateful frown for judging me. Her makeup has smudged under her eyes, and dying raindrops sit calmly and still on her cheeks. There is a strange crease in the side of her face growing up from her neck: the seatbelt, I guess; it looks red and sore. I see her reach up to touch it somewhat tentatively. I half expect to feel warm blood beneath my fingers before she flinches and lets her hand fall. The silence pulls me away from her glare as I realise that my earphones are silent too, and I pull them out of my ears as they lie tangled in my long hair.

The small light at the front of the car shines dimly as doors open: Nathan is grabbing his bag out of the footwell whilst Dad starts rooting about in the boot. My brother frowns at me as he slams his door with a little more effort than needed, and I swear at him under my breath. Dark window Emmy is smirking now, and I smirk back at her before letting it fall as Dad ghosts in the image behind her with a smile.

"Come on then, Sweet-Pea. We are here now." He says warmly as he opens my door.

I do have to be careful with what I say around Dad as he does get upset. He just doesn't get it though. Nathan is ...well, I hate him.

"I've left your pillow in the boot, if you wouldn't mind bringing that in, Flower?"

His hair is all skew-whiff as he balances a huge backpack on his shoulder, another five or so bags in his free hand. I can see, even in the dark, that his fingers are white and strained as he holds them.

"Whatever," I shrug, and turn away from him, stuffing my phone into my small shoulder bag and wrapping up my earphones. My stupid phone had died, not the music, and I keep my back turned till my heart stops racing and I feel him move away. He is struggling up the drive once I dare to look back.

It's not that I don't love my Dad – I do, I guess. It's just that he needs so much more from me than I can give him now; like when he tries to give me a hug before school or when he tries to say goodnight to me like he used to, coming into my room to smooth the hair from off my forehead. I find myself building that wall around myself and shutting him out. A cold wall of iron – the one *she* taught me to build. One to shut them all out. It's for his own good, I know that. And for mine. He needs to get over it anyway - hugs and things are stupid. They mean nothing in the end. But I can't help that bubble breaking in my stomach when Nathan runs back to help as the large backpack falls from Dad's shoulders.

I grab my pillow from the boot and slam the door.

I don't know why we bothered leaving so late on a school night. I guess some people struggle to say goodbye. Due to the time, an old lady greets us at the door, a large heavy wooden door painted a strange mauve colour, a bronze knocker in the shape of a lion or bear creature on the front. She lets it swing heavily behind us straight away as we squeeze past her into the corridor. It's lit by a little old-fashioned looking lamp clinging to the outside wall; it had made the door shine like a beacon as I shuffled up the driveway. She had only opened it a crack, and Dad had struggled the most, squeezing that ridiculous backpack through.

The hotel itself is alright, I suppose. Dad had said that it used to be a manor house of some kind, having been converted many years ago into a large hotel after the original owners fell to poverty. That had at least made me smirk. The family who had owned it after that had lived here too amongst the guests, but in a converted apartment on the very top floor. After it was passed down over many years and sold on again, the apartment became empty. Wasted space. Fitting that we were to be living in it now, I suppose. Dad had assured us that it had been made 'modern' though. Said it was a real 'steal', whatever that meant. Cheap I guess, as surely no one else would want to live where other people were only residing temporarily. I look around bitterly. It is grand, I suppose. In another lifetime I may have been excited to be here.

A large spiral staircase grows out of the corridor and disappears to the floors above and old looking lamps hang from the walls. I stand awkwardly as Dad explains to the receptionist who we are, and hold my pillow to my chest, resting my chin on top. Nathan smiles at his phone, probably texting his girlfriend – is that a picture he just took of himself? He holds his phone up and stands next to one of the strange lamps, pointing at it like a weirdo. I try and put an annoyed expression on my face, but my heart is beating too fast. I feel like I need to sit down. How is he being so normal about all of this? The old lady continues to stand near the door as if guarding it; her gnarled hands on her hips and a toothless and cracked smile on her lips. 'Mrs Locklea', I read from a little name badge she wears pinned to a little woollen cardigan, and she nods and taps her nose when she notices me looking. I raise my eyebrows and quickly look away.

The carpet is fairly new, despite the place having an old feel, and there is a strange chemical smell in the air, as if it is at the start of being changed or renovated. It's spongy beneath my feet. Maybe those lamps could go next? Dad smiles at me from the counter and waves goofily. I squeeze my pillow tighter. It smells like home.

There's no lift, and Dad has to stop three times on the way up. His cheeks shine a sweaty shade of pink as his breath comes loudly between his lips. I could have taken one of his bags, I suppose. As soon as we open the door, Nathan runs into one of the bedrooms and throws his bags down before flopping on to a floral sofa in the large lounge area as if he has always been here, whilst Dad fiddles in the small cubby kitchen trying to figure out the oven. He has even found the radio and is humming along to some seventies classic.

How are they both so...ok with all of this? They seem ok anyway. More than ok. I hold my pillow closer as Nathan laughs at his phone, sticking his tongue out in such a way which could only mean he is still picture messaging his girlfriend, and when he catches me looking he sticks it out further still. Yes – I could quite easily smack him in the face. I smile sarcastically, realising I am still standing next to the front door, and walk to the room which is to be mine for the foreseeable future with heavy legs. Dad winks and points at me as I pass, singing now to the chorus of his song, but I can't lift my cheeks in return.

The walls are an off-peach colour. The bed linen matching the frilly curtains in a strange mint green with lace fringing the outside; the bed frame, a tarnished metal that creaks when I sit on the edge. Who had even decorated this room? Probably that old lady from downstairs – there is a clear hint of old lady about it, even in the smell. The carpet is burgundy – even better – and I slip my shoes off and bring my legs up to rest beneath me on the bed. I haven't let go of my pillow yet.

"Knock, Knock!" Dad appears around the doorframe, waving a frying pan in his hand, flour on his face. "Look! They've even left some pots and pans and plates! Isn't that great! I knew it was furnished, but isn't that brilliant!" he laughs as he wiggles it about. The handle is loose and crooked. "Now, I know it's a bit late, and that we've already had dinner, but I was going to make some pancakes if you would like some, Blossom? Thought I would test these babies out!"

I roll my eyes and turn away from him, pushing my lips hard into the edge of my pillow.

"I'll make some spare and leave them on the counter for you, ok?" he waits for me to reply. I don't.

"I-I shall see you in the morning then, Ems. It's a nice place this, isn't it? Better than I thought – we've been quite lucky really! Right...well, ok, Petal. Get a good night sleep. I love you very much..."

He waits for me to finish our rhyme before continuing himself, his voice quieter.

"...like sprinkles of stardust and lollies and such. Okay. Night, baby."

I look up as the door gently closes, and purse my lips into my pillow. The silly rhyme we had made up when I was little... I can't believe he still remembers it. From a time where I was obsessed with the stars and would say that their star dust sprinkled down from the sky and made the world wonderful. And, well – lollies were great too, I guess. What a joke now. As if anything could make this world worth anything. I push down the ache rising in my chest and hold my pillow closer, hold it as tightly as possible and rock back and forth. How are we here? What is life going to be like now? Maybe if I close my eyes...focus on that stardust...maybe this will all go away, and the world will be ok again. But when I re-open them all I can see is the closed door, a dirty off-white colour, as Dad and Nathan's voices float through from the lounge, laughing about something.

Maybe if I close my eyes a little longer? A little longer...

Broken glass

This isn't even a school bus. My bus doesn't stop near the hotel, so I have to walk twenty minutes to the nearest stop this morning after refusing a lift from Dad. Nathan's friend Paul had called by on his bike; racing off red-faced and panting with Nathan sat on his handlebars after promising that they would be careful, and they cheered at me sarcastically as they flew past. A long ride for Paul to come just to see Nathan, really.

It's busy, and I have to sit next to an old man that smells a lot like cut grass and cigars after I pay for my ticket. He smiles and sniffs when I sit down, wiping his bulbous nose with an old hanky and I raise my eyebrows with what is more of a grimace than a smile. He wears a very grubby woollen jumper, purple and green, with a flat cap covering his wiry grey hair; and after grumbling something and spluttering a laugh, I turn my body away from him to stare at the chewing gum on the floor. The only other children on this bus are little ones sat on their parent's laps; Nathan and Paul must have cycled the whole way to school. Not that I am looking for them.

They chatter away, the little kids, in high-pitched choruses of made up words and gurgles as their parents coo and boast. I shrug my shoulder bag from my arms to rest on my feet as my stomach grows tense. It only contains a lunchbox that Dad had made ready for me this morning; I had left my books in the box in Dad's car. Surely our current situation is enough to excuse me for not bringing in my homework. Or a pen.

There is one little boy in a green shiny waterproof coat with yellow ducks on, sitting on the two seats the other side of the aisle from me. A bit silly really, as it isn't even meant to rain today. He squeaks that annoying squeaky plastic noise every time he shuffles on his mum's lap, and he leans back into her chest now whilst sucking his thumb as she calmly strokes his flyaway blond hair. He closes his eyes as she kisses him gently on the forehead and after a few seconds she too closes her eyes, smiling through his hair. A bubble rises quickly in my chest and I bite hard onto my lip, fixing my stare onto that stained and trodden chewing gum again until we stop near the school. The old man smiles again at me and winks in what is probably meant to be a friendly way, but I don't attempt to mask my scowl this time. I grab my shoulder bag and swing it onto my back, almost knocking that little duck boy as I stride off the bus. His mother starts calling out to me, but I shove in my earphones and the guitars drown out her complaints.

School is always the same lately. People never really know how to react, and always start off by tiptoeing painfully around the situation. It's like standing in the middle of a frozen lake or on fractured glass. If they come too close or speak too loudly, you and everyone close at the time might fall through, getting cut on the way. So...to keep you safe, they keep their distance. They watch from a-far, they 'give you space'. Or, at least that's how it starts. Soon, they start to get frustrated or forget. Soon, when before they were ready with smiles and sympathy, they hold annoyance in the lines on their faces. They judge. They whisper. They carry large, heavy stones in their hands ready to throw at where you stand alone on that fractured glass, not the large safety net they may have held before. And instead of preventing you from accidentally falling down into the dark, they do the work for you. Harsh words and judging eyes like a grenade. You end up tumbling down and down by yourself. With no one to reach out a hand to save you. No one at the bottom to catch you. Just you, in the dark. Falling.

Mr Stephens is my main teacher, and supposedly the one I am meant to go to with 'personal or emotional problems'. As if. They always assign you to a certain teacher – usually the one you end up having the most lessons with as they are supposed to 'know you better'. Tough chance of that. He has been treating me just the same as before. There is no way I am going to talk to him about anything. Lately, he seems to be of the opinion that I need to 'show more passion' or something. Seriously, what does that even mean? I turn up. I sit down. I do the work. Yes, I may not stress over it like some others do, and yes, I may not decorate my exercise book with wrapping paper to 'show my personality and originality' – but seriously, what will that do? What possible point does that have in my education or life? Oh right – so Amanda has covered her books in foil and drawn on pictures of swirly flowers with biro. Oh yes, you're right Sir – that clearly means that she is going to do better than me at school and in life. That she has 'drive' and 'passion'. And if that is what solidifies his opinion of me, well - I am definitely not going to work to change that. My books will remain blank. He can think what he wants of me. They all can.

"So, Emmeline," he croaks from behind his desk. My

stomach clenches. He knows I hate being called that.

We were meant to have been taking notes on a film clip we had just watched about the Romans. I had been lent a small pencil with teeth marks on the end as well as some brown 'spare' paper. It feels more like that supposedly grease proof paper you get your fish and chips wrapped up in.

"Can you please name two of the English cities where the Romans chose to build baths during the resettlement of England?"

I look down at my page. Blank except for a few doodles. I have drawn eyes and stars in the corner.

"Well – Bath, cuz it's called Bath obviously..." I grumble, still looking at my paper. One of the eyes I have drawn carries a teardrop, just teetering on the edge.

"Yes, I think the class probably knew that one already." He's followed by a cluck of laughter.

Wow – can these kids suck up more to a teacher if they try? I look up and see Sophie, Kate and Jemma sat together near the front. We used to be a group of four before it happened, but I can't imagine talking to them now, as I sit near the back of the class on my own. They are leaning in and whispering before shooting me a glance. My stomach knots and I look back down at my paper.

"Well, Emmeline?"

I can tell that Mr Stephens is drumming his fingers on his desk now, leaning on one hand as the other rests on his hip. The classic 'I am waiting, young lady' pose that he does. I shrug again.

"I don't care." I whisper, feeling that bubble rise again.

"I'm sorry?"

"I said I don't care." I say it louder this time; spit it! Then bite my lip and focus really hard on not letting the ache in my chest grow up and into my throat as my eyes start stinging.

Mr Stephens sighs.

"You really need to start thinking about your attitude problem, young lady."

Yes – there is that 'young lady' part.

"Currently it stinks. So...Anyone else? – Yes, Laura, the answer was Exeter! Of course, it is buried alongside the cathedral which was also erected –"

Blah. Blah. Blah. So what? How are the Roman baths and where they were built ever going to do anything? Who actually cares?

I scribble over the eyes on my page till the pencil breaks through the paper.

I eat alone on one of the benches, in a shaded area on the grassy bit. Not on the playground and not on the field, but sort of in-between some of the classrooms, away from it all. Just a large triangle of grass surrounded by some trees. At least Dad's lunch is nice. I am drowning out the loud hum and screams of people playing and laughing with my music. We aren't technically allowed phones out during school time, but no one ever bothers me here. My own lonely place. Me, and my music. That's all I need anyway.

A small stone hits me on my shoulder and I yank my earphones off and stand up defensively. It's only Nathan.

"Hey loner! Do you want to swap? Dad gave me peanut butter and honey! Do you have egg or ham or something? I think these were meant for you."

I slowly sit back down, raising my ham and lettuce sandwich to my lips over exaggeratedly before taking a big bite. I then smile and wave nastily.

"You are such a – ugh! No wonder you're sat on your own! Saddo!"

"I WANT TO BE!" I scream back through my full mouth, standing up again so forcefully that my lunchbox tumbles off the bench and spills out on to the floor.

Nathan laughs and walks off. I pick up my apple from the floor, wet and bruised, and hurl it into the trees behind me.

* * *

The old lady is hanging about the front of the hotel when I walk back from the bus stop. She is just staring up at the side of the house, her back bending forward despite her neck reclining, and she rests her hands on her waist to support herself. She stops to watch me as I get closer, my shoes must be making noise on the stony driveway, and she smiles a toothless smile and mouths something.

"What?" I say loudly, taking out my earphones. She just giggles and taps her nose before looking back up the side of the house. I frown at her and follow her glare. No, nothing that I can see. Just the windows of the rooms and a small weather vane on the very top of the roof. Green from rust, a small horse caught frozen in a gallop stands atop, as the arrow points stubbornly to the south. I look at her again, feeling the firm ridge above my nose as I glower at her. She holds that weird smile and cackles quietly to herself as I walk through the front door.

Dad has been given time off from work since our 'circumstances' have changed. "Compassionate leave", they had called it. He is due back soon. Apparently, a few weeks is all you need to sort your life out. He has clearly been working hard all day today though, making this place feel a little bit more like *our* place. He must have made a trip to storage, as there seems to be a little bit more of 'us' in the living area now. Pictures hanging almost merrily on the walls and random ornaments dotted around. He has even brought our TV over, getting rid of the ancient square monstrosity that had been sat heavily on the cabinet in the corner of the lounge area when we got here last night. Not that I spend much time watching TV now anyway; but Nathan will be pleased I suppose. He must not be home yet, otherwise he would have been spread across the sofa like old laundry hogging the remote like he did back home. Even the rug from our old lounge lies calmly down the little corridor towards my new bedroom too. I can make out the little hot chocolate stain from here, and something stirs within me before I stubbornly push it away. Dad comes floating at me now, with his arms outstretched before stuttering and putting them back to his side, the crinkle around his eyes wavering.

"Well – what do you think, Ems?" he beams, raising them again to take in the room.

"Yeah, great." I say bluntly, dropping my bag next to the door and making my way to my room. No, not my room. My room is back home. I have no room.

"I brought back the cushions – and the sofa throw that you like. The fleecy one!" he continues grinning – I can tell he is trying really hard.

"Yeah. The fleecy one's good." I say without looking.

"And...and how was school? I hope Nathan kept you company on the bus, he said that he would. Were they ok getting Paul's bike on? Sometimes they can get funny with that, can't they?

Hope they didn't have to pay any extra. Nice of Paul to cycle out and meet Nath though, wasn't it? Will your friends be popping over to see the place? Oh! And I found your school stuff still in the car – I've put it in your bedroom."

I start walking faster.

"Nathan is a mean idiot, I have no friends, and that is not my bedroom."

I duck into the small kitchen, grab an apple from the fruit bowl Dad has carefully arranged, and carry on.

"Now, sweetie – don't be like that, it's a tough move for all of us," he says breathlessly following me. "I've asked the manager of the building if we could maybe paint in here, due to us...well, and he said that he would think about it – so we can make it into your very own room! You can even choose the colour!"

"I don't want to paint the stupid room, ok Dad? I don't care. I really couldn't give two –" I bite hard into my apple. The juices run over my hand. I open 'my' bedroom door and hesitate. Dad has changed my bedsheets to the ones from back home. And my curtains. My chest aches and my knees buckle. "– I just want to be on my own, ok?"

I don't wait for his reply before I slam the door.

Nathan comes back a couple of hours later. He clanks about in the small kitchen helping Dad with dinner as they both sing along to the radio. Another seventies classic by the sounds of it. I am sure that Dad has played us this one before on his guitar, I do recognise something about it. They sound like they are having fun anyway. I have been listening to my own music, but my phone has been playing up. The wire keeps crackling and cutting off the music when I put the cable into the port, but it has also started playing strange electronic notes down my ear instead of the chords I am used to. Sometimes only the words come out; ghostly and lost without their musical companions, and sometimes give way to nothing but silence. I had hit the whole thing against my hand until my palms had gone red before giving up and plugging it in to charge. Maybe the whole thing just needs resetting.

I creep out of my room just as Nathan and Dad begin singing some eighties power ballad at the top of their lungs. When I walk past they are both pointing to each other, holding wooden spoons in their other hands as microphones. I roll my eyes and wander over to the sofa. I grab the fleecy throw and wrap it about my shoulders despite feeling warm. Dad was right; it is my favourite. I turn on the TV and bunch the blanket close to my neck; watching the pictures as I run my thumb back and forth along the soft material. I can almost imagine I am home right now, and I close my eyes for a moment to breathe in the fleece's smell.

There are some frames and ornaments resting on the TV cabinet too – I hadn't seen them earlier, and I feel kind of impressed with Dad's effort. I would never tell him that though. I shuffle forward on the sofa to have a look. That little glass globe he used to have on his desk – the kind where it looks like different coloured bubbles are residing within, trapped and unable to ever reach the surface. A plate I had made when I was little, with little mosaic bits stuck on to make what I think is meant to be a gold fish, and an egg cup that Nathan had painted. The chick is blue and looks more like a blob than anything else.

The frames hold the classic photos you would expect to see in a 'happy' family home. Me and Nathan when we were tiny, all smiles as I sit on his lap as his arms wrap around me. A picture of us from the zoo a few years back; looking grumpily at the camera as we stick our head through holes turning us into tigers and zebras, Dad in the middle as a smiling large orange orangutan. He has even put out our first school pictures in a joint frame. Had my hair ever been that curly? It is like I wear a strange wig. And Nathan's fringe! It looks like a bowl has been placed on his head for his hair cut. And – what?

"Dinner is served, oh smelly one!" Nathan sings, carrying a tray to the small round dining table tucked into the corner of the lounge where a serving window lies cutting into the kitchen beyond. I can see Dad through it, smiling as he sorts the drinks.

"What is this?" I screech, holding the latest picture frame. My hands are trembling and the blood rushes loudly in my ears. "What on earth is THIS doing here?"

Nathan's mouth drops and he gently puts the tray down on to the table. He then shuts it again quickly and shrugs his shoulders.

"What do you mean?" he asks. His stupid squeaky voice gives him up.

"THIS!" I scream again, tugging the fleece from off my shoulders and throwing it violently on to the floor; brandishing the frame high above my head. "Who put this here? This has NO right to be here!"

"Hey, happy campers – what are we squabbling about now?" Dad chimes, coming around the corner holding three cups of squash.

"Dad, did you bring this picture here? Did you honestly think that that was ok?"

Dad's mouth falls in the same way Nathan's had, but goes tight in the corners. He carefully lowers the drinks down.

"Now, honey...just calm down for a second." His hands are

raised in front of him defensively as if I hold a gun. I wish I was.

"I will not calm down! Whose idea was this? What are you playing at? Are you trying to hurt me?"

Dad advances then, hands still held up in front of him.

"Look...Ems, you need to calm down. I know this is all very strange, and difficult and...and I know you aren't dealing with it very well..."

I launch the frame at the wall and it shatters, raining glass to the floor followed by the clatter of the heavy frame. The picture within is torn; shredded by the broken glass.

"*Dealing* with it?" my whole body is shaking now. I have to get out of here. I have to get home. No – I have no home. "Don't you *dare* talk to me as if you know what is going on in my head – you have NO idea!"

"Emmy – this is hard for all of us, Dad's just trying –"

"Well he isn't trying hard enough!" I spit back at Nathan, and Dad recoils visibly as if I hit him.

I storm past, smacking my knee hard against the corner of the sofa but I don't let the flinch stop me. Dad moves out of my way silently whilst Nathan swears and punches his fist on to the table. I slam my bedroom door. No! NOT my bedroom! And run over to my phone charger. I can hardly see. My breath comes in heavy shudders and my shoulders heave painfully as I push at that bubble – push it right back down in to my stomach. My hands fumble with my phone as I try to put the cable in.

I can't – I can't do it. I thought I could shut off – I *want* to just shut off – but I can't! Why did they bring that here? Bring *her* here?!

I can hear Nathan shouting and Dad crying – I can't, I can't do it! I need my music, I need to escape. I put them into my ears.

"Come on!" I cry, hitting my hand against the phone case as the music stutters. "I can't – I can't do it, come on please..." I curl on to the bed, grabbing my pillow and shoving my face into it, screaming, crying. The music stutters. Stutters. "I can't do this anymore..." I whisper, my pillow already wet, but I hold it tighter. "I can't..."

The music stutters. Stutters. Then falls silent.

I sit up, pushing the pillow away, gritting my teeth so hard that I bite my cheeks as I push down the sobs – push them down, down. I hit my phone against my palm again. Again. Again!

"Please...you've got to help me..." I squeak with a sob, "I can't do this anymore. Please! COME ON!"

I let my phone fall to the bed and shake with crying, hunched over my knelt knees, gripping my duvet in my clenched fists. How could they have brought that picture into this house? HOTEL! How are we even in a hotel – how has this whole thing happened? I rub my hands roughly over my face. I know exactly why we are here. We are here because of her. I am swollen from crying and I hate myself. I said I wouldn't; said that I wouldn't cry. I look at the black makeup on my wet fingers and rub my eyes again, when my phone catches my eye. The screen turns blank and shines white. Bright white. I pick it up and press on the keys. Nothing. Just a white screen. Great – and now a broken phone! Just fantastic. I swear loudly, when something whispers through my earphones. No, probably just the blood in my ears – but enough to make my own cries fall silent. Something again. Is my music still playing? I press on the volume key; hold it down till my thumb hurts and hold my breath. Listening.

I will help you.

I yell out and yank the earphones from my ears, my phone dropping to the bed as I push myself frantically away from it. My stomach squirms and the hairs on the back of my neck stand up as if cold fingers move up into my hair. The screen shines white and blank. It comes still, dully through the earphones as they lie tangled in the duvet:

I will help you.

Willow

After being too scared to move for what must have been at *least* an hour last night, I had wrapped my phone up in my ugliest pair of socks and stuffed it under my mattress. When lying down, and swearing that I could feel ghostly fingers poking at me through the material, I stuffed it in the bottom of the small chest of drawers and put my box of school books in front of it instead. Dad had put a little post-it note on the front. A smiley face and three kisses.

I eventually crept out into the lounge too, once the small crack of light beneath my door went out. I held my breath and moved like a shadow though; navigating silently through the dull moonlight as it came through the curtainless window, bathing the room in grey. I don't know what I expected to see or why it felt weird that everything had been cleared away as if nothing had happened. Just that I had walked quickly back to my room after hiding my earphones down the back of the sofa; the feeling of someone uninvited watching me from the darkest corner of the room chasing me away.

* * *

It's been two days without my phone now. Two days; and its unbearable.

I bounce on my toes anxiously on the bus, determined not to look at anyone as I wring my hands in my lap. School is even worse. I am met with the continuous drone of laughter and talking during break times, despite sitting alone in my lonely little corner; filling my head with pretend conversations and images of normality which I can usually lose with my music. Too many thoughts swirl around in my mind now, so fast and bumping in to each other that the voices in my head rival the volume of those around me. I've been finding myself desperately pressing my hands to my ears to strange looks from others, but they come just as loud. I can't even find the will to eat. Despite avoiding him, Dad is still leaving me out lunches, and todays is peanut butter and honey on soft brown bread. He would always make it for me on toast when I was little and feeling under the weather. He would say '*the honey is to make you sweet, but the peanuts are to keep you nutty*'. It would make me laugh and laugh, and we would cross our eyes and pull stupid faces. I always used to think that there must have been stardust in there somehow too...as whenever I would have them I would feel warm inside, as if I was glowing. Dads are made of magic when you are little after all, aren't they? They can do anything! And I know that he would have found a way, if he could have.

I put these ones in the bin.

Nathan isn't talking to me either. Not even to taunt or attempt to annoy me like usual, but walking straight past me without looking. Well, at least that is something positive. I *have* noticed however, since forced back into this loud world without my music, that Sophie, Kate, and Jemma – the girls that *used* to be my best friends – watch me quite often. If we are walking to different classes or as we leave school, they are always quite close by. Probably stalking me or something. Probably planning on doing something nasty or creating a wild rumour to spread. As if they haven't done enough since it happened! Well, they have done nothing - not said one word.

I walk back to the hotel today. I take one look at the bus, packed due to it being a Friday, before turning away and back down the street with a huff and roll to my eyes. The bus driver notices and frowns, of course. Good - I want him to notice! There is no way I am going to squeeze myself to stand uncomfortably under somebody's armpit for twenty minutes whilst being sneezed on by someone else. Although, that would probably be an improvement on my life currently.

It takes me an hour to get home. No, not home. I keep reaching up to my ears as phantom earphones sit in them; I can even feel the weight of them as well as the cord around my neck, and when my fingers can't find them I get that rush in my stomach as if I am suddenly out in public naked. I focus on the traffic at first; the rumbling noises, the tyres on concrete, the beeps of the crossings and the smack of heavy shoe on the ground; create a rhythm and tap my finger. Anything to keep me out of my head. Rumble, tap, beep-beep, screech. Yes. Again. Rumble, tap, beep-beep, screech. Grumble, grumble, smack-smack, squeak.

Once out of the buzzing of the town centre however, the road to the hotel peters out to a wide and quiet country lane with high hedges and grass verges, and I feel nervous at the sudden silence. I keep the rhythm going though – try to keep tapping my finger, but words start to fill my head. Things that I don't want to think about. Things people had once said and things I never got to say. The bird song is a welcome relief, and I hum harmonies to their melodies and tap a new rhythm on my thigh. They fly out to startle me every now and again, before rustling the leaves as they lie deep within the hedges. One even holds a large family of sparrows. I count eight of them.

The old lady is standing in front of the hotel again, this time throwing seeds onto the ground. Not onto the grass to plant flowers, but just onto the dusty stones in front of the door. She cackles and waves at me as I approach.

"Alrigh', Mrs Locklea?" I nod with a fake smile as I step over the seed. It looks like bird seed. It is just sprinkled in front of the entrance. She grins back and continues to throw them, looking up excitedly into the sky with expectance and hope. I don't bother waiting to see if her hopes are answered.

Dad's going back to work on Monday. I half expect to see him with those arms out wide now, trying to force his hugs onto me, the crinkles around his eyes happy and hopeful. Yet, despite my resentment towards him, my chest does tighten when I see the empty and quiet lounge area before me. I close the door as quietly as I can however, and swiftly make my way to my bedroom when I jolt. A pile of clean and folded laundry has been left on top of a freshly made bed, and curled up amongst the underwear on top, are my earphones. Dad must have found them down the sofa and thought that I had lost them. Thought that he was being helpful or kind. I stand staring at them for a bit and calculate what to do. My neck starts squirming as if something has walked right behind my back, and upon looking down the empty corridor and the lounge beyond, I quickly close the bedroom door.

"Right..." I whisper aloud to myself.

Talking to myself when scared sometimes helps me to feel like I am not alone when freaking out like this. Or, if I'm *not* alone... the thing creeping about will hear my voice and run away scared. Not that *I* am scared. What is there to be scared of?

I knock the earphones off with a pair of balled up socks and start to put my clothes away, but there *it* is when I open the bottom drawer. Wrapped in my thick green thermal socks: my phone. My stomach knots for a second and I quickly check that my door is still closed. It is, of course. I let out a long breath through pursed lips and sit back on my knees. Why am I being so silly? The whole thing will have just been my phone acting up and my overactive imagination getting one over on me. It's just a phone. My phone – with my music on it. The music I need. The music I am missing so much.

I force out a laugh; again, to prove that I am not afraid, and pick up the socky block and begin unwrapping it. I pull it out, the back cover facing me first, with its silly little sticker in the top corner by the camera of a unicorn. A bit stupid and kid-like really, but I had tried to peel it off before and it had started to rip, so I left it on there. Sophie, Kate, and Jemma have the same sticker on their phones. Well, they had done. I don't know if they do now, and I don't care.

The phone vibrates as if turning on, and my stomach lurches again. I haven't touched any buttons. Turning it over in my hands steadily the screen shines white and blank again and I immediately drop it and slam the drawer. My heart races. Come on! Why am I feeling so weird about this? This is just my phone breaking...doing a weird 'data reset'. Or maybe the socks were wrapped too tightly around it and were pressing on some buttons? And when I unwrapped it, it freed them – making it turn on? I cannot settle my swimming stomach.

"Come on...stop being stupid." I breathe. I stand up and shake my hands and move from foot to foot, breathing deeply to settle my nerves, as if preparing for a race at sports day. I laugh loudly at myself, picturing having to explain if Nathan or Dad walked in, and put my hand to my forehead.

Yeah, so my phone is talking to me.

Yes – I know that's what usually happens with phones, but I haven't called anyone.

No I didn't pocket dial.

No, no one has called me.

*No, my **phone** is talking to me.*

I sigh, the remains of a goofy smile left on my face, as I shake my head and open the bottom drawer again. There it lies, the screen blank and white but this time I push down the butterflies and pick it up. If it *is* doing a data reset thing, I will just have to figure out how to get it working again. Get my music back. Just think logically.

I hear the apartment door go and Nathan call out to see if anyone is home. I keep silent and soon his rustling subsides to the sound of the TV. He probably knows about phones...he spends enough time on his; he'd probably know what to do with mine. His girlfriend goes to a different school than we do. She is supposedly 'clever', so goes to an 'all-girls grammar school' type of place. He has her picture proudly as his screensaver. She just looks stuck up to me. With her dark green blazer and golden tie, pinstriped skirt and the 'badges' she had been awarded for 'excellence in class'. She has like seven. She always used to show Dad when she would come over, to his enthusiastic congratulations. Then she would smile at me. As if *I* want a stupid badge, show off. No; I don't want to ask Nathan. He will probably just mock me or make me feel stupid. Or maybe break my phone on purpose, even if he *does* know how to fix it just to spite me.

My phone vibrates again and I jump. Am I getting texts now? No; no one text me anymore. The screen remains blank.

"Oh come on..." I mutter, pressing the buttons on the side, holding down the 'off' key for three seconds followed by the down volume key – that's meant to do something, right? Reset it or something? I would check but my laptop is in the lounge too. I feel myself getting more frustrated as a sudden flush of heat spreads across my cheeks. A few days without my phone is enough...I need it back.

"...just work, come on."

Another vibrate. A long one this time, as if I am getting a call. Is someone calling me? The icon to answer isn't on the screen – nothing is. This is ridiculous! I grab my earphones and shove them violently in to the port, losing patience now, and the vibrating cuts off.

Hello.

The voice speaks calmly through my earphones. Have I answered it? Has someone called me? I bring the phone closer to my mouth.

"Uh...Hi? My phone is all messed up, I can't see who has called me. Who is it?"

You can call me Willow.

Willow? I don't know a Willow.

"Uh...well I think you have the wrong number there, Willow. Makes sense, no one calls me."

Your friends would call, but they fear what you would say.

What? A sudden sickly thump to my chest.

"Uh...I'm sorry?"

Your friends. They miss you...but you are pushing them away.

You have pushed them away since it happened. They would call you, but they fear what you would say.

Who is this? Is this some sick prank from someone at school? From Nathan?

"How did you get this number? Who put you up to this?"

I know Nathan is in the lounge, but I cannot stop my temper raising my voice. My heart races unevenly.

That's the problem, Emmy. You think the worst in people. You never used to.

"Right – that is enough! I don't know who you think you are, or how you know my name or got my number! But don't ever call me again!"

I press any button – all the buttons – to try and end the call and drop my phone to my side, my heart pushing up into my throat trying to get away from my bubbling stomach.

That's the thing...

comes the voice. I freeze.

I didn't call you.

Those cold fingers in my hairline at the base of my neck again, and I squeal out as I bring my hands to my mouth, dropping my phone completely. It yanks on the earphones still attached to my ears and hangs there near my knees.

You don't need to be afraid, Emmy, that is not what I want. I want to help you.

I rip the earphones out and the phone goes crashing to the floor.

* * *

I only realise that it is starting to get dark when I hear a knock on my door. A knock so tentative and quiet that I definitely wouldn't have heard it if my earphones were in. I wait for a bit, and it comes again, no louder than before. I rub my eyes, and push myself off of my bed, stepping over my phone which still lies on the floor. I open the door a crack; the landing light stinging my eyes for a moment.

"Dinner is ready." says Dad gently. He doesn't look at me when he speaks, his head downturned to the floor and hands held together in front of his stomach as if nervous.

"I know you haven't wanted to eat with us the past few nights, but it is your favourite. Cheesy pasta bake! So thought I would make extra and let you know. You can eat it in there if you want, but I would love for you to eat with us."

Purple flecks beneath his tired looking eyes as if someone has flicked a paintbrush at him; the lines around them tight with stress and tension, not silliness and joy. A twinge of guilt, which I quickly brush aside.

"Um...S'pose." I mumble, I too diverting my gaze to stare at the floor. The door creaks as I lean my weight into it.

I hear an intake of breath and dare to look up. Dad is beaming.

"Great! I'll – I'll tell Nathan that you get to choose what we have on the TV – we can keep it on and you can have your programme on whilst we eat if you'd like!" he starts darting towards the kitchen, his eyes barely visible from his wide smile. His hands are moving about excitedly. "And what squash do you want? Oh! – tell you what, that it is Friday – we can all have a fizzy drink! How does that sound? I do have some lemonade that I brought with us! Maybe we can add it to the squash and make up our own fizzy cocktail! It might not be as fizzy actually...it did move around a lot in the car –"

"No. I meant I suppose I will eat it...but in my room."

Silence then, as his face drops.

"Oh...Oh, ok. Yes...sure thing, Sweet-Pea – uh...right. Well, I will fetch it from the lounge then..."

"Just leave it on the floor." I grumble, pointing to the spot next to my door frame, and I turn back into my room and shut him out. It is really dark in here now and my eyes struggle to adjust. I sigh and turn on the light.

I can imagine Dads face now. Can almost see it; his mouth turning down dramatically at the sides as he tries hard to hold on to a smile. His shoulders slumping. His eyes filling up. I lean against my door and close my eyes. Push that bubble down. It is fine for him to feel upset...for him to feel hurt by me. I don't care. He has no idea what pain feels like.

I hear his footsteps and a gentle jangle of cutlery on a plate, a pause, and then footsteps leading away again after a few minutes. Yes. Cheesy pasta bake is my favourite. He has even put it on the plate I used to always want at dinner times when I was younger. I would cry and cry if Nathan accidently got given it, as it has a little bear on the bottom. Not even on the actual plate itself, but on the bottom; as if a signature or logo by the company who made it. I had called the bear Alfred. I can't believe he had kept it for so long. Stupid really.

I sit crossed legged on the floor leaning against my bed, using my knees as a table. Laughter drifts in from the lounge in reaction to something on the TV, and I grit my teeth stubbornly. I eat it all, tasteless in my mouth, and turn the plate over in my hands. Alfred is all faded...almost gone completely. I place my finger carefully where his face used to be.

Perhaps if I just stay in here, shut myself away and turn off all of the lights, then maybe I could fade away too? Just like Alfred.

Painlessly and peacefully...forgotten and old, and covered in dust. Like a child's teddy bear left in the loft. Loved once; needed and comforting, but just as easily lost to time and to memory. I am perfectly fine being on my own, perfectly fine being left in that way. I am.

I turn the plate over so as not to look at the bear anymore and glance to my phone, playing with my lip.

Bubbles amongst the flowers

My phone vibrates again early this morning. The screen shines that bright white, and it spins in mini circles on my bedroom floor. I don't touch it though. I stay and watch it from my crouched position on my bed; feeling as if I so much as dangle my feet over the edge, that the boogie monster will grab me; that, or some other kind of monster.

I really am going mad.

I still don't know who that was who called me, nor how they seemed to *know* about me. I've been thinking about it a lot, actually. One of the girls prank calling me? Maybe they had been staying at Kate's house and I was at the receiving end? Or someone Nathan had put up to the task – his girlfriend maybe? To get one back on me after my explosion at dinner the other night? Or a ghost? A ghost in my phone...Yes - that is where my mind had ended up at around 3am when I found that I couldn't sleep last night. I laugh exasperatedly as I rub my eyes now, before squinting at my curtains as a pain spreads deep within my head. I'm really not getting enough sleep lately. Not since it had happened.

My mind had thought of many things during the night without my music, and I had ended up shoving my head completely under my pillow just to listen to my muffled and echoed breathing. I even tried to create a rhythm from that to focus on. Anything to focus on. Perhaps I should get a clock? One that ticks really loudly? My jaw creaks as I yawn, and I finally plonk my feet on to the floor. The phone is silent now.

Nathan's door is still closed when I amble sleepily past the kitchen. Dad must have washed up my plate that I had left outside my door last night. It is drying in the small rack next to the sink, and I feel that twinge of guilt again. I hadn't even said thank you. I shrug my shoulders and pour myself a large glass of water whilst watching a faint Alfred with water droplets in his painted fur. He looks like he could be crying; or as if he had been. I take a deep sip and go into the lounge.

Great. A Saturday. No school is one thing I can be positive about I guess, but at least at school I can be on my own...or pretend that I am. It's going to be harder to pretend today.

I sit in silence for a while, running my thumb along the cool glass as small water droplets condense on the outside. It makes me think back to the night that we had driven here; with the dangerous wet road and the water droplets on the window. How we had left, finally, for a 'new life' and a 'new start'. Strange how it feels like we have been here for a long time already. A long time...but also no time at all. As if we are stuck in some weird time lapse; one that flitters between super speed and slow motion. One that toys and teases. Where even am I, on a scale of time? Where am I now, and how long ago had it happened?

My thumb starts to ach from the chill of the water, and I pop it into my mouth. We are here now, at least. Here for our *new life.* But when this new life is meant to start, I don't know. I don't even know how I am supposed to start living it. Nor if I want to.

I shake my head before taking a large gulp of water again, and quickly turn on the TV. Wow – it *is* early. These cartoons are meant for small children – the kind that sleepy parents can dump them in front of whilst they make milky breakfasts, half asleep. There's a little digital clock that lies at the bottom corner of the television screen, one flagged with cartoon stars and rainbows that reads 6:27am. No wonder the pain behind my eyes is pressing – only three hours sleep.

I pull the fleece down about my shoulders and put my head on to the cushion. Its soft, and I am instantly warm. Nice, and warm.

Only three hours sleep.

Dad was right...this fleece is my favourite. My eyes flicker and suddenly get very heavy.

Only three hours sleep?

It's so soft against my neck, against my cheek. Dad was right...this fleece is my favourite.

Dad?

Yes, Dad – in the car, with those raindrops on the window as we leave for our new life. Dad's eyes, smiling in that mirror – and I smile back as I laugh along with Nathan. Our new life, like a sun peeking through a storm cloud, and we head towards its bright white light as it floods into the front of our car. It feels warm. So warm, and we squint happily into it. Nothing can stop us – for this new life calls to us with arms open ready to take us in a safe embrace, and I can't wait! Can't wait to live again.

But the engine suddenly falters. Stutters, like my music. Stutters and creaks, - stalls - as if something is holding us back. As if we can't move forward.

The light falters too and grows dark, the rain heavy on my window. Dark; and I can see my pale reflection, that dark window Emmy, and her face is contorted in pain and fear, as the water starts to pour into the car.

Dad? What is happening?

Dad's eyes in the mirror, not crinkled, but wide – the whites showing more than his sugary brown. Nathan – leant right around not to play or tease, but to stare open mouthed out of the back window. He raises a trembling hand and points. Points out of the back window.

The engine falters. Stutters.

No. No, I can't look. Where is that light? That one we were heading towards? I can barely see, but I immediately know what it is – the *thing* keeping us back. The thing stopping us from moving forward. It grips onto the bumper of the car, it screams and it wails. It begs – begs for us not to leave it behind. Says we can't – says we can't live without it.

Dad shifts the car, desperately trying to shake it off. Trying to just loosen its finger nailed vice grip, for it to go crashing to the muddy ground below for us to flee – to find that light again! The three of us! That's all we need! Leaving us free.

My clothes are getting wet; the raindrops keep coming. They are in my hair, on my face. Nathan, pointing still, his face morphing from his own, to Dads, to a face I cannot recognise.

Dad? Come on, Dad! Find that light! I can't see! I am scared! I don't want to see...please, don't make me see.

It wails. Screams. Begs.

Can we though? Just let it fall to go crashing to the mud? Leave *her*, our life, behind? It cries now, in a voice that shakes my very chest as the rain starts pouring from the ceiling. The water gets higher, and higher. Nathan, hair sticking to his face as he thrashes in the water, shouts and swears and points out of that back window. Dad, his eyes not wide but closed now. Scrunched so tight and his white knuckles gripping the steering wheel. He doesn't want to see either...he can't see, won't see. I won't either – you hear me? Do you hear me? I don't want to see! The water swishes around my neck, becomes hard, like ice, starts to choke me.

No! I won't! I don't want to look at her!

I grip onto my legs and start to scream as the car drifts.

No – I'm not ready! I'm not ready for my life to end!

I jump as the sofa cushions beneath me move. My whole body ripples, and goose bumps flood my arms as my heart surges into over drive; ready to run or fight. It's Nathan; plopping down onto the sofa next to me, popping his feet noisily up on to the coffee table in front and grabbing the remote. Well, either fight or flight would work here. It only phases me for a second as to why his clothes are dry, before I cannot remember why I would have even thought that in the first place.

I rub my eyes. My headache pounds more than it did before. He shoots me a look as I push myself up, flattening down my hair and pulling strands out of my face. The bottom of my hair is soaking, as is my pajama top. I had spilt my water.

"You do have a bed to sleep in, you know?" he says sarcastically as he changes the channel, casually sweeping the damp fleece aside unaware of the empty glass.

8.58am now. Wow; I am sure that I just closed my eyes for a moment. He looks at me again and laughs.

"Wow. You look as rough as a donkey's as-"

"-just shut up, Nathan." I snap, standing up and taking the fleece with me. It trails on the floor behind me, and I hitch it up higher onto my shoulders and gather it up in my arms. Dad is in the kitchen now, and as he opens his mouth to say something I turn my face away.

"Hey – I was only joking!" Nathan calls, as I slam my bedroom door.

* * *

After chucking on some clothes and grabbing an apple from the kitchen, I sneak out of the front door. Nathan is still in front of the TV, stretched out further still, whilst Dad sits at the small dining table having a cup of coffee by the smell of it. He smiles at me weakly when I catch his eye through the closing door. He looks like he hasn't slept much either.

I have decided that just walking around will be better than being in there. Maybe the rest of the hotel is nice and noisy with it being a Saturday, or maybe there is more traffic on the roads. Hotel? I am still not used to saying it.

There are three more doors on our floor leading away from the large staircase as I close ours behind me. Dark wooden doors with golden numbers and golden door handles. It gives the illusion that there should be other rooms beyond our door; as if we are simply just another floor full of guests escaping the mundane lives that we've left back home. Well, escape certainly is right. Maybe a design choice? Something that managers long gone thought would disguise the fact that they were living here? Not that I mind that disguise. The whole thing for me still feels weird and embarrassing. I am fine with guests not knowing that I live here.

I spot a young couple from the floor below as I lean on the

banister, and they giggle as they run down the stairs. They can't be much older than late teens or early twenties; maybe a first weekend away together? Their voices echo up as he chases and tickles her, she spins on the spot to push him playfully away; her long hair trailing behind her just like her long skirt. Her feet are very close to the edges of those steps though. She could fall backwards and take him with her if she wasn't careful. Her face wouldn't be so pretty then.

I can see all the way down to the reception floor from here. Not as tall as some of the hotels I have been in before, but for an old converted house, it is truly huge. I guess people choose to stay in a place like this for its 'character'? I hear old people say that about old buildings all the time; that they have a certain charm or character. I guess you have to be of a certain age to notice those kind of things; it doesn't look anything special to me.

The house seems to be as wide as it is tall, only going up four stories it spans out really far to the sides. Probably has about 40 large rooms at a guess? Well, perhaps a few less due to our apartment.

I walk over to the stair opening, dragging my hand on the banister so that it makes a horrible screeching noise, and hesitate for a moment. It does seem to go smoothly all the way down to the bottom...in a perfect spiral almost. My jeans are tight, but I manage to lift my right leg up and over the banister, holding on tightly with my hands as my back faces the sheer drop. I feel a small rush in my stomach and my cheeks lift as my teeth bare in a smile. Now; I haven't done *this* since I was little! I carefully push up with my left foot as it teeters on a toe for balance, lean forward with my body and begin sliding. Slowly at first, and my hands continue to screech on the polished wood, but as I loosen my grip, the danger rising in my stomach –

"What do you think you are doing? Get down from there this instant!"

I close my hands tightly and come to a screaming stop. A man in a tight black business suit has come out from the first door on the next floor. It's the weekend...why is he wearing a suit on the weekend? Surely that's the time *not* to be doing business things? He looks ridiculous with his little clipboard. He stares up at me angrily.

"I was trying to have some fun." I retort sarcastically, and test him as I slowly loosen my grip again.

"Don't you even think about it." He warns. He points a pen at me threateningly and I can't help but to raise my eyebrow mockingly. "Are you even staying in this hotel? I have a right mind to call the police."

"Yes." I sigh. "I am staying here."

"What room?" he takes his pen to his clipboard now.

"I don't have to tell you! You could be a weirdo!"

"What room?"

"My Dad says not to talk to strangers."

He smiles then, his own mouth holding a mocking quality.

"Ahh. You are from the family that have *moved in,* aren't you?"

I swing down from the banister and cross my arms. Although I am looking down on him from above, I suddenly feel very small.

"Yes, thought as much." He scribbles something on his clipboard. "Your father spoke to me about making some adjustments to your room. A new colour maybe. Nice man, your father seems."

"He is." I growl through gritted teeth.

Why is he still smiling that smile? I feel my blood boiling.

"I am the manager of this establishment, by the way, in case you hadn't guessed." He pulls on the bottom of his blazer top as his chest puffs out. "I have my own place off of the estate. You may have passed it on the way in." He smirks now too. With his baby face he looks no older than Nathan. Nothing intimidating about him at all.

"Right, and that means?"

"That *means*, young lady –" what is it with men thinking that they can call me young lady all the time? "– that I am in charge around here. What I say, goes. And I can tell you one thing: if you have left grubby fingerprints all over *my* banister, then you can kiss goodbye to that pretty pink bedroom you want."

"I hate pink." I spit back. I can really feel my blood getting hot now. What makes him think he can speak to me like this? Like I am a *little* girl? Why are my eyes starting to water? I push the bubble down and bite on to my lip.

He makes another note on his clipboard and glances up at me over it.

"I don't want to see you on the banister again, ok? It is dangerous."

He watches me for a while waiting for a response, and after I avert my eyes, arms still crossed, I hear another door open and close and he is gone. I quickly wipe at my eyes before walking down the rest of the stairs.

It isn't noisy at all. If anything, it seems quieter. After the initial bustle of people leaving in small families or couples to go off for the day, the area around the hotel grows almost silent.

And no, I can't even hear any traffic from here. Nothing at all.

I have found a stone trough that is full of flowers to sit on. There are five of them running along either side of the main mauve door against the walls of the house, each holding purple and light blue flowers in them. I sit on the one right on the edge, away from the door but close enough to listen in on any conversation. Not that there is much to listen to; I grind my feet into the gravel beneath me just to give me something to focus on. The stone edges are just wide enough for me not to get my bum muddy in the soil, but not comfortable enough to rest my whole weight on, so I lean against my trough precariously, twirling one of the flowers around in my fingers. A purple one – I hadn't meant for it to come off in my hands.

"Nathan upstairs?"

One of the petals comes away in my fingers as I lurch on my stone seat. Paul calls over from near the main entrance. He is wearing his oversized dark blue hoody, and pulls the hood down now to uncover scruffy hair. He frowns over to me, but diverts his eyes as I look up, as you would do a stranger.

I remember when we were all that much younger, how we would all play together; him and Nathan, me and his younger sister. I hadn't seen her in years...she must have gone to a different Secondary school. Paul used to have this old cart, one that he would attach to his bike at the time; red, if I remember correctly. He and Nathan would take turns in pulling me and Christa along in it, us girls being small enough back then to squeeze into it together; our legs tangled up and arms wrapped about each other's shoulders, as one of the boys would pedal with the other sitting wobbling on their handle bars. A bit like him and Nathan still do now, really. They hadn't changed much.

Paul's hands are stuffed deep into his pockets now as if really uncomfortable, a tight quality to his face from what I can see. Isn't like *we* are pressed together in that old cart; there is probably a good fifty meters between us. Do I give off that much of a vibe?

"Yeah." I say in my most monotone voice I can muster.

He shuffles his feet then, bringing one of his hands out of his pocket to run through his wavy hair as if he is going to say something else. His eyes look nervous. Is he starting to move towards me? His feet have definitely changed direction.

"What? I said yeah! Go on then!" I shout.

He becomes still, his eyes narrowing as his hand goes firmly back into his pocket.

"Wow, Emmy. Nothing, don't you worry."

I can just make out a frown and what looks like a sigh before he strides through the doorway and out of view. What? He feels the need to say something now? Offer words of comfort as I sit here all by myself? He hasn't said *one* thing to me since it happened, not one. Oh no, sorry – he has done. Words like *loner* or *loser*. He has scoffed along with Nathan when seeing me by myself, or chosen to turn away completely, as if I don't exist. So, forgive me if I am not up for chats with an *old* friend. Like *he* even cares. I can't care less what he thinks of me. As if he would try and be nice in front of Nathan anyway. I don't need anyone saying anything to me – offering me anything. I am *fine* being on my own!

I then realise however that I am not.

"Um. Hi?"

Mrs Locklea is leaning against the side of the house to my right side where my trough ends. She waves the fingers on a gnarled hand as the other twirls its own purple flower.

How long has she been there? My stomach clenches from awkwardness. I am fine on my own...

"Um...do you want to sit?" I shuffle up and she smiles, putting her hand to her chest as a thank you gesture and totters over, almost creaking as she bends her knees to sit down. They are bare, and peek out of her floral dress. It looks almost identical to our sofa pattern.

We sit here for a while in silence. I can just about make out some of the song birds calling from the country lane down the path and my stomach settles slightly. The old lady looks towards that direction too, and she holds a peaceful smile on her weathered face.

"So...you work here then? Or...or live here?" I say to the floor with a cringe. I'm really no good at talking to strangers. I don't want to talk, really. When she doesn't answer I glance over to her. She is sat pretty close actually, and I subtly slide myself along a bit further to increase the gap.

She is smiling that big toothless smile and nodding, still twirling that flower around in her fingers. Huh. Maybe she doesn't really want to talk either. She *could* leave then, really...

She looks up and points at me then, and gestures to her name badge.

"Sorry?"

She shakes her head, still holding that smile, and points to me and then to her name badge again. Her smile is warm, despite being gappy.

"My name?"

She nods and laughs.

"Oh. Emmy."

She tilts her head and looks forward, looks thoughtful. I try to hide the look I can tell is starting to creep onto my own face, the kind of look that makes others aware that you feel terribly uncomfortable. What is her deal? Does she not talk? Could she not?

She points up towards the top of the house and then back at me, her smile fading slightly. Funnily enough, I feel like she doesn't need to speak a word.

"I'm the one living here, yeah." I reply. "With my Dad and brother."

She nods, that hint of sadness becoming clearer now. What does she know? Had Dad told her something? Not like she could repeat it, I guess.

We sit in silence then for a long while. Paul and Nathan had come out and gone somewhere on their bikes, a couple had come out with a wicker basket probably full of picnic foods, and that horrible man-child in the black suit – clipboard still in hand. He glanced over at us, lifted his pen as if to say something like *'get off that flower bed, young lady!'*, but as Mrs Locklea waved at him, he lowered his pen and walked towards the flashy black car parked close by. Why did he need to drive if he had a place 'just off of the estate'? Probably just to show off.

I sigh, and Mrs Locklea knocks in to my arm, points towards where he had walked and raises a rude middle finger. I can't help the splutter that comes out of my lips, and she holds her stomach and laughs too, tapping her nose cheekily with her finger. She smiles then, the sadness held to her eyes this time, and reaches out and places her hand on top of mine. Despite their gnarled appearance, they are soft, and I feel a bubble rise in my chest. She nods solemnly, and places her other hand to her chest above her heart. I feel my eyes water again; what is wrong with me today? And I wipe at them quickly as she taps my hand gently. She places her purple flower behind her ear with a wink, and then with a sigh of her own and a creak, she gets up. One last sad smile, a nod, and then she disappears around the side of the house.

I *am* alone now. And that bubble comes up hard and fast.

Can we talk?

I didn't see Mrs Locklea again. In fact, I haven't even opened my mouth to speak for the rest of the day. I changed sitting positions a few times as my legs went numb; even walked around the house grounds as they stretched behind the house itself – the same direction Mrs Locklea had gone. I couldn't find her though. Not that I was looking.

There is a really pretty and long garden area around the back of the house, where more purple and blue flowers grow in flowerbeds cut out in patterns in the grass. Probably kept from when it used to be a Manor house, I guess. I bet it looked amazing back then.

The grass now is very short and very green as if it is well looked after. It is all very pretty, actually. Maybe Mrs Locklea could be the gardener? I had spluttered at that idea at first, as I imagined her with large sheers sitting astride a giant motorised lawn mower – cackling away and chasing that business man in his posh suit. Maybe threatening to chop his head off? I had pictured myself following her too; waving my own war banner or flag, crouched in Paul's old red cart flying along behind her. The war banner had a picture of me, holding up that rude finger, and I would shout out profanities as the manager would cry and beg for us to forgive him – that we could *both* slide down the hotel banisters if we wanted!

No, she couldn't be the gardener.

A few benches are spread around the back too. I can imagine it being a place where people come to sit as the sun sets; maybe snuggled under blankets with arms wrapped around each other. They had all been empty though when I was there. I had sat at one of them for a good while however, and watched a squirrel running across the lawn and up a tree. It had stopped and stared at me too, before darting up; I thought for a moment that it might have come over. It didn't though. I even came across a small swing hanging from a large branch from one of the trees, and had rolled my eyes at the thought of a time where I would have run over to it. Trying to slide down that banister was my last attempt at making myself smile. I don't know why I had even bothered now – it just isn't worth it.

I wonder if I would had been stopped if I had tried to throw myself down them instead.

I have been starving all day, having had nothing since that apple this morning. I focus on the feeling though – telling myself that the ache I feel relates to my empty stomach, rather than my empty company. When I begrudgingly climb all those stairs back to our apartment, the sun has already turned pink on the horizon and the wispy clouds around it go golden.

Yes – those benches would have been a nice place to watch it set.

I only jolt slightly when I see the table arranged ready for dinner. Nathan is just setting down a bowl full of salad in the middle as Dad brings in the plates. He smiles when he sees me. My plate is already set, and I grab it and make my way to my room without a word or a glance; but the look I think I see on Dad's face out of the corner of my eye though is enough to make my hands tremble.

The sky really is red tonight – it is bright enough to shine through my closed curtains, and I open them to sit on my wide windowsill to look out. I actually have quite a good view out of my window which I hadn't noticed, seeming as I always keep my curtains closed. The sunset is beautiful; and I eat my spaghetti bolognaise in silence as the edges of the sky start to turn dark purple.

Today has lasted ages. Like...it feels like today has been forever. The bubble suddenly rises to my throat as I realise I have to do it all again tomorrow, and a salty tear falls onto my fork. I just don't know what to do. Push it down...but it doesn't work, and I start sobbing so hard I have to put my half eaten plate down on the sill so as not to drop it. I have to do it all again. This day, again.

As the sky darkens, I start to see my ghostly reflection in the glass. That Emmy has a purple flower in her hair.

Nathan's girlfriend has come around for pudding; I can hear an annoyingly chirpy knock on the door and lots of happy voices including her squawky one come floating above the loud TV. They are putting on a Saturday night film – just like we always used to – and the microwave is whirling now accompanied with the popping of popcorn. Still I cry. So hard that my throat starts to hurt; starts to feel so raw that I almost can't catch my breath. Feels as if it could almost start bleeding. My stomach aches more than it used to from laughing. When was the last time I had laughed so much I ached?

Images of people pop into my mind, people laughing – people I love. No – *had* loved. No! Never loved! And I rest my head against the cool glass and wrap my arms around myself and squeeze; trying to hold myself together. I feel like I am on the verge of just falling apart – shattering in some explosive way so that there will be no pieces of me left big enough to recognise. No matter how I feel – no matter what has happened, the world carries on. It just carries on. Laughter from the lounge - what is wrong with them?! If they saw the world, the true world as I see it now, they wouldn't want to live. They would be just as broken as I am -

A buzzing that make my sobs cut short. I hiccup as I try to push the sobs away as I listen, wiping my drenched face on the back of my hand. It is dark in my room now except for one light; one bright light, coming from the buzzing sound on my bedside cabinet. My phone.

My loneliness feeds my curiosity; feeds my need for contact. Need to talk – just to talk to someone. Someone who doesn't know, who can't judge; someone who can't say 'I know how you feel' or 'that must be hard' when they have *no* idea. Maybe this is still all in my head? My phone, whirling around, a white and blank screen shining brightly from its face. I suddenly launch myself at it, my fingers fumbling with the earphones as I press them into my ears. I curl up onto my bed, my back pressed against the windowsill and bundle up my fleece into my lap. I hold my phone in front of my face, my hands trembling, my breath coming short and hard. The phone stands still. I wait.

"Willow? Are you there?"

Hello Emmy. Yes, I am here.

My stomach cramps uncomfortably, and I fear for a moment that I might bring up my half eaten dinner. I take a deep breath and swallow down the lump in my throat.

"Are...are you real?" I laugh through a sob.

A long pause. My heart starts hammering. The bright white light hurting my eyes.

If I wasn't real, we wouldn't be here together, talking. I am as real as anything.

I take another deep breath.

"...who are you then?"

You can call me Willow.

"A-Are you from my school?"

No, I am not from your school.

"Right. Um...has someone told you to call me? To...be here, or whatever this is? To talk to me? Kate or Nathan? Dad? Or..."

No one has told me to speak to you. Only you. You needed to talk, Emmy – you need to talk. So here I am.

Okay, this is all very weird. My mind races. My heart flutters like a small bird in my chest, making my throat feel funny as my breath trembles up my neck.

Don't over think this, Emmy. This isn't a trick. This isn't a test. I am here for you, and you alone. You need someone, before it is too late. So here I am. I am here to help you.

Ok – this most probably is me going mad. I rub my hand roughly over my face. I take an earphone out to listen – yes, the film is playing loudly from the lounge but their talking has died down. I huddle down into my bed, wrapping my fleece about me, bringing the phone closer to my face.

"Ok."

Maybe if I am going mad....if I am dreaming this - maybe that's ok? I find that the fear I had initially felt, the first time I heard this voice from my phone, is ebbing away into comfort.

'Before it's too late', she had said.

Just like how it had happened.

It could be too late for some people...had it been going in that direction with me? Is it going that way? Am I just the same as her...? I shudder and pull my fleece about me closer.

"How...how can I stop it from being too late?" I ask aloud. To myself? Or to this *Willow*? Either way, perhaps it did need to be spoken about. With anyone...with myself.

I can't give you that answer, Emmy.

I shift uncomfortably, horrible images coming into my head – playing out into scenes from back home.

But I can tell you that it starts from talking. To talk about how you feel. To not shut yourself away, to not fade away.

I bite down hard on to my lip and scrunch up my eyes. To fade away? No – No I can't think about that – I can't see it again, I can't! I've been working so hard to keep it far from my mind's eye. Focus on the pain. I taste blood on the tip of my tongue.

No – no it won't end like that. I am here now and I won't let it, Emmy. Do you hear me?

The image is still there; foggy, but still there. I feel that hard bubble pound at my chest.

Listen to me. Focus on me, Emmy. Focus on me. Tell me about school.

I can see her, how she used to be; and I feel myself failing again.

Tell me about school, Emmy.

I fumble, trying to bring new images into my head. Images of school. Sat at my desk. The doodles on my page, the eyes... the cold, staring eyes on that dank brown paper.

School, Emmy. What are you doing at school lately – tell me.

"Uh..."

Come on, focus! Screw up that piece of paper and look up

from your desk. Yes. Look up.

"Mr Stephens – my teacher."

Yes, good Emmy.

"He...well, he is annoying. He makes me feel stupid."

Ok. How does he make you feel that way, Emmy?

I feel my shoulders relax as I focus on her voice, on school. Yes – Mr Stephens. I open my eyes and lick away my bleeding lip. Focus on anything. Mr Stephens will do. My old home, the darkness surrounding it – that day – start to slowly fade.

"I guess...I guess that I feel like he just doesn't give a crap." I start, moving myself to sit up again. I bring my knees up and rest my phone on them as I wipe at my lip with the back of my hand. Still wet.

How come? What has he done?

"Well...well nothing, really. He is supposed to *be* there for students who...well, who need to talk –"

But you haven't wanted to talk.

I jolt then.

"No, no I haven't..."

So how has he been treating you, Emmy?

I picture him then; leaning against his desk, tapping his finger with his *'I don't appreciate your attitude, young lady'* look.

"I don't know...Making me feel bad for not doing the work? Making me look a bit like a fool, I guess. Acting like nothing has happened – still expecting the best from me. I can't concentrate on work though – I don't care about the Romans, or about letters being used instead of numbers in math. I don't care about what colour magnesium shines when burning. I don't care what comes after this year. What's the point?"

There's a pause then, and I find my stomach rolling in fear that my phone has cut out. No, the screen is still shining brightly, but I hold it tighter in my hands.

Would you want him to treat you differently? Would you want him to act differently around you?

I jolt again, frowning against the light.

"Uh...I don't know."

I think hard about it. What are my expectations? I don't want people with their looks, like they had done when first hearing the news after that assembly. I don't want stepping on egg shells. What do I want?

"No...I don't really know."

A pause.

It might be worth you thinking about what you want or need from school, to help you. You don't need to do all of this alone, Emmy.

"But I don't mind being on my own – I don't care." I say it confidently, but even I don't really believe it. I think back to that look Paul gave me, how I got emotional at being told off by that manager man, how I have been eating alone in my bedroom for almost the last week.

Well, you aren't on your own any longer, Emmy. Don't isolate yourself in a way that forces people to not see you. Don't be unseen. Don't get lost.

Don't be unseen? Well, I could easily go a whole day without making eye contact with someone at school as of late. Would they notice if I wasn't there? If something had happened? Would they look for me? Tell Dad? I tremble at the thought, and pull the covers back and go right beneath my duvet, creating my own little den with the light of the phone bouncing off the covers as I pull them over my head. I am probably glowing.

There could be others in school who feel that way...the ones who get missed or forgotten. Would I notice? I know for a fact though that when the person does *not* come back...everyone notices. And it hurts more than humanly possible. But is it preventable? Could we have stopped it?

"Can...can you stay with me, for a little longer?" I whisper into the phone.

I feel the corner of my eyes moisten, and a lose tear streaks out and onto the bridge of my nose.

I am here as long as you need me, Emmy. You are not alone anymore.

I smile and place the phone upright onto my pillow and watch the patterns it makes on the duvet above. Yes – I probably *am* glowing. My own little nightlight. My own light from within the deep dark. Like a star...sprinkling stardust down onto the world to make it wonderful.

My last thought is of Dad as I close my eyes.

Mr Stephens

I wash my plate myself this morning. I feel a punch to my stomach when entering the small kitchen though, as bowls of left over popcorn lie scattered on the work surface as well as empty fizzy drink bottles. I feel myself going sour, thinking of them all having fun last night and wondering whether Nathan's girlfriend has stayed over. I really don't want to have to deal with her. She asks too many questions. I manage to push the bubble I feel forming angrily in my stomach down instead of letting it erupt, but can't help the nasty thoughts. Like her coughing on a popcorn kernel until she turns purple, or the TV exploding in a harsh bang; raining glass down upon them all and screams filling the room instead of their laughter.

I place the plate a little over zealously on the counter top.

The day ends up not being too bad in the end. My phone is nestled next to my pillow, and I glance at it every now and again with what is almost a hint of a smile, choosing to stay indoors instead of being on my own like yesterday. I even leave my bedroom door open; just on the crack. Nathan avoids me like I hold some deadly disease or if I am a bad smell, obviously, but Dad stops to poke his head in and smile at me as I sit reading on my bed. *Of Mice and Men*; I found it at the bottom of my book pile. He doesn't come in though, or attempt to talk. Just a quick smile. Good. I don't want to talk. Not to him, yet.

I haven't spoken to Willow again, yet I have been thinking a lot about what she had said. Or rather, what I had said to her in consequence. I have really had a think about what I want from school. What I want from Mr Stephens. I have played with the idea of talking with him...or at least saying I need to talk at some point, but stubbornly keep putting that wall back up. He doesn't deserve to be let in after all...to see me vulnerable. The thought of how he could possibly help is laughable. Would he even want to hear what I have to say? Does he even care anyway? Still, Willow's words hold some impact, as I do keep thinking about it. Thinking about what I might say. What he would say in return. That is what frightens me the most though...that and the look on his face.

* * *

The bus journey Monday morning flies by in a misty swirl as I stay rooted deep within my own head; playing out different scenarios and possible conversations that could happen at school round and around. Mr Stephens breaking into a fit of laughter and telling the whole class what I have to say. Me opening my mouth and no words coming out; my throat closing up to the point of choking. Mr Stephens sitting down with me and listening to what I have to say; being sensitive and caring. Me actually talking about it, for the first time, since it happened. All of these outcomes are just as bad as each other, I feel, and my stomach twists anxiously the whole journey there. I only realise my stop as Nathan and Paul press the button. Paul taps my shoulder as he awkwardly pushes his bike down the aisle. He had taken it right to the back of the bus instead of the spaces at the front, of course. Probably because Nathan had insisted they sit back there. It's where the 'cool' kids hang out in American teen movies anyway – isn't it? As if anything could make Nathan cool.

Paul nods to me as I gather my shoulder bag up before jumping off the steps, already swinging his leg onto his bike.

I spend a lot of my time in the girls' bathroom before my first lesson with Mr Stephens. I have just finished double science where I spent my time daydreaming whilst others did the experiments. People were used to me not contributing lately anyway, and they didn't bother saying anything anymore. I could have very easily not have been there, and I shiver at the thought of fading away like a shadow in the dark. Like Willow had said. A few new scenarios had popped into my head before the bubble bomb they were making exploded, landing me back to reality with a harsh bang. Funnily enough, an explosion had been one of my new scenarios. Except, I was the bomb. And I took this whole school down with me.

Break lasts twenty minutes, and the first bell is already ringing. I still stare into the mirror though; the florescent lights really showing the bags under my eyes and the pale quality my skin holds as of late. When was the last time I had washed my hair? I pull it back into a scruffy pony tail and it lies all matted over my shoulders. After a small attempt to make it look neater, I give up; feeling stupid at the thought that I could maybe look a little bit pretty. I push the bubble down.

Not *one* girl comes into the toilets on her own. They all come in pairs, or flocks of up to seven. There's always that awkward quiet that ripples over them when they notice me, standing alone. As if they all catch a draft at the same time, or if I am something dangerous that they don't want to disturb. That's fine girls – you can think I am dangerous if you want to. I am stood on fractured glass, remember? Don't come too close.

How they think I can't see their glances to each other or the words they mouth though, I don't know. And no: squeezing into a cubicle together to whisper does not make you sound proof.

'Is that *the* girl?'

'Yeah...Poor thing.'

'The girl whos...?'

'Yeah...*that* one. Can you imagine? I think I'd just die if that was me. I mean...can you believe it?'

'Should we talk to her? Ask if she is ok?'

'No...I hear she is weird now. Like...gone all dark and stuff.'

'Yeah. Not surprised.'

Yes, that's right. I am standing on thin, fractured glass. And even more so; I am holding shards in my hands so you better not reach out to 'save' me. Better to just whisper behind closed doors and smile at my reflection awkwardly as you wash your hands and fix your perfect hair. I resist the urge to punch the mirror before I leave. I slam the bathroom door behind me though. Slam it as hard as I can.

My heart is racing when Mr Stephens starts the lesson. I have changed my mind countless times as to whether I am going to try and talk to him. Or, at least to let him know that I would be up for the subject of talking. Maybe. How I would *maybe* talk to him...about things...someday. I don't know. I have this funny feeling about not wanting to let Willow down or disappointing her in some way, despite the fact that she is most likely in my head as I suffer a colossal breakdown.

The brown spare paper is left in its usual place on his desk and I laugh to myself as I swipe a few pages. Yes. A colossal breakdown describes my life quite nicely.

We are looking into Pompeii today in our '*historical and geographical tour of Italy*'. I guess mass devastation from an erupting volcano is something I can at least relate to. Oh, not the fire and burning lava, of course. But...the suffocation bit. Yes. I can relate to that. How something as small and seemingly innocent or harmless as ash or a cloud...can creep up on you and take your breath away. Literally take it away. We watch a video depicting how it happened; clips of actors dressed in historical clothing running, gripping at their throats, and throwing themselves on top of loved ones in their attempts to save them. My stomach flips as a woman grabs her young child by the hand and runs. Yes; mothers protecting their children in any way they can, at any cost. At least the people of Pompeii saw their ash cloud coming. I had no idea until mine was raining down upon me; stealing my breath and leaving me completely empty.

"Now remember class, tomorrow we are going to be starting our Pompeii display - so don't forget to bring in an old t-shirt that you can pop over your school clothes as we will be using papier Mache. Yes, thank you Ryan – very 'morbid' –"

Did he glance at me then?

"– but this is an important topic to demonstrate just how devastating our natural world can be and how we need to respect and protect it. The whole school is dedicating itself to the *Protect the Planet* theme, and all the work from the different year groups shall be displayed around the school for the public and parents –"

Yes, he definitely shot me a look then.

"– to come and look at. We have many live volcanos left around the world, so it will be great fun to attempt to make one of our own. You shall be linking up with this topic in science over the next few weeks to make some *lava* – so watch out!"

A small giggle ripples around the class. That boy Ryan and a few of his friends bang on the table excitedly with their hands. Some people just like to watch the world burn, I guess. The bell begins ringing.

"Right! Get out of here then, you lot."

People are already packing up their bags. I stay seated.

"Remember – T-shirts, ok? No, leave your one with the 'buff chick' on it at home, Simon. Just a plain t-shirt will do. One you don't want to get ruined, ok? Yes – any extra credit you want then a write up on '*How could we prevent Pompeii from happening again*' is due next week! Thanks for the reminder, Sarah."

Only a few people left in the room now. I shuffle in my seat. My palms are sweating. I can somehow tell that he is avoiding looking at me now.

A few chimes of 'bye, Sir' and 'thanks, Sir' as the last few children leave the room till it is just him and me. I lift my hands from my desk to clench them on my lap. Sweaty imprints lie on the polished surface for a few moments as if someone invisible is standing over me; leaning heavily over my head and crouching as if ready to pounce. Maybe protecting me? From Mr Stephens? Or preventing me from doing something stupid?

Mr Stephens finishes fiddling around with some pieces of paper before turning to his laptop and turning off the overhead projector. I stay seated. I feel sick.

"Everything...alright there, Emmy? Do you have a free period?"

Oh god, this is it. Is it? My stomach seriously cramps now as my heart hums in my ears. Do I feel dizzy? Maybe I should go to the nurse – just leave here and not talk. Never talk.

"Uh...no, but...um..."

Mr Stephens stops his fussing to look at me. I look away and back to my desk. The handprints are fading; slowly evaporating away.

"Uh..." oh, come on! "Could I talk to you?"

My heart throws itself at my chest cavity so forcefully I think I am going to head-butt the table with the momentum. I panic. Feel it rising. Feel that hot bubble pushing up my throat – like a volcano.

"No – f-forget it, never mind, sorry, Sir – I have to go to... um, art. Uh..."

I gather up my bag. The strap is caught under my chair and it almost falls backwards as I pull it from beneath the table. I swear accidently. The tears are coming. I have to get out of here.

"Emmy?"

"No – no, it's alright, Sir. It was just about that extra credit – nothing important. I think I've got it sorted. Pompeii. Death. How to...*stop* people dying..."

The tears start bubbling over now. Hot. Like lava. Images come in to my head. My own images...not replaced by actors in costume. Real. Too real.

"...Yeah, sure thing. We can prevent things like that – or *should* be able to. Should we? But what if...what if they do it anyway? Die, I mean? Just *die* in a way that we didn't see coming?"

My bag is free. I throw it over my shoulder, knocking another chair over. I can't see. I wipe desperately at my eyes.

"What if despite it all, they die anyway? And – and it is put down as an *act of nature*, or an *accident*, or used as some story that people learn in classrooms but don't *feel* anything when they hear it. *Who* was that person who died? *Who* did they leave behind? None of that matters, does it, Sir? The world just carries on. Who cares about *Pompeii*, really? Who cares about – about any of it?"

I trip on something, crash forward; something hard hitting into my stomach taking my breath. My head is spinning.

"And - and what about the people they leave behind, Sir? What do they do? How do *they* get over Pompeii?"

"Emmy," I feel large hands around my shoulders then, almost holding me as my knees sag beneath me. My head lolls. I can't see. I can see *her* though...

"Even if we *could* see that ash cloud coming, what would we do if they didn't want to be saved? Huh, Sir? What if they didn't call for help? What if they, instead of taking our hand – *ran* towards that oncoming cloud? Huh? What could we do? What if despite it all, they *wanted* to die?"

"Emmy – look at me."

My whole face is wet, and my eyes almost stick together as I try to open them. I feel both empty and heavy inside; as if the lack of anything is painful. Or that I have too much inside and I am threatening to explode. To erupt. Everything blurs as things tumble together and merge in my head. The ash cloud. Her face. Empty eyes drawn on scrap paper. Children holding their mothers hands. The door to her bedroom...back at our old house.

He holds almost my whole weight now...I'm not even trying

to keep myself up anymore. I can't.

"Hey – Emmy, come on...come on, let's sit down...here look? Just here. That's it..."

I feel myself being lowered into a chair. Then silence and darkness.

* * *

I have never been to the nurse's office before. How embarrassing. I am glad that I hadn't really been aware of what was happening around me, as Mr Stephens had propped me over his shoulder and slowly walked me there. I could still hear the whispers though. That and feel all the eyes.

He stays with me while the nurse looks me over. She is a young woman with a friendly smile and corkscrew hair; so blond it is almost white, and her dark eyes look misplaced in her pale face. She makes me eat a chocolate protein bar and drink a whole pint of water before she's happy for me to sit up unaided. The bar's so chewy I still have bits left in my teeth.

I watch Mr Stephens as the nurse checks my temperature and blood pressure; sitting in one of the waiting chairs just outside of the small curtain I sit behind. I can just about see him through the gap. His legs are crossed and he plays with his lip as he leans against the arm of the chair; his forehead furrowed and his eyes staring. I am in here for a while, a long while, and not once does he look at his watch.

Once nurse Lilli is happy that I'm not at the immediate risk of fainting again, she said I have the choice to either go home or stay in school but to take it easy.

'Do you have any friends who can keep an eye on you?' she had

asked. I had asked for another protein bar.

When Mr Stephens comes in to the small partitioned room after nurse Lilli draws back the curtain, my stomach swims nervously. I am so embarrassed. How had the idea of 'telling him that I *might* be up for talking' turn into *that* catastrophic episode? He must think I am a complete nut job.

He sits down, somewhat tentatively, in the chair next to the little camp bed I sit upon. Even though I keep my eyes to my knees, I can tell that he is looking at me.

"Hey. How are you feeling?" he asks gently.

He leans forward slightly on his own knees. His eyes look soft and worried when I glance up. I look back to my knees and shrug, and I hear him take a deep breath and sigh. Not an 'annoyed' sigh...but a sad one.

"Oh, Emmy. I really wish you had come to talk to me sooner. You know that I am here whenever you need to talk – you know that, right?"

I shrug again, and he shuffles in his chair.

"Look..." he starts softly. "I cannot even begin to imagine how difficult these past few weeks have been on you and your family, so I am not going to pretend that I know how you feel. The whole school is here for you though, Emmy. I do hope you realise that..."

Huh. No they weren't. They whisper. They joke. They judge.

"...and if you need to take a step back or have some time off, you can do. I was just trying to keep some of the...uh...*normality* for you. Give you something to use, something to focus on. Don't think for one moment that it wasn't for a lack of caring. You have a lot of people around you that care about you."

I shuffle then, crossing my legs awkwardly and then uncrossing them. Pulling my long ponytail over my shoulder to twirl in my fingers; throwing it back behind my back again.

"Um...will I get in trouble for missing art?"

He laughs ever so softly then and I look up. His eyes are still soft, but that furrow remains in his brow.

"Of course not. I will say it was my fault – ok?"

I feel my cheeks rise a little. That weight in my chest lifting ever so slightly.

We sit in silence then for a bit. Someone pops in to say that the school has arranged for a taxi to come and pick me up and take me back to the hotel. Something about not wanting me to walk to the bus stop and wait for an hour. That is nice of them, I guess. We talk about just normal things as we wait, for a bit. Mr Stephens tells me about his wife's new 'health kick', and how he has been banned from eating chocolate. I say how when I am older I want to go to Canada to see the humpback whales. He says how he has *seen* a humpback whale.

"So...um, Sir?" I start up again. I feel nervous bringing the topic back to this. Do I want to? Should I leave it?

"If I don't feel so...um...great...are there things I can do from home? From my hotel? I just..." no come on, swallow that bubble down. "...I just feel very alone at school at the moment."

He stays silent and looks intensely at me, as if he is trying to read something written beyond the glass of my eyes.

"Tell you what," he starts cheerily. Is this what he meant about trying to make things 'normal'? I guess it is better than the judgemental eyes. No...there is no judgement in *his* eyes.

"You can pick *anything* you like from Italian history to contribute towards your class grade. Anything. You can write about it, you can draw...make. Anything you like! Just promise me something, ok?"

I shrug.

"Use it as a distraction. Pour yourself into it and forget your life, for a moment. Just...press a pause button, and let yourself be free. Does that sound like something you might be able to do?"

I shrug again, but smile ever so slightly.

A distraction...just like my music. Yes, that sounded ok. Something to help...to think of something else. Anything.

"Are you ok here by yourself for a second whilst I get a handout from the classroom?"

He hesitates after I shrug, but smiles warmly and runs from the room. I don't think I have ever seen a teacher run before. Is that the last lunch bell? Mr Stephens hadn't had any lunch. He is back within moments, and I can tell he is trying to talk normally through his lack of breath.

"Here – all the topics we have covered currently, and ones that are extra. Have a look and pick from the list. Oh – and this is another little something."

He hands me a thick envelope. I frown and flip it over to open it, but he puts out his hand, still smiling.

"This is a little something to...look at when you are feeling alone. To open when needed. Maybe I should have given it to you before, but it all felt a little too..." he frowns and rubs his eyes.

I guess I forget how difficult my situation can be for others too.

"...just know that you have it now. You can open it when you are home, you can never open it. It's yours though, ok? To do with as you wish." He grins showing his teeth and nods. His eyes hold that sadness though. Everyone's does now...even when they do smile.

The last warning bell – the one meaning students should be

stood outside of their classrooms ready for lessons. He flinches and rubs his temples.

"Uh...I am sorry Emmy, I've got to – do you want me to wait for your taxi? It shouldn't be too much longer –"

"Nah its ok." I say blandly.

He nods and gets back up, spins on the spot and then hesitates by the door.

"I'm...glad we had a chat, Emmy. I look forward to seeing your project...and I'll tell you more about those whales next time we have a chat, ok? My email is at the bottom of the hand out if you have any questions from home and...uh...well, just take care of yourself. Ok?"

He waits for something back from me, and upon not getting it, smiles and nods again before disappearing behind the door. I put the handout and the envelope into my bag and stare into space until the reception lady comes with her fake smiles to lead me to my taxi.

Schools out

The reception lady had given me another letter as I left the school gates and got into my taxi. This one said that I was 'excused from school with no need to call', with an added note saying that I was welcome back at a time I was 'well enough'. She hadn't even attempted to make her smile reach her eyes when she had passed it to me, nor wait till the car door closed before walking away.

I think that the taxi driver had tried talking to me on the way home, although I cannot find any words in my head now that he might have said. I know that I had stared blankly out of the window though; looking at the world and seeing nothing. It was as if it were hiding somewhere beyond a white fog, and I have no memory of seeing anything beyond the glass nor as I had walked up the many steps back to the apartment. It was as if the bubble that usually plagued my chest had grown so big that it had consumed me completely - keeping me numb, deaf and blind within.

I sit silently on the sofa now with my bag still over my shoulder. I am staring at the letter as it sits alone and slightly crumpled on the table top, slowly becoming aware of my vision again. I thought it the best place for Dad to find it, and I had placed it next to the coffee stain he had already made.

The colour of the room starts to prickle at my eyes as the mid-day sun streams in, and I slowly become dully aware of other sensations that my bubble had been keeping me privy to. Such as the grumble in my lower stomach, the thoughts that ghost on the surface trying to make me react to what I had done today; even my eyes start to sting.

When was the last time I had blinked?

I sit for a long time until my stomach is all I can feel, slowly totter into the kitchen, grab an apple, and move silently into my bedroom.

I curl up on my bedroom windowsill wrapped in my fleece until Nathan comes home. He starts when he sees my bedroom door wide open, and comes to stand in the doorway swiftly and silently. I hadn't even thought about closing it, to be honest. I hadn't thought much about anything. I don't even stir to look up at him until he starts shuffling uncomfortably.

"Uh...hey." He mumbles.

His school shirt is buttoned up wrong; it has a long tail poking out of the bottom and his collar is all crooked. I pull my fleece tighter around my neck as something within my bubble stirs.

"Someone in my year said that Mr Stephens took you to the nurse today? That...you didn't look good?"

I glance at him emptily, yet as soon as I catch his eyes my stomach cramps and my bubble wavers. His arms are crossed as he leans against the doorframe. His eyes are the same colour as Dad's in this light. Hazelnutty brown with flecks of green. They look tight in the corners. A small crease between them.

"You...you ok?"

"I'm fine."

He fidgets again and pulls at his shirt.

"Well, it didn't sound fine to me. Sam said you had fainted or something? That you were sent home?"

Great – so the whole school knows. Another thing for everyone to talk about behind my back. Another tremble on my bubble's walls.

"I came home, yeah. So what. What do you care?"

He pulls at his shirt again, harder this time.

"Uh...because you're my *sister*."

I turn my face away coldly.

"Fine, Emmy. Because I hear from my mate that you've basically been dragged to the nurse's office, but that when I get there you're gone. Because your phone doesn't seem to be working as I tried calling and calling you but it kept going blank. Because I've been wondering what the hell is going on with you all day - so much I couldnt even think straight."

Even the giant bubble can't prevent my stomach from jolting when he mentions my phone, and I dart a glance towards it. I hope he doesn't notice. He is frowning when I look back and I feel myself harden.

"Sure, Nathan. I am sure you were *really* worried."

He tugs harder at his shirt. One of the buttons come off.

"Just leave me alone."

Another tremble. Thoughts of the two of us laughing from another lifetime, drifting on the outside of my bubble; playing like a film projected in water. Distorted. Comforting. I can feel myself reaching out to it, ready to tear the bubble open with my fingers.

"Emmy...people are worried about you."

Pop.

"*Well they don't need to be!*"

It all comes rushing back now as I yell. Why did I do that?

Put it back up...put the bubble back up...

"I don't need their *sympathy* or whatever, Nathan! It's all fake! No one actually gives a shit!"

I feel it all, feel it all again, like I did with Mr Stephens.

"We are just good gossip! I can't *believe* that you are *actually* falling for it all! No wonder you seem completely fine! You over it all, yeah?! Just care about what your so-called friends or your girlfriend think of you?"

A punch to my stomach and a grate to my throat as Nathan's own eyes fill then, but I don't stop.

"You were probably more worried about your reputation when people began talking about me - about how embarrassing your sister is, right?"

I can picture them all; whispering in each other's ears as I am dragged through the corridors. Can see them pointing, rolling their eyes, laughing, joking. Even as my face goes ashen, my body lifeless...falling to the floor. They laugh. They move on. They walk over me. No one bends to help. No one sees me anymore; as I lie there, cold.

"Well, if you care *so much*, Nathan, probably best to just tell people that you don't have a sister. I don't care! That is *perfectly* fine by me! You don't *have* to have a sister anymore!"

The two of us laughing; it had tumbled into me once the bubble had burst and my chest hurt with holding it. When even was that moment? Was it real? When had I loved my brother? When was it ok to?

Nathan brings his arms tightly across his chest after quickly wiping at his face. He scoffs, but the kind of laugh that doesn't reach the eyes. The kind that sounds hollow in the throat.

"Look, Emmy." He sniffs. "I know that things are crap, right? And I know they will probably be crap for a *really* long time, but you need to stop being such a cow to everyone. You get that, right?"

A thump to my stomach.

"What?!" I screech

"A cow, Emmy. A moody, nasty, spiteful, cow. You sit there and watch the world crashing and burning around you, right? But I don't get how for the *life* of me that you cannot see that others are hurting too. That you are *not* the only one burning. This whole place is a furnace; and it hurts so much." His voice is cracking now as his tears come fast, but I am stone. "We are trying *so* hard, me and Dad, to put the fire out and try and be ok...to help *you* be ok – but *you* aren't trying, Emmy! You aren't trying at all!"

"Stop thinking you know how I feel!" I scream, and I run over to the door and slam it as hard as I can in his face.

I stay there, panting for a while, my hand still pressed firmly against the wood in some weird fear that Nathan will try and come back in. I wait for the resistance; get ready to push back. But it lies still and dead beneath my fingers.

I picture *him*, now. Nathan...ashen faced, lying in our corridor, covered in scars...in burns. My stomach jolts in a sudden panic to open the door – reach down and help him – but I turn away stubbornly. Maybe it would be easier to picture that I don't have a brother, as well. That I have no one. You can't burn when there is no one close by to strike the match.

* * *

I lie in bed the next morning, listening to Dad and Nathan getting ready. Dad is firmly back at work now, so I knew I would be alone today. Really alone. Their voices are low, and all I can hear are rumblings and grumblings as they talk. Probably talking about me.

I have been awake since first light, having left my curtains open all night long to look at the stars. The window is open too, just a crack, and I can feel the breeze on my face and the smells wafting up from the kitchens below.

I think we forget sometimes that the rest of this house carries on functioning as a hotel; guests taking a break from their lives flocking down to a breakfast cooked for them by another person. Helping themselves to things they would never bother cooking for themselves, as they share idle chit-chat about absolutely nothing of importance. I guess we came here for a similar reason; to try and escape from our lives for a moment. Except, we are not going back.

There's a quiet knock on my door. I guess it must be around 8:30ish, as I have already heard Nathan leave with Paul and both he and Dad have been up for at least an hour. I pull my fleece over my face and snuggle down into my pillow, trying not to make a sound, and footsteps fade away followed by a click to the front door. I stay here for a bit; under the fleece. The bright sunlight through the window casting my vision in a soft white light, as the material ripples over my face like water. It tickles; and I focus on that feeling instead of the pins in my chest. I stay, until I can no longer ignore the twisting hunger pains in my stomach. I yawn, simply because I feel I should, and stumble to the kitchen. Someone has left a cereal box out, accompanied by a bowl and a spoon, ready to be used. My chest stirs as I picture Dad gently knocking on my door to no answer, and quickly grab some toast instead; leaving the bowl and box where they are.

After staring at the TV but not seeing the show that is on, I start to wander around the apartment. Dad has made a real effort, I guess. It looks like our very own place. Every little detail now is *our* detail; from the ornaments, the pictures, the sofa throws and the cushions. Is that even a plant from back home? It sits in the middle of the dining table, surrounded by little placemats that are definitely something I recognise. I haven't sat at that table since coming here, but still – three placemats sit neatly in front of three chairs. Only three.

Both Dad and Nathan's bedroom doors are closed, but I go to Dad's first. My breath shakes as I push it open, but when I see what is inside, my heart slows. In fact; I feel nothing, and I have to search within myself to check that it is still beating.

Back home, before any of this...Dad's room had always been so busy and colourful. Full of brightly coloured pillows that laid smattered on the bed, picture frames covering the walls – both of family smiles, weird art, and old film posters. Clothes would be hanging awkwardly in an open wardrobe almost to the point of looking messy, but so organised that you could cross reference a particular colour with an item and find just that, perfectly in place. A full length mirror had stood within, hidden - so that you had to part a few long dresses to look at it properly. It was covered in shiny pins and buttons, with long necklaces hanging off the corners – always making your reflection seem that bit more interesting as you almost sparkled. As if surrounded by stardust. That is what *she* had said anyway.

Dad's bedroom here, just *his* bedroom now, is bland. Plain. Cold. White bedsheets and one single white pillow. A large suitcase that is propped open – his clothes folded neatly inside with the occasional thing spilling onto the small chest of drawers next to it or on top of a small hamper he has sitting in the corner. No colour. No sparkle...no stardust. Just empty. There is nothing of *her* here. Nothing of him. Nothing; and I search within my chest again as my heart suddenly picks up. The starkness becomes pressing; so pressing in fact that I feel like the room is closing in on me. No, not closing... getting bigger. Stretching out so far and wide that I lie tiny and trembling in the middle, panicking. The only bit of colour, the only bit of warmth; until I too start to turn white. The colour leaking out of me as if I am made of ink and am dashed into a vast bowl of water. Just ebbing away – myself, ebbing – spreading – drifting – fading. Just like Dad is doing.

I grab my breath and hold it in my lungs as I tumble out of the room, quickly closing the door behind me. I pat myself down and hold up my hands in front of my face. Yes. The colour is still there. I am still here. I let my breath go. My stomach still squirms though as I think of Dad, alone in that room. Cold. White. Colourless.

Just like *she* had been; in the end.

I shake myself and walk towards Nathan's room.

Now, if I were to walk through any door anywhere in the world, and it looked like this on the other side, I would know that it's my brothers. It looks almost identical to the one we left behind. Band posters all over the walls, that weird material flag thing he has hanging from the ceiling that sags in the middle, clothes – mainly odd socks – strewn all over the floor. It even smells like Nathan. How he had put his smell into a room so quickly is beyond me. Did he spray his scent like some sort of wild animal? I wouldn't put it past him. Maybe it is safest not to touch anything. And to breathe through my mouth.

I wade through socks, imagining that they are alien eggs

and that if I so much as touch one, it will rattle and hatch – launching to my face and suffocating me where I stand. If my feet were any bigger, I'd have no hope. I can barely see the carpet. The comparison from Dad's room is...scary. Dad seems completely lost; on standby almost...as if this place, this place in time even, is temporary or alternate. Alternate to the life we are supposed to be living; so he has just created a cell for himself in which to wait it out. Wait until our time – our timeline – is back on track. But Nathan? Looking at his room now as it has always been, how it had been before...is he truly not bothered by any of it? Is he stuck somewhere on our old timeline? Or is he merely trying to get back?

I stub my toe on the edge of his chest of draws and shout out, hopping madly before falling to the floor. The socks fly everywhere. Well – the aliens will surely get me now, there is no way out! I furiously check my large toe; picturing that the whole nail has come off and I end up bleeding out on this dirty floor, alien socks eating my face. My breath comes hissing between my clenched teeth. Bleeding, but not bleeding too much. Just a black nail, I suppose. I hold it in my hand for a moment and rock back and forth.

It's funny isn't it? How when sometimes you are in such a sudden amount of pain, that the pain envelops everything else for a moment. Masks any other pain you might be feeling, as if it is trying to be the centre of attention; as if it is the star of the show. Well...my big toe has a spotlight on it now, and I stay rocking on the floor cradling it in my sweating hands until the throbbing dulls enough for the chorus line to start up again. They wear faces I don't want to see; sing things I can't bear to hear. For me, they are the real stars of the show, and my show is in constant encore. Maybe I should stub my toe more often.

I pull myself up using his chest of drawers, they too having socks scattered on the top, and test putting weight on my foot. Seriously, how does Nathan have so many socks? Does he just buy new ones instead of washing them? Is he breeding them?

Some of them come away with my hand as I start to move back towards the door, and something catches my eye. The socks are covering other things on the table top, and I push them off onto the floor to have a look. The chorus starts getting louder in my head as my heart punches nastily at my chest. Pictures. Photographs – loads of them. Scattered on top of the chest of drawers like some nasty collage. Photos of us, *all* of us. My throat begins grating. Why does Nathan have these? My fingers fumble as I try picking one up. It is creased...dented all over, as if it has been screwed up and smoothed out again. The two of them, standing together, followed by little me and little Nathan in front. I think that was from when we went to Spain. A memory forces its way in and plays on my mind's stage before I can put up my barriers; Dad trying to explain to the man at the beach how to use his camera, *she* trying to get me and Nathan to stand nicely next to each other. It had taken a while to get us all smiling at the right time, and we fell into arguments afterwards. You wouldn't have thought that though, looking at this picture.

Another one finds its way in to my hand: from a wedding; *their* wedding. Dad without glasses – I can't help the little flip to my stomach as I smile at how handsome he looks. His eyes weren't as crinkly back then, but they still held their warmth. More, actually. And her? Well. It is like seeing a photo of myself, almost. Hair, not as long and scruffy. Eyes, a different colour: but me. She isn't looking at the camera; her face is turned almost completely to look at Dad. Her mouth open in a still laugh. She looks happy. As if she was the happiest she had ever been.

Another. In a swimming pool. I don't even know who would have taken this one. I could not have been much older than a baby, as I float, chubbily, in a little ring as Nathan sits on Dad's shoulders as *she* throws the ball. It had been captured, hanging in the sky like a bright striped moon; droplets frozen as they rained down. They look like stars. She looked happy here, too.

I don't know why some people get so precious over photographs. How they honour them, protect them. How they say 'they are the first thing I'd grab in a fire!'. How they trust them, completely and utterly, for support in times of difficulty or loss. For memories and moments. Because none of those moments are real, not really. They are posed. Constructed. They may capture a moment, yes – but a moment is all it is. She looked happy in these *moments*...but that doesn't mean that she was. She couldn't have been. Photographs lie.

Another one, this one just her and Nathan this time, and I put it down quickly as if it burns. It has been screwed up too. *Her* eyes, scratched out. Nathan's face, marred to the point of holes appearing through the paper. And as I flip it over in my hands, scrawled on the back in angry pen is the word...

Why?

I grab a handful of socks and smear them over the pictures as my stomach clenches to the point of being sick. I turn to leave, quickly adjusting one as her face is still showing. I almost miss the sock completely due to my shaking hands. I don't want to see her – don't want Nathan to see her. I stop myself reaching for a pair of sharp looking scissors on his bedside table and shredding them all, and close the door quickly behind me in fear that she may somehow follow me out.

I sit down, slowly sliding my back down the wood, and hold my knees. My breath quakes harshly, and I hold it in my mouth for a moment and close my eyes, pushing my tongue to the roof of my mouth to stop the bile that sloshes angrily in my stomach from coming up. My throat burns as it creeps, and I grip my stomach and put my head to my knees. Swallow it down.

The scissors float into my head, and I can't help but think how sudden pain pushes down other constants. My stomach knots again and I bring my knees in closer. I take hold of my swollen toe and squeeze it till it stings.

Apollo

"Willow...are you there?"

I only stay in my clothes for a short while before changing back into my pyjamas. I have a hot shower and stay in there till I can't see for the steam; my whole body shining bright pink as I try to scrub away the things I had seen as well as how I felt about them.

It's interesting...what people keep behind closed doors. I wonder what they would discover about me if *they* came snooping about. I know that I would be mortified, if they came into my room when I wasn't there. What if they found all my school books, untouched and now pushed under my bed? What if they found my phone, if they found Willow? What if they found me, in those moments that they thought I was doing ok, *not* doing ok?

Nathan certainly didn't seem to have noticed that anyone had been in his room though. I was primed and ready for him to come bursting in – enraged at my nosiness – furious that I could undermine his trust like that! But he didn't. I had listened; my ear pressed hard against my door till the sounds of the TV distorted any other secret speaking's that may have been going on. I must have covered my tracks well! Yet, that only made me feel more guilty, and I pick at my fingernails to give myself something else to think about.

I can still hear it now, the TV, as I sit on the edge of my bed, my pyjama bottoms tucked awkwardly into some fluffy socks, my hair still damp. It transitions smoothly from children's silly cartoons to the evening news and beyond and I shuffle, suddenly panicked that he isn't even there- until there is a gentle knock on my door.

Dad holds a plate of steaming food with a tired smile, and closes the door without prompting as I take it and make my way back to my bed.

His eyes are definitely looking different. I burn my mouth on the rice as I shove my fork forcefully into my mouth.

"Willow? You there?"

It is almost half way through the next day now. I have spent all morning in bed, just staring up at the ceiling drifting in and out of sleep. My night had been plagued by horrible dreams: the kind I would have screamed out from; Dad running in all raggedy, ready to calm me down and take me in his arms. But this time...I had awoken in cold sweats and with stifled screams; biting my tongue so as not to yell out and wake others. I have forgotten them now, as I hold my phone to my face with earphones pressed in deeply. They are merely marred visions of odd and shifting colours, shadows and faces. Enough to still make me nervous though, and I am yet to open my bedroom door.

"Willow?"

Yes. I am here.

My shoulders relax.

Are you ok, Emmy?

There is something oddly comforting about the white screen now. I know I am imagining the warmth I feel from its glow on my face, but that is ok. Not everything has to be real.

"Um...I don't know."

I ruffle my hand through my hair. It's all wavy after my shower yesterday. My fingers get caught in the tendrils.

Tell me what's on your mind.

Wow. What a question. Too many things. Things I don't know how to put into words. Stupid things, pointless things. Profound and frightening things.

"Uh...I don't know. I am tired, I guess."

But you want to talk?

My stomach flips anxiously.

"Um. Yeah...is that ok?"

I am always here, Emmy. Whenever you need me.

Right...good. Why have I picked up my phone again? I'm really conscious of my heart in my chest now. Why do I want to speak? And what about? I had been fine about not talking to anyone before; about being alone. My stomach swells as another voice whispers in my ear; laughing at me, criticising me. 'Fine'? Yeah right.

What would you like to talk about, Emmy?

The scissors on Nathan's bedside table flash into my head, along with that picture where his face lay scratched away.

Are you worried about something?

I consciously try to hide my thoughts now, as if my earphones are little microphones; burying into my head and eavesdropping on my most private thoughts. Relaying them back so that Willow knew every deepest and darkest secret I held. The scissors stay though.

"I don't know...maybe."

About your family?

I build that wall higher; desperately placing brick on top of brick.

"Uh – I don't know. They are probably fine."

Dad – his colour expelling into the air. Nathan, bloodied hands gripping silver scissors.

It is easier not to worry, isn't it? You don't really want to think about how they are doing.

I jolt.

"What do you mean?"

A pause.

Well. It is easier – thinking that they are fine. Focusing on yourself.

I feel my face tumble into a frown.

"Myself? You saying I have been selfish?"

A pause.

Do you think you have been selfish?

A pause that I hold now. I feel myself getting angry. Cautious.

You've been angry with them.

I laugh defensively. I can feel a heavy weight in my stomach; the kind you get when you are lying, and quickly run my hand through my hair again to act causal. Not like Willow can see me...

"Yes, I've been angry with them! They crack on with their popcorn and film nights – laughing and singing in the kitchen – acting like everything is fine. Of course I am angry at that."

Acting? Acting like everything is fine?

I stumble again. Wow...if this is me talking to myself in a strange mental breakdown I am having, I'm not holding back.

"What do you mean?"

I know what she means.

Does it mean that they are fine? If they are acting *like everything is fine?*

I put my phone down on to the bed and play with my earphones. Mirages from my dream swim around in my head. Faces, photographs. Shadows and silences. Why had I picked up my phone? Why had I wanted to talk?

...just like you say that you are fine on your own? Acting like you are happy to be alone. To not talk. But that isn't true, is it?

Despite myself, I feel myself getting stubborn as a different type of wall builds up around me. I cross my arms tightly across my chest; push any feeling down. My stomach gets heavier.

"Don't be like them – don't act like you know how I am feeling. You don't – they don't. They haven't a clue. They *are* fine. They are better than me, anyway."

But you are worried. Aren't you?

Those scissors. The photos.

"No."

It is like I feel a sigh then – an exasperated sigh – from somewhere that isn't me, even though I don't hear it from my earphones. Guilt pricks up, and I push it away, gritting my teeth.

If you wanted to talk today, Emmy – you may find it wasn't me you wanted to talk to.

I keep my arms folded, my face set.

...Talk to him, Emmy. Talk to your brother.

* * *

Sat in the lounge at the small dining table, I have my laptop, a pen, a pencil, and a scruffy piece of paper in front of me. I had felt a horrible pang to my stomach when smoothing it out and noticing his email address at the bottom; Mr Stephens had given up his lunch time for me after all. It is the project handout, and consists of a typed up list of all the things we have covered in class.

- Italian agriculture.

I can't think of *anything* more boring.

- England.

That is about the baths and the walls the Romans built, isn't it? How I can make a whole project about that, I have no idea. Build a brick wall in place of my bedroom door? ...that might work. Or stay in the bath tub for years, until I turn into a blue prune.

- The colosseum.

Fighting and violence. Hmm. Maybe.

- ~~Pompeii~~.

Mr Stephen's had already crossed this one out for me, and I drew over the line harder just for good messure.

- Venice.

Dad had gone there on honeymoon.

And an extra topic at the bottom; one we hadn't covered yet. Mr Stephens has drawn a little star next to this one.

- *Ancient Rome.* *

I get up numerous times from the table to pace the apartment. I get another drink, go to the bathroom, tie my hair up, take it down, turn on the radio and turn on the TV, turn them both off again. It is like my bones are itchy, and sitting down for too long results in tremors across my whole body. I certainly bounce my legs up and down now as my hands tap a drum beat on the table. I go to get an apple this time, and stand leaning on the kitchen surface, looking at my laptop through the hatch window while I eat.

I wonder who lived here before we did. Had it been a happy and bustling apartment? Or a cold and quiet one, only used for sleeping in. I kind of hope that the horrid manager hadn't lived here at all...I don't like thinking of a version of him standing where I do, eating an apple of his own. Or caviar I guess now, in his special 'place off the estate' like he had boasted about. Maybe Mrs Locklea used to live here?

Suddenly, I put my half eaten apple down on the counter and make a panicked dash for my bedroom as I hear keys outside, pushing my door to and looking through the gap. Nathan's bag is already off his shoulder and he holds it in his hand, the bottom of it dragging along the floor. He pauses – probably noticing all the stuff I have left on the table, and makes his way towards his room. I move away from the gap, pressing my back against the wall with a hammering heart. A shuffle, a slight bang which must have been him throwing his bag, and his feet again – walking to and away from my door. Then the TV.

I blow out air between pursed lips in an attempt to slow my breathing. Would I have felt this way if I hadn't seen what lay hidden in his room? Would I even be trying to talk to him? Had I been selfish?

Another deep breath as a different kind of voice screams in my head and pulls back at my clothes in protest, as I firmly open my door and stride towards the lounge area.

He doesn't even turn to look at me. He stays fixated on the TV, but his shoulders tighten. They are almost touching his ears. I stutter, and quickly sit down at the table, busying myself with my laptop. My stomach is squirming as if a bucket full of worms lie crawling about inside me, and the image of that is enough to make me almost give up. I feel so awkward! I turn to look at him over my shoulder, pretend I am stretching. Yes; the classic move you make when you want to take a sneaky peek at someone. His shoulders are even tighter, if that is possible. At least he clearly feels uncomfortable too. I take to another approach: I begin sighing.

"Have I got something on my face? In my hair? Coming out of my nose?"

He catches me mid-stretch, and I put my arms down quickly and snap my face to look at my laptop. My heart pounds in my ears so hard it makes me momentarily dizzy.

"Well? Have I turned into an alien? A yeti? A warthog?"

I giggle, still facing my laptop.

"A warthog would certainly explain the smell."

A patterned cushion goes flying past my left ear and I spin defensively to find Nathan smiling too, a second cushion in his hand ready to throw.

"You know I never miss twice." He laughs before his eyes turn dull, and he puts the cushion slowly down onto his lap, wrapping his arms around it and turns back to face the TV. I feel a pang in my stomach.

'*Talk to him*', that's what Willow had said. How *did* I talk to Nathan? I mean, how did I used to? We had never really talked about anything....*meaningful* before. Not really. We were mean to each other...that was our dynamic. Brother and sister who hated each other. Another pang as I feel the guilt from that word. How often have I said that to myself? That I *hate* him? I really am horrible.

"Uh...did you...um...do the Italy project when you had Mr Stephens?"

He doesn't answer straight away, and I am almost ready to get to my feet; shifting to make a run for it back to my bedroom. He shuffles, moving his cushion slightly.

"Yeah. We didn't do Pompeii though – we did Gods and Goddesses."

I keep my eyes on him, wondering if he will turn and give me the eye contact I am actually quite desperate for. He still stares at the TV. I can't blame him though. He probably has his own wall up – maybe even higher than mine.

"The school must have a tick box to fill out regarding the environment this year. Everyone's class projects are a bit intense it seems. Death this...destruction that. My year are doing Hiroshima, if you can believe it. Talk about morbid. Just what we all need..."

I feel my lips curl and my eyebrows knot as my mind stutters over the word, and he finally looks at me, his own eyes going soft as he smiles at my contorted face.

"*Hiro-shee-ma.* It's a place in Japan where a really big

nuclear bomb was dropped. Really bad stuff has happened to the environment because of it...shocking, really." His eyes go to another place, and I'm glad I can't see what he does. Pompeii had been enough for me.

"At least you've gotten out of having to do that." He says as his eyes clear and he refocuses.

"Actually...Mr Stephens has set me my own project. I need to choose something from Italy to do my own thing on."

"Ohh! So the laptop isn't just a ploy to look busy." He mocks. He turns to face me though, keeping the cushion firmly on his lap. My stomach starts to settle.

"No, I actually have some work to do." I mock right back. "But...I don't know what to do it on."

"Gods was a good one – loads of different things with them. And they are quite fantastical – so it's not like it is boring or close to real life."

His eyes go elsewhere again.

"It's nice, not to focus on *real* sometimes, isn't it?"

We look at each other, properly then. I forget how to breathe for a second.

"So...what would you find interesting to do? What would hold your focus or make a project fun?"

I swallow before speaking.

"Um..."

"You always have those earphones in. What about something to do with music? Dad might even have our instruments in storage. He didn't say you had to *write a paper* for your project, did he?"

I stumble.

"No. No, that I could do anything, I guess..."

"Great! Uh...type in 'music' and 'ancient Rome Gods' in

together – see if anything interesting comes up."

I give him a sceptical look in which he replies by sticking out his tongue, and I cannot help but raise my cheeks in a big smile as I type the words into a search engine. Is this how we had been? Before it all had happened? I can't remember.

"Um...*music. Rome Gods*. Ok..."

Lots of different pages come up and I scan through them. I can feel Nathan's eyes on the side of my face, and he is leaning on his cushion, smiling.

"Uh...well some planets have come up..."

"They are the name of the Roman God's, you muppet!" he laughs, and throws his new cushion at me. "You know – *Jupiter, Mars, Venus!* Ha! Have a look...scroll down."

I sigh and tut over exaggeratedly, making sure that he notices me roll my eyes.

"Fine. Um...well, the planets...uh. *Roman religion and mythology...similarities between Greek and roman gods*...Oh!" I turn excitedly and point at my laptop, Nathan grinning as if he knows something I do not. "*Apollo making music!* And here – *Apollo. The god of the sun, art, poetry and music!* Did you know that already?"

He tuts and rolls his own eyes.

"Do you not think I would have just told you if I knew?" he laughs again before turning back to the TV.

"Glad to be of service!" he waves his hand dismissively, a big smile still on his face.

I feel one on my own too – a big one.

Looking blue

We are still in the lounge when Dad comes home from work. He looks like he is ready to fall down when he sees Nathan and I, sat on the sofa watching some American sitcom. We both splutter at his expression before he cheerily strolls in to the kitchen to start dinner. Stir-fry I guess, as I hear lots of chopping and the searing of things in a wide pan.

Nathan hands me the remote and gets up to help, and I stutter as my body moves to do the same before I stop myself. No... things *aren't* back to normal, no matter how much Nathan may want to pretend.

I choose a different channel and bring my feet up underneath me to prevent them from trying to walk off again. Just one step at a time. It's a big deal that I am still sat here – my bedroom certainly does scream for me. I wonder if my phone is glowing? No, come on - baby steps. Maybe I can eat with them tonight? Just for a bit?

I haven't done much more to my project apart from jot some ideas down with Nathan's help. I really like the idea of creating something brand new...like whether I could make a song or a poem of some kind? After reading more about Apollo, it seems that he is also recognised as the God of truth and healing. I had squirmed at that after thinking how much truth I had accidently shown Mr Stephens, and the lack of truth going on between me and Nathan this afternoon. No...not too sure I could be brave enough to link *truth* in to my project. I would have to see. Nathan's suggestion had been that I take up archery and scare people at the school – seeing as pictures of Apollo show him to be holding a harp, and a bow and arrow. Hmm. Something else to consider, I guess, even though he had clearly been joking. Would certainly give me a good entrance when I went back to school! If I went back.

"You want this in your bedroom, Flower? Or...?" Dad lingers with two plates in his hands after Nathan sits down at his spot with his own. I had already moved all my things away and back in to my bedroom, choosing to come back in instead of staying in there. Why had I done that? My stomach certainly is crawling from nerves. Maybe too anxious to eat? Nathan looks to me, fork frozen half way to his mouth.

"Um..."

I stammer, looking away from Dad to the floor, but I can feel Nathan's glare in the back of my head.

The wall...it is hard to climb over sometimes. I'm not ready to break it down...but perhaps I could perch on the top for a bit? Just a bit?

Dad's hands begin trembling. The plates do look hot. I feel myself being pulled back to my lonely dark bedroom; a version of myself stood shadowed in the dark with tears staining her cheeks – a rope held tightly in her hands that ends up tied around *my* neck and she pulls and pulls – bringing me into her dangerous company.

"Oh come on, Ems. Look, sit down – you're taking forever." Nathan breaks the silence and I feel the nose loosen. Dad smiles hopefully.

"Um – yeah ok, but I can't stay for long. I want to look at my project..." my stomach swells as Dad grins, placing the plates down carefully. His fingers are red when he picks up his knife and fork and I twinge.

We sit in silence for a little while. Well, I say silence – Nathan is a very noisy eater – until Dad breaks the tension.

"So...Petal, you are doing a special project whilst you are off school? That sounds wonderful." His eyes crinkle.

"Uh – yeah." I say shortly around a mouthful of noodles. I am eating so fast my plate is almost empty.

"She is gunna do it on Apollo – aren't you, Ems?" Nathan splutters, his own mouth brimming.

I can't help my mocking smile, and he opens his mouth disgustingly to show me the mushed up food inside. I nearly spit mine out in a coughing laugh. Dad ignores the behaviour, too busy smiling at me. He has hardly touched his own dinner. Is his face looking thin?

"Oh, lovely! – What do you think you are going to do? You have creative license, I assume?"

I look away from his face, his cheeks are definitely looking gaunter, and push away the images of his bedroom and play with the colourful vegetables on my plate.

"Uh – yeah I guess. Mr Stephens said I can do what I want. I dunno – might do a poem or write a song as part of it – I guess. Or draw something..."

"Sounds just perfect. You were always so good at art." Dad beams again, holding his gaze upon me, before finally taking his fork to his food. Mine and Nathan's plates lie empty.

* * *

There's a note left for me on the dining table the following morning in Dad's handwriting. I had gone into my bedroom after dinner and stayed in there until I heard them both leave this morning, having a quiet midnight shower once they were both asleep. I felt both relieved and sad, once having closed my bedroom door, and found myself listening to the TV from my little seat on the windowsill until they both went to bed.

Why did I feel the need to leave them? To be alone? Well, I know why. It was too much – being around them all the time. Seeing them *hurt* me. Like...physically hurt. The balance between feeling good – feeling happy when with them, was shifted very easily by the feelings of hurt and anger at them for even being here. About *me* being here, really. Did we deserve it? How was it fair – us carrying on as normal? That is why I'm not. I don't deserve to; and the scales always tip in favour of punishing myself in some way, rather than forgiving and forgetting. My phone had stayed both dull and silent all night too.

'The manager has agreed that you can change your room. I will leave tester pots for you at the reception in my lunch break. Maybe an idea for your project too? I love you very much - like sprinkles of stardust and lollies and such.

– Dad x'

I wander down in a baggy sweatshirt and my pyjama bottoms once the clock hands hit half past one. I don't have the urge to try and slide down the banisters again, but I run a finger along the polished oak. Run it all the way down the stairs to a lovely ear cringing squeak. They polish things well here – the tip of my forefinger is shiny when I reach the bottom.

There's a very plain and boring looking woman sat behind

the small reception area. She wears a tightly fitted grey top and a face that look as if it has never smiled. I strut, over-exaggeratedly, to the desk and lean my arm on the surface, the sleeve of my sweatshirt trailing over my hands and lying awkwardly in front of her. I grin sarcastically and flick my hair.

"Do you have the package?" I ask, feigning sudden caution, casting a quick look behind my back.

Her face goes blank. More blank – if that is possible.

"The package..." I ask again, leaning in closer, knotting my eyebrows the best I can. "Has it been...*delivered*?"

"I'm sorry?" she asks.

Wow. Her voice is almost as boring as her face.

"The package!" I suddenly shout – placing my baggy arms over my head and flailing them about dramatically. "The package, woman! The package! It is of utmost important that I have the package! I can't take it anymore!"

I try hard not to smile or laugh and hold on to the look of anguish I think I have going on. Her faces changes ever so slightly – I'm guessing the face she pulls when she is worried? Confused? Or needs the toilet? It's anyone's guess.

"I-I'm sorry, young lady – I-I don't know what you are talking about. Are you in the right place?" she starts looking about her now and leans in close, lowering her voice to a whisper.

"Perhaps...perhaps this *package* is waiting for you outside? Uh...is it a *contact* that has brought it for you?"

Huh. I must look pretty 'street' in my sweatshirt and PJ bottoms. I can't help the laugh now and my act falls.

"Nah – my Dad brought me some paints? Do you have them?"

She continuous to look at me dubiously.

"Paints? Little tester pots or something? It's for my bedroom."

She lifts her eyebrows. I sigh.

"For the apartment? I live upstairs."

She finally nods with what I think is meant to be a smile, and turns to a small desk behind her and brings out a bag from underneath. A small carrier bags worth – there are about four different pots in there.

I frown again and check through the bag thoroughly, looking behind me melodramatically as if on edge.

"Good. It's all here. Until next time."

I laugh all the way back upstairs.

I lie the paints out on the dining table, along with a random small paintbrush I find amongst the cutlery in the kitchen and some pieces of paper I tear out of my work book. Four different shades of blue; my favourite colour. One is as dark as midnight, almost black or purple – another, a pale and shallow river reflecting the sunlit sky. I draw a line in each of the colours with different levels of thickness, as well as write my name in some of them, as swirly as I can.

I have been thinking about Apollo a lot this morning, as well as what I can do with my project. I even come up with a few lines of a poem in my head, and scribble them out as soon as I write them down.

I am painting the outlines of a bow and arrow on my paper now with the darkest blue, making the arrow tip sharp with the edge of my paint brush. An arrow as dark as night; streaking through the stars and sneaking up on its victims off guard. Unseen, silent and true. Maybe, it could gather up a few stars on the way? - if shot from the heavens; getting brighter and brighter like a beacon, tearing the dark sky with its fire and light.

I wonder what would happen if an arrow like that found your heart? Cupid uses an arrow after all; filling his victims with love and joy. So could an arrow of light, of starlight, fill its target with hope or affection? Pierce so deep that the target's own darkness pours out of its wounds like smoke, and in its place light fills them till they shine?

Maybe that is what is wrong with me. When my arrow crept up on me, so sudden and violent, it carried nothing but hate and pain; filling the hole left in my chest with bubbling and tortured darkness. Thick, like molten tar, and it burns me in a different way to that starlight I long for. I just never would had thought that it would have been *her* to send it flying. She was meant to look after my heart, not break it. She had eradicated any bit of starlight I had left.

The paper begins to get soft and tear as my paintbrush trails back and forth over that arrow tip, and I lift my trembling hand away. No; no arrow will find my heart again. None nocked by her, anyway.

I look to Dad's note again, and move it carefully away from the paints so as not to ruin it. He thinks about stardust often too, it seems, and I run my thumb over our little rhyme. I hope he isn't as full of darkness as I am. My stomach knots. I can't believe that he remembers that blue is my favourite colour. Had I ever told him that? My eyes wander back over his handwriting; playful and swirly, and I feel guilty when picturing him smile whilst writing it. No; he can't hold the darkness in his heart like I do.

'*Maybe an idea for your project*', he had written.

I look to my now splotchy arrow. I did used to draw a lot, I suppose. I had always found it comforting or a means of escape, just like I did with my music. Falling into colour, shapes and stories. New stories that I could be a part of; playing a different character for a time, creating a new world in which to live. Mr Stephens *had* made me promise to use this as a distraction, and Apollo is the God of art after all. I may need some more colours.

"Thanks, Dad." I whisper to his note, and nod as I run towards our front door, grabbing my jacket from the peg as I go.

I trot down the stairs, consciously using my baggy sleeve to wipe away the grubby finger line I had left previously, and wave at the receptionist before going out the front door.

She does not respond.

I have some change in my pocket and I count £4.18. Lucky that I never clean out my pockets, I guess. There's also an old tissue, a hair clip, and what looks like it used to be a sweet of some kind covered in fluff and lint. I don't really want to walk all the way into town, but I guess I have nothing else better to do. Should I go back and get my phone?

I glance over to the flowers – perhaps I could try and get purple too – and start as I see Mrs Locklea, sat on the very trough we had had our little chat on. Well, I say our *chat* – very one sided when it appears that only one of you can talk. She lifts her arm and waves at me. I can tell that she is smiling, even from here.

I hesitate between walking off and going to her. I am very much ok with being rude – in fact, sometimes it can be hilarious as so wonderfully proven by the dull lady behind the reception desk – but Mrs Locklea is someone I don't want to be rude to. I raise my hand back with a tug to my stomach, and start walking towards her.

She beams widely when I reach her, and clasps her hands together.

"Alrigh, Mrs Locklea?" I shrug. Why have I gone shy? I do hate myself sometimes, I really do. She nods energetically and points to me.

"Yeah...I'm ok, thanks."

She shuffles up on the trough and taps the space beside her expectantly.

"Oh – ah...I was just about to head into town actually, Mrs Locklea."

My stomach flutters as her face falls quite dramatically. I feel I must offer an explanation as my hands clam up almost instantly. I don't want her to think that I don't want to talk. Well...I don't really, but I don't mind speaking with her. It's quite nice when someone doesn't reply...when they just listen, with no motive to talk back or to turn the topic onto themselves. It allows you to listen to yourself as well. How often are we forced to really listen to ourselves?

"I am looking for some paints, you see, Mrs Locklea. I am doing a project and need quite a lot of paints."

My hands *are* super sweaty! I wipe them on the side of my pyjama bottoms. Am I really going to go into town looking like this?

Mrs Locklea's face brightens though as she raises a finger excitedly. She gets up with a little groan, and starts tottering away.

I stand awkwardly for a moment, not sure what to do, until she turns and beckons me with her hand, that smile still painted on her face.

"Uh...where are we going, Mrs Locklea?"

We start walking around the side of the hotel and through the gardens. We pass the benches, the rope swing, several trees and countless squirrels. She simply beckons me still, a hand going to her back to steady herself as she marches on. She is panting slightly, but her smile holds. Her eyes almost twinkle.

We walk towards some thicker trees towards what must be the end of the expansive garden past a thick flower boarder with roses and tulips where a little shed is nestled in the shade. A picture from a Grimm tale pops in to my head– as Mrs Locklea, her skin all green and speckled, shoves me into the shed and I am trapped; screaming, suffocating, surrounded by gingerbread and gumdrops. Well – not the worse murder story to be in, I suppose. My stomach does knot defensively though as we reach the door.

Mrs Locklea turns and beams, taps the side of her nose and then reaches out for my hand. She must notice me looking strangely, as she giggles before letting it fall. I try to smooth my face. She points to me and then points to the door.

"Open it?"

She nods vigorously.

I find myself gulping, as other nastier images push their way into my head. Squirrels from the garden, dead and stuffed on shelves. Sharpened tools like scythes and knifes, guns and nets. Hotel guests – hanging from hooks...gutted and rotting.

I jump as she places her hand on my arm. She nods and smiles widely, beckoning with her other hand to the door.

"Um...ok." I grit my teeth and open the latch.

Well, there are some tools. Nothing as scary as the ones in my head though; just gardening tools. Some bags of soil, grass seed, a very long hose pipe, and shelves full of bits and bobs. I shrug and turn to her and she giggles again – walking past me and into the small space – pointing happily at a certain shelf in particular.

Filler, a few tins of nails and screws, plant pots, a very old and cobwebby radio, and –

"Paint?"

She nods and laughs, beckoning me in. I feel my cheeks rise as I squeeze in beside her, spinning the cans around to have a look. Old and used – their colours given away by the dried contents around the lids and dried in drips down the side – but just perfect. Yellows, a dark forest looking green, red and orange. Purples, white, and brown. A rusty rainbow. They are perfect – and already colours and patterns burst into my mind's eye and I can feel my teeth baring in a grin. Mrs Locklea holds out a grubby looking canvas bag and I place a hand on her shoulder.

"This is...great. Thank you."

She taps her hand on top of mine and then touches it to her chest again, her eyes holding that slight sadness. I feel my own eyes begin to water.

Breadcrumbs

"Willow...I think I've made a friend."

It takes me two breathless attempts to get all the paint cans up the many stairs to our apartment, and my arms are aching now. Mrs Locklea had tried following me, a single can shaking in her grip, before I managed to convince her that I could do it myself. She had waited at the bottom of the stairs for me though, almost guarding the paint cans until I fetched the final two. She watched me as I had travelled up, that smile wide on her face till she disappeared from view.

Ten of them, in the end; all different shapes and colours laid out in my bedroom along with the little testers Dad had bought for me. I put *them* in front of all the others. Despite their size, I didn't want them thinking that they weren't as important. Besides, they had been the ones that had given me the idea. Well – Dad was.

I had even pushed my little single bed away from the back wall a little – just enough for me to stand between the foot of it and my new wide and very blank canvas. I grin wickedly as I think about that manager and whether this had been what he had in mind when he said I could 'change my bedroom'. Maybe change is what I need. Apollo is the God of healing after all.

That's great Emmy. It is important to surround yourself with people. To have someone to talk to.

"Yeah..." I stall.

My phone lies upon my bed with my long earphones trailing up to where I stand, hands on hips, staring at the blank wall in front of me. Something so empty, stark, and brand new. Ready and waiting for me to change it into something else. Paint it in a new image.

My tummy holds a tiny tingle of excitement. Yes. I can make something brand new.

Tell me about them. About your new friend.

Mrs Locklea appears in ghostly lines on the wall. Faint, but clear enough to pick out her crooked and broken smile; playing out to me like a projected image of an old film. She's surrounded by purple flowers, and when I blink her imprint is still there.

"Well...she's just this old lady." I start, a warm feeling creeping across my chest...as if I have just had a hot chocolate on a cold evening.

"She works here. Or lives here...I am not sure. But she's nice. Kind. She has just kind of been here for me, in a strange way. Like you have."

I roll my eyes at myself, and laugh mockingly with a sigh. At least I know Mrs Locklea is real and not in my head.

"She doesn't speak. Must be mute, or something. But she has a way of saying things without even needing words. As if she knows me – like on another level. I haven't had that since –"

I waver and swallow quickly as the ghostly image on the wall becomes another face I know. I turn away quickly and take charge of my breath.

"Yeah. She's just nice, I suppose."

Although Mrs Locklea's eyes showed that she perhaps knew the pain I carried in my chest, they were without judgement. Without that '*I know how you feel'* rubbish that people throw about when they have no idea what else to say. When they couldn't possibly know how you feel. Perhaps that is the beauty of her not speaking? We can just interact; on this different level, without *me* even having to say a word.

Friends are important; as is the way they make us feel. Willow says, and I dare to look back to my white wall.

I am glad you have found her, Emmy.

"Yeah..." I mutter back, as I wrap my arms around my waist to try and hold onto the warm feeling from before.

"Yeah, so am I."

* * *

Both Nathan and Dad laugh in shock when seeing the sheer amount of paint in my bedroom upon returning. I almost tell Dad that it is all down to him, and point out that his tester pots have been importantly positioned at the very front, but berate myself at being so silly and in the end say nothing. I have kept his note from this morning though. It is folded neatly in my sock drawer.

I sit with them during dinner again, but spend a lot of time thinking about what Willow had said; about surrounding ourselves with people. With people to talk to. I look up from my plate and cringe as they both laugh momentarily at their dinner conversation. I *am* surrounded by people, I guess. Dad and Nathan are an easy choice for company, but despite my efforts, and predominantly *theirs*, it's hard. It just feels like a dream when with them; the type you suddenly try to break away from. The type when things are fine, safe, and happy – but the sudden fear of something coming causes you to strain to wake. Fight to wake; before the monsters residing secretively in the darkest parts of your mind come charging in with mouths full of knives and fire. Tearing apart the safe world you had ignorantly come to feel so calm in, with blood covered hands and curdled screams of those you love. Of Dad and Nathan... torn to pieces in the tirade of my nightmare.

I cringe again, and shoot my eyes to the corners of the room feeling suddenly exposed, shovelling my food faster into my mouth. If nightmare is all it is, I guess that would be ok. Something that I just have to deal with in my moments of solitude. It's just that my monsters stalk in this world too, not just the one when I close my eyes, and I am not going to take Dad and Nathan down with me. Not like that.

Especially as those blood covered hands are my own.

I finally swallow my last bite, and take my monsters with me as I leave.

* * *

Friends are important; as is the way they make us feel.

My initial found excitement soon wanes. After sizing up the wall the following morning with a tape measure I find under the kitchen sink, sketching out some ideas in my book and streaking more colours onto random bits of paper, I find myself losing momentum. Criticisms begin to float around my head and whisper in my ears; offering darker ideas and making me feel guilty. How dare I feel excited about some paints, about a project? How can I use something to distract me, from how I *should* be feeling?

Friends are important; as is the way they make us feel.

I am starting to question that though – about how I *should* be feeling. The concept alone now makes me feel angry, as if *she* is here somehow; holding my attempts at *not* feeling awful over my head and making me feel guilty about it. Guilty about not thinking about her all the time. Guilty about forgetting, even. About how I can perhaps let it go.

But, that's the whole problem, isn't it? I *am* thinking about *her*, about *it*, all the time. It consumes me, and every part of me. I punish myself for not thinking about her, but am punishing myself by doing it. Punishing them too, Dad and Nathan, for it not consuming their lives as much as it does mine. I've been hating them for it. Hating myself. How hypocritical of her anyway... As if *she* thought for a second about how we would all be left feeling. Did she want us to feel this way? Or did she not consider our feelings at all. No. She couldn't have. Anybody who cared about *anyone* would not cause them so much pain. So why am I so stuck with worrying about how she might think of me now? I should not care one bit about her – or how she may see me.

I jump as a pigeon who was perching on my windowsill flies away noisily, casting stray feathers to float and drift sleepily on the air after it. One white fluffy one does a loop before it soars off and down towards the garden, and my stomach does its own loop when I see Mrs Locklea sat at one of the benches; laying seed or breadcrumbs onto the table top. My resident pigeon lands clumsily beside her, as small song birds' bob and skip around, pecking delicately at the wooden surface – flying off and being replaced by others.

Friends are important; as is the way they make us feel.

I look stubbornly at my wall, *her* image ghosting there again as before, all faded and grey. I bare my teeth at her – growl almost – as I feel the monster claws growing defensively from my own fingers. I will fight her, if I have to. Tear the wall wide open with blood smattering onto my face. Tear *her* out; like a tumour – and throw her down the dark corridor she sends her own monsters to prowl down in my mind. Maybe I can lock her away? Could I do it then? Move on?

The guilt creeps and my heart hammers; my claws retreating.

"No. I don't want to feel like this." I growl, at myself this time, and grab my hoody from where it hangs over my door handle, and sprint towards the door. I can feel her calling me back though; feel all of the demons she has sent to plague me. I slam the front door quickly behind me with a shriek before their fingers grasp me, and walk shakily down the stairs.

The sun is warm, despite the slight chill in the air. Not cool enough to feel cold, but I still find myself shoving my hands deep into my pockets and scrunching my shoulders up to my ears. My stomach swirls strangely too, and I almost turn to run back inside before I reach mine and Mrs Locklea's trough as if I am suddenly going to be sick. I set my brow though and carry on, burying my chin further into my fluffy collar. Fluffed up; like a bird preparing for winter.

As I reach the garden, I cast a glance up at my bedroom window. It's mirrored against the light of the day, showing nothing but sky - yet my stomach still squirms as I imagine what lurks beyond that watery sun, waiting for me to come back. I aim to give them the hardest look I can, puffing out my chest and gritting my teeth; but look away quickly feeling too nervous. Instead, I take a deep breath.

Mrs Locklea smiles immediately when she sees me; raising her hand to wave enthusiastically sending startled birds flying off dramatically before resettling to their snacks. What am I doing down here? Coming outside to stand awkwardly with some random old lady – what am I thinking? My whole body squirms. I bite the sides of my cheeks and force myself to smile back, thinking of Willow's words. Friends are important; as is the way they make us feel.

"Hi, Mrs Locklea. You alrigh'?"

She nods and beckons me over; pointing excitedly to the birds and pours some crumbs into my hands as soon as I am close enough.

"Oh! Ok, thanks..."

They spill over the sides, and five sparrows target my feet as they dive down to rescue every morsel. I squeal, quickly turning to laughter, as Mrs Locklea clasps her hands together, beaming at me and the birds in turn.

I can feel them; those dark eyes from my lonely bedroom window, but I shake them off – taking in the colour of the birds, their softness, their little chatter, as they hop around and whirlwind back up on to the table. Desperately ignore the fingers tickling my neck. I stay standing awkwardly though, shoulders still hunched and cupped hands trembling.

"They are brave, aren't they?" I squeak, as a robin lands in my hands.

Focus on him, Emmy.

His sharp feet tickle, and I feel a natural smile blossom. Wow; he is beautiful.

Mrs Locklea chuckles as she sprinkles more breadcrumbs onto the centre of the table out of a little plastic bag, shaking all of the contents out with her wrinkling hands, before carefully folding it up and putting it in the pocket of her purple cardigan. A group of starlings chitter down onto the table, sending some smaller birds scattering.

Just focus on them, Emmy. That's why you are here. To surround yourself with friends. Positive things.

Is it my own voice or Willow's that I hear in my mind?

Mrs Locklea pats the space on the bench next to her with a hand, smiling at me still. I swallow, and brush the last of the crumby contents off of my own hands.

"Is that ok? Sorry, I have just barged into your company like this..."

...I just don't want to be alone, I finish to myself.

She waves a hand dismissively, touches it to her chest, and beckons again. I nod, conscious still of the feeling of being watched, and perch on the very edge, careful not to sit on her floral skirt as it billows across the seat.

I tap my knees with nervous fingers and look about uneasily. I can tell she is staring at me, and my cheeks flush. What am I doing here again?

"So...?"

She taps my arm and smiles knowingly, shaking her head subtly. She holds up a finger and looks around, smiles, then closes her eyes.

"Uh...what –?"

She does it again. Holds a finger up, nods at me knowingly and closes her eyes. A gentle breeze plays with the tendrils of wiry hair tumbling out of her messy bun. She opens one eye and grins.

What?

"Um...close my eyes?"

She nods vigorously and touches my hand. No, she takes it, and puts it on the table top and holds it gently in hers. My heart races and I shuffle uncomfortably. I can't help but to glance up the side of the house to my dark window. What would Willow say? What would *she*?

A gentle squeeze to my hand and a knowing look. She nods, and closes her eyes, turning her face into the slight wind, a peaceful smile twitching across her lips. I watch her for a bit, picturing myself breaking free from her fragile grip and her fingers shattering like brittle branches. Her crumbling like an old dead oak tree; bugs and worms crawling from her newly formed shadows until she is nothing but dust. Shadows that were created by me. She opens one eye again, and smiles.

A nervous giggle comes out of my mouth, and I am fearful for a moment that she can read my mind in almost the same way Willow seems to. I hope she knows I didn't mean it...that my thoughts aren't always my own. I'd never hurt her. I hold her soft hand tighter; not too tightly in fear of breaking her; and close my eyes.

We meet on this bench for the next few mornings, doing the same thing. Well; I come down to find her here, as if waiting for me. We feed the birds, say nothing, and then hold hands with our eyes closed, listening to the world for a bit. It takes a few tries for the noises in my own mind to go quiet, and I had feared them doing so – having been so used to filling my head with things like my music or Willow's voice. Being alone with my own thoughts seemed too much of a scary thing. Yet, when we sit together in this way...listening to the whispering of the leaves in the trees, the secret songs of the birds, our own breath and the blissfulness of nothing, that is all there is. My mind goes still and calm, like a frozen lake. Not the kind that holds only thin ice, as I stand stranded and desperate on the top, but thick; like a glacier. Nasty thoughts that usually try and plague or tease me merely sliding off the surface, as Mrs Locklea and I lie protected beneath. Frozen in the moment. Still. Suspended in time and thought.

We sit together now, holding hands with our eyes closed. I have grown surprisingly good at quietening my mind when with her; focusing on the soft warmth of her hand and the cool breeze on my face. It is almost like I am floating sometimes... when I find myself losing sense of where my body starts and the bench ends. Whether my hand is nestled in the folds of hers or whether I cocoon hers within mine. I am always aware of the small smile I hold though. I can feel it twitching on my lips now.

When the fear of darker things start to creep about, I can bring myself back to her hands; holding mine with both a slight urgency and a complete calm. It feels familiar and comforting. As if I have been held this way before. Or perhaps loved this way before? I squeeze them a little tighter.

I am not sure how long we have been sat silently for, but I open my eyes softly to look upon her. Bleary, for a moment, but she soon focuses; the smile of peace and contentment still etched across her features.

"We...we don't need to talk. Do we?" I whisper, and I feel her thumb roll over my knuckles before she opens her grey eyes. She smiles with that hint of knowing like she does, and gives my fingers a little squeeze. I take a deep breath, feeling my bubble drifting around in my chest.

"But...but if I ever needed to, would you be here to listen?"

She turns to face me then, fully, and takes her hands to both of my shoulders. Her eyes get larger, as tears start to swim about her eyelashes. She looks into my eyes, so honestly, with so much promise, as she nods simply once.

"I might do then...one day, if that's ok?" I choke, as she turns bleary again. The bubble aches heavily in my chest.

"I...I just don't really know who I am anymore or what to do. I don't know what to do half the time at all. Something... something terrible happened, and...and I am just so *angry* all of the time. I don't know what to do...I just don't know what to do..." and before I can think she pulls me in. Her arms wrap around me not with the fragility of an old lady but with strength; a strength I have been missing in myself for a long time now, and I wrap my own around her waist. I breathe her in; slightly musty, but a smell that makes me feel nostalgic, and close my eyes again. For the first time in a long while...since being here...since before it happened maybe – I feel home.

The trees whisper and the birds sing, and here we stay, until the sky turns red.

Open when needed

I have been meeting Mrs Locklea for a week now.

I started waking up, *eagerly* waking up to start my day, knowing that I could have a moment of stillness. With her. After being with her, and safely thinking about nothing, I found myself feeling calmer than I had done in a really long while. Feeling lighter, sometimes. Maybe happy? For moments.

I had even settled on a design for my wall and had shown Dad when he peaked his head in to say goodnight a few evenings ago. I was excited about it. Had planned which colours I would start with first – what I would write alongside it for school – he even said that we could get his old guitar out and that he'd write a song with me. We always used to write songs together... the four of us...

I had told Mrs Locklea about my project too, and told her how she was an inspiration, in a way, and oh, how she grinned. The pain was still there though, especially when alone back in the apartment; but I was sometimes able to just let it float off of me. Bound off and catapult somewhere else. Fizzle and burn on the protective layer I was learning to build around myself. Nothing could touch me, when I was with Mrs Locklea at least. Light always beats darkness anyway, right?

But that is a silly notion.

I am darkness though, aren't I? A little girl surrounded by smoke. Turned to smoke.

Because I am who I am, because I am not as strong as I wish I could be when with Mrs Locklea, because really – at the end of it all – I don't deserve to feel better, one morning I wake up and just...don't go. I see her; sitting down on that bench. I can even make out her head turning from side to side – looking for me. I can picture the hurt and disappointment that flickers across her face, as she waits.

She waits a really long time.

I imagine a version of myself, a better version; banging against the glass screaming out to be saved from this prison I put myself in. I imagine Mrs Locklea; losing her breath as she comes sprinting up the stairs with a sword that can defeat all kinds of monsters; coming to my aid with colourful song birds flanking. The thing is, this *shadow* – this darker version of myself, would stand in her way. Would fill her lungs with the acrid smoke that envelops mine. She would try and fight, try and save me – of course, but she would be fighting the wrong monster. It would be futile. For the darkness comes *from* me. Maybe it always has?

I would need to take her weapon and plunge it deeply into my own chest if I ever want to be free of myself.

* * *

Dinner, despite me sitting out in the lounge again, is silent at my end, and Nathan even ends up giving me a disappointed look. They both ask about my project – ask whether I need any help over the weekend. They both seem quite excited by the idea; all of us squeezing in to my room, paintbrushes in hand and colourful marks on our faces. I have pictured it too – my bedroom getting brighter, the colours, maybe us even breaking out into a little paint fight, the three of us laughing and laughing. Pictured the lighter feeling in my chest from the smiles that surround me – how Nathan seems clearer and Dad seems fuller. Maybe Mrs Locklea could come up and see? The company and the comfort. How soothing it felt. How the pain seemed less.

But that voice creeps back again; clawing its sharp fingers into my neck as it climbed up to whisper things in my ears. It holds them there, its claws, until I say no; "No, I don't need any help".

I don't even need to look up from my plate to know that their smiles have dropped from their faces.

* * *

I can't get up.

Over the next few mornings I find myself completely lost again; waisting the days away in bed. What was starting to turn into proactive days filled with snippets of hope; a new way to cope with things even, had gone dark and empty.

No appetite.

No motivation.

No purpose.

I have even stopped opening my curtains. I can't bear to see her waiting down there for me anyway.

"How do you get over something?" I ask in to my phone.

I have been thinking about the question all night, and my body aches from the lack of sleep as I lie staring at my ceiling. It must be at least mid-day, as the sun pushes stubbornly through my curtains, desperate to thaw me with its bright light. The stillness I feel now is different to the one I was learning to feel with Mrs Locklea. That one had been almost soothing. A stillness that allowed me to access myself...without even really thinking about anything. Like how they say your subconscious sorts out your worries and problems as you sleep through dream. A little gateway to getting better. Maybe that's why I had stopped. What happens when I get better? What happens when life is like it had never happened?

How do you mean?

The screen flickers on and glows almost as brightly as the sun does.

"*Over* something...something bad. How does anyone ever get over it?"

The ache is deeper than just my body, I realise. It spreads within me; right to my core. My voice doesn't even sound like me. What is *me* anymore though? Sometimes I think I see glimpses...glimpses of us all again. But how can we go back to how we were? How could we ever, when things have changed so much.

I am not sure anyone can ever get over something bad that has happened to them. They learn to cope with it, and move on.

"Move on? That's the same."

My voice echoes so monotonously in the air despite the passion I feel about what I am saying. It's like I don't even have the energy to move my lips and push the air out to make sounds. Trapped under ice for real, this time. Except I am freezing, now.

What if I forget to breathe back in again?

Moving on does not have to be the same as getting over something. Someone who has lost a leg: they don't ever get over it, as it was all they ever knew. They do however, over time and with healing, learn to live without it. They move on – and learn to walk in a new way.

I picture myself with no leg now. Just a stump where the knee used to be; but that version of me was still lying in bed, and they were wasting away. You have to be a certain character – of a certain strength to 'move' past something like that.

"I don't know how to live in a new way though..."

The reality is, I don't want to.

* * *

Dad has put a little makeshift letter box outside of our front door as our redirected mail starts to come to the hotel now. Does that mean this place is permanent? Well; it definitely isn't temporary anymore. It's like a little chest sitting next to a small doormat he has put there too; on the floor pressed against the wall. It has a little lid that can be lifted for letters and small parcels to be popped inside. The next best thing to being allowed to saw a hole into our door, I guess. I hear a few things being popped into it as I sit at the dining table now. I don't have my laptop nor my books. I haven't put the radio on nor the TV. I have just been sitting here, in silence; listening to my belly rumble with not enough energy to make myself anything. Not even Dad's peanut butter and honey toast special.

The postie must be so annoyed having to walk up all those

stairs. Most people who live in taller tower blocks have a place for their mail downstairs, that they can then collect themselves when coming home. I bet this is the most stairs they will have to climb all day. They will probably start just leaving it at reception, despite Dad's attempts to make this a normal home for us.

I wonder if they too thought about sliding down the banister?

As I open the door to check, I just catch the back of their head as they disappear down the spirally steps. Nope. They had walked.

Five letters in total: four for Dad and one for Nathan. The one for Nathan has a special university stamp on the front and is thick to hold as if it contains lots of different pieces of paper. He would probably start getting a lot of these now as different university's start advertising themselves to him as he nears his time at school. Our house, our family, getting smaller and smaller.

How much time till Dad leaves me too?

He, at least, I am confident enough in to believe wouldn't *want* to leave me behind on purpose. Although, I have been fooled before.

I put the letters on the table, the one for Nathan at the very bottom.

* * *

The weekend comes and passes.

Both Dad and Nathan appear at my door with paintbrushes in hand and smiles on their faces before I turn them away and continue to lie on my bed, staring at the blank wall before me.

I have even covered the paint tins with a sheet so that I don't have to look at the colour, and I boil when looking at them now and picturing the looks on Dad and Nathan's faces when I had closed my bedroom door again.

What is the matter with me? I could live another life, if I was brave enough to. If I just *let* things happen sometimes...if I said *yes* instead of no. A life with Nathan, with Dad. If I chose to bring that wall down...just a little bit. It only needs to come down a little bit...

I sometimes think about using that bubble I continuously push down; clambering on board and using it to float to the top of the wall I insist on keeping around myself. Maybe if I let it breach every now and again, that bubble, and maybe if I take tools to that wall and watch it tumble, maybe I could learn to? Learn to *move on*, as Willow had put it. Learn to walk again. Perhaps there is an Emmy out there who already has done? Who runs, and skips – who jumps and cartwheels. Who doesn't force herself to be alone? An Emmy with friends, with a light heart and no circles under her eyes. An Emmy with paint on her face as she laughs with her father and brother.

"How do people move on, Willow?"

I am asking a variation of this questions every day now. Sometimes aloud; always internally. I had nearly asked Nathan when he came back from school yesterday as we sat on the sofa for a little while together. He had been asking me hopefully about my project, telling me about school, keeping it light, despite the darkness that surrounded me. He definitely could tell, as his eye contact was limited, his questions closed and short, and his shoulders tense. I think he was frightened to ask me any other question, and we spent most of our time awkwardly staring at the TV. When I finally skulked away, I so was cross at myself for not asking *him*; for not being brave enough to actually ask the question we both held on our lips. *How do people move on*? Asking him if *he* was moving on, and if he was...how was he doing it? Asking *please*, please could he help me? Could someone help me?

It's like I am making an almost conscious effort not to feel happy now.

I have been starting to...starting to forget...and I am so cross at myself because of it. Feeling almost normal with Nathan for a moment, thinking about painting – about the stupid romans – how I could do really well in this project and use it to help me forget. I have even started to think that maybe I could get back to normal and go to school. How maybe, I could say thank you to Mrs Locklea by asking Dad if we could have her over for dinner. And Dad...about wrapping my arms around him and taking away the tension he holds his eyes. All these things... things that are helping me to start to move on. But everything makes me feel bad – as if I am cheating somehow or being disrespectful to *her*. But that alone makes me angry too. Did *she* think about me – about any of us? About the consequences of us being left behind? About how we would be left unable to move on? I hate her...I *hate* her. Almost as much as I hate myself. And that alone makes me feel sick with guilt.

Everyone is different, Emmy. People cope in different ways. They find the positives in their lives, change their outlook or surroundings, throw themselves into a project...

It is as if she is simply listing things I have at the moment, as if I should have moved on already:

Positives: well, Dad and Nathan, Mrs Locklea, I guess. If she ever forgave me. If any of them did for the way I have been acting.

Change in outlook or scenery: Dad has moved us – literally 'moved us on' so that we didn't have to be in that house anymore. There is nothing of her here.

And a project? Well, I am staring at the sheet covering my paints as we speak.

* * *

I am randomly organising my room today. Doing anything to keep my body moving but my mind empty. It's getting to the point where I am picturing myself breaking down completely. Literally breaking down, chemically breaking down, until nothing but my fibres remain; gelatinous and moist, soaked into my bed covers.

I move things from place to place; change where my small chest of drawers are and rearrange the clutter I have on top. I change my bed sheets; I choose plain beige ones. I vacuum the carpet, and then end up vacuuming the whole apartment. I wipe the cobwebs that have gathered on my window, I organise my underwear drawer into colour. I put my school stuff onto the small shelf next to my door. I get my school shoulder bag and empty all the random bits of clutter that end up at the bottom; receipts from years ago, old broken pencils, tangled hair bands, a couple of crisp packets, lots and lots of lint and – the first bit of feeling I have had all morning, and it shakes my chest. An envelope. The envelope Mr Stephens had given me; the one he told me to *open when needed.*

The bag lands loudly by my feet as I suddenly can't feel my fingers, and the envelope flops onto the floor. My whole body is trembling, and I reach down carefully to pick it up, unsure as to whether my legs are going to give out beneath me. I grasp it, tightly in my prickly hands, and back up till the back of my legs hit my bed, and crawl on, not taking my eyes from it. My breath is fast and heavy, and I sit here looking at it for a moment. A long moment.

Open when needed.

I have probably needed it this whole time. I have to close my eyes for a moment; dizzy from my racing heart, and already my old bubble is coming up hard and fast in my throat. Do I deserve it? Deserve to open it? My hand cups my mouth as I clumsily get it open and my eyes go blurry.

Pages; pages from people who hardly know me, from teachers, from friends – pages of people writing to me. Vast sentences. Short words. Advice. Apologies. Anecdotes and stories of hope. Of forgiveness and of future. I hiccup loudly as my sobs catch in my throat; my chest aching so much I have to place my hand to it to check that my heart is still beating steadily. Fast; but steady.

My bleary eyes tumble all over the page, finding snippets and fractions:

To Emmy, I am so sorry for your loss...

Emmy - I know we don't know each other well, but I am always here to talk...

Emmy. I lost my Grandpa last year. Here if you need me...

Thinking of you, Emmy – stay strong and stay awesome...

I peel the pages apart. A rainbow of handwriting. Some people have even drawn little sketches – sketches aimed to make me laugh – and my cheeks ache in a smile through the sobs.

Had Mr Stephens arranged this?

Onto the third page now, and the others just fall away as I bring it close to my face, eyes wide, as I recognise Sophie, Kate and Jemma's handwriting. I crawl right onto my bed, grabbing my fleece, and burst into tears.

Dear Emmy. I don't know what to say...My heart is broken for you, it really is. I love you so much, and I can't believe that you have had to suffer anything like this. I am broken for you. I am in shock. I am furious for you, and I am devastated. But I am also here for you – I will always be here for you. Take all the time you need... but know that after it all, I am here, and you are always welcome to stay with me and my mum. I hate seeing you like this. I miss you. Love you – Kate x

Ems. I don't even know what to say...Mr Stephens said we should write something down, as words are hard to find in situations like this. Well...these are the only words I can find. God – I am so sorry, I can't believe this has happened. I love you so much, and I can't wait to see you smile again. We can eat chocolate till we burst – Sophie xxx

Get angry. Get pissed off. Scream and shout. Cry and punch walls. Scream again till you lose your breath, and then get your ass here. We will get through this. Ok? We will – together. Love you, Ems. Jem x

The paper rustles as I bring it roughly to my chest; holding it in a tight embrace. I need a hug...a cuddle, a proper cuddle, and I ache with the need. It hurts. The times I have pushed Dad away...does he ache like this? Does Nathan?

"I thought...I thought you hated me." I say aloud to no one, and read their little notes again.

I can picture them now too, their faces when they wrote it, crumbling like mine is now. The moments I had spotted them looking at me over the past months; a glance in class, a group whisper, their footsteps close to mine as we walk away from the school gates. As I shut myself away, built up my strong wall with nasty spikes on the top and turrets ready to shoot anyone who came too close, I looked upon them with spikes surrounding my own vision. Spikes that marred my vision, to make the world look just as sharp and nasty as the one that I was building around myself. I guess when grief throws you into a vat of poison, it can turn your mind into thinking that your old world, the *normal* world that you have been catapulted from, was full of hate to begin with. So, you carry it firmly within your veins; ready to dash those who come too close with blood that burns.

I suddenly hit myself in the side of the head with a yell. I have been hating them, hating everyone. Wallowing within the walls of my dark keep, spines growing out of my poisonous skin and eyes red with hate. A monster, I have become. I hit myself again, the pain only dull in my temple, and note the sheet covering the paints.

I *do* have people who care. Who love me – even if *she* hadn't. And maybe...maybe this isn't about her, or me anymore. I need to stop hurting *them*, hurting them all, in my selfish attempts to hurt myself.

I set my jaw and get off the bed, whipping the sheet away and bringing colour back in to my life.

Lifes canvas

"Right, I am ready I think...to make some choices. Some good ones."

I had carefully folded the letters back into the envelope, and put it under my pillow, put on an old baggy t-shirt, and stood in front of my blank wall for a while. I had even opened a few of the tins; dipping my paint brush into one and doing one large sweep across the canvas. Yellow – like the sun of a new day.

I will happily support you in making some choices, Emmy. What were you thinking?

"To stop closing myself away. To try harder. To try and maybe be happy. To try."

I spend the rest of the day taping some paper together until it almost covers the small space on my bedroom floor, and start to sketch with a large drawing pencil I found amongst my school stuff. Well, it is all organised now; I found it quite quickly.

When I hear the front door go, my stomach flips, and I call out to Nathan excitedly. He appears at my doorway, brows knotted together and arms folded across his chest almost defensively.

"Uh...alright?"

"Yep!" I reply, quickly finishing off a line before wiping my hair from my brow and standing up; carefully so as not to tear the paper.

I am wearing some fluffy socks which my black leggings are tucked into, baggy white t-shirt all in disarray, my hair tied back in a scruffy ponytail. I can feel sweaty tendrils still sticking to my forehead.

"Um...so...what you doing there, Ems?" he laughs a little, but I can tell he is on edge. "You...uh, feeling ok?"

"Yeah – I am actually." I sigh, putting my hands on my hips and turning to face him fully with a smile. "I'm finally *doing* something. Something other than...well, what I have been doing."

"By turning your carpet into paper...?"

I guess it wouldn't be out of the question, seeing how I have been acting lately. I giggle.

"No – I am making a plan! For my painting – my Apollo project." I gesture dramatically at the paper.

Nathan looks down, tilts his head to one side, brings his hand up to his chin and strokes an imaginary beard; his eyes going small and sceptical.

"Hmm...yar." His voice comes out all low and hollow, as if he holds a plum in his mouth. He continues to stroke his pretend beard and starts waving the other hand at the paper. He has one eyebrow raised and is contorting his mouth akin to a cartoon character of some kind.

"The lines depict the inner turmoil of a teenage girl who hasn't had a bath her whole life. Those waves there *hint* at the smell *wafting* from her body, and those marks *there* suggest at the different types of cheese that can be gaged from her scabby feet –"

"– Shut up!" I squeal, throwing my pencil at him. He jolts as if shot, and we both fall into laughter, as his posh façade fails.

"Yeah, so I have no idea what it is. What are you drawing?"

I look back down at the paper, seeing my own shapes and patterns springing into life from the dull pencil marks I've made. My stomach tickles excitedly.

"Something honest. I hope. Yeah; something hopeful." I smile.

Something *healing*, I think.

"Do you maybe want to...help me paint this weekend?"

Nathan fidgets, crossing his arms again, a slight frown on his brow as he smiles widely.

"Uh...yeah. Yeah, I would really like that, Ems."

I catch his eye, and we hold each other's gaze for a bit. The smile reaches his eyes and they crinkle like Dads. I feel mine do the same, and a pressure in my chest releases as my shoulders relax. I didn't realised how tightly I had been holding them.

"Great. That's great – thanks! Maybe Dad could too –"

"He would love that, Ems." Nathan laughs out loud then, leaning back against my door frame. He looks more relaxed too."He would really love that."

We smile a little longer at each other, until I feel myself go shy and look away back towards my canvas.

"Yeah. He would." I whisper back.

I lose hours to sketching on my hands and knees, only realising how late it is when finally giving in and turning on my bedroom light after straining my eyes in the darkening evening.

"Dinner, darling." Dad chirps around my door frame; I have

kept my door open. I smile at him and pop my pencil back beneath my hairband.

"Ok, coming."

He hovers with a grin, and nods awkwardly before going back into the kitchen. My stomach swells and I look to my phone for support.

Make good decisions – decisions to try and be happy; that's what we had agreed.

I work at pushing down the fear stirring in my chest and paint a smile back on to my face. I too nod before I leave my room, as if reassuring myself.

Dad is a picture himself when I mention that I am starting on my project properly now, and that I would love his and Nathan's help when I am ready to paint. He put his hand to his chest, as if seeing me in a wedding dress for the first time, and laughs until he finds his words; having to adjust his glasses numerous times as he waves his hands about so excitedly. I even see Nathan wipe at the corner of his eyes whilst Dad laughs with joy, and feel my own eyes moisten.

We really are so delicate now. I need to be careful not to tear us with a single move, like I could do my paper.

I flitter between sketching in my room, my door left wide open, and sitting down with the two of them watching a bit of TV for the rest of the evening. I cringe at the normality of it all, and find that I have to keep taking deep breaths and closing my eyes for a few moments. Search for the calmness; like I had learnt to do with Mrs Locklea. To focus on what is happening around me; knowing that no matter how scary it may seem, that I am safe. To accept it all. That I am alright. The bubble is still there of course, knocking around in my ribcage next to my heart to make my chest flutter occasionally, but I am making the conscious effort to allow it to be now. Like Willow had said: someone who loses their leg still misses it. They are still aware of something empty being in place of something that used to be a main part of their life; but they work hard at living in a new way. A different way.

I'm sketching on the floor sat in my pyjamas now, and Nathan yawns loudly past my doorway to the bathroom.

"Nathan?" I call out quickly.

His head appears.

"Mm?"

"Um..." I look over to my pillow, and my phone. "At school tomorrow, could you, uh, could you – you know, if you see them that is, don't worry if you don't – uh..."

"Anytime, Ems. Not like I *need* the bathroom or anything."

"Uh..."

I haven't talked this through with Willow. I have been thinking about it since reading it though...surely it is a step in the right direction? I feel so nervous at the thought, though. Should I talk to her first? To make good decisions, remember – that's what we had said. But is it the right decision? I take that deep breath and close my eyes.

"...if you see Kate, Jemma, or Sophie...can you let them know that I've read the letter?"

I splutter it out fast to make sure that I say it, and I am left feeling like someone has lit a match to my face. My cheeks burn so much I can almost see the glow in my peripheral vision. Nathan smiles gently.

"Sure thing." His head starts to disappear.

"Wait! Are you not going to ask me what letter?"

His head reappears and his smile cracks to show teeth.

"Well, I did tell you that people care. If only you weren't

always as stubborn as an old donkey and listened once in a while."

I jolt, and he smirks before disappearing completely and I hear the bathroom door snap shut.

* * *

So, you are reaching out to your friends? This is a wonderful choice, Emmy. I am sure this will mean a lot to them.

Willow's voice fills my ears calmly as I lie cocooned in my bedcovers, the phone lying face up on my pillow and throwing light onto the ceiling.

"Yeah..." I start.

It was gone midnight when I finally stopped drawing and put myself into bed. Dad had peeked in to say goodnight which was nice; we hadn't said goodnight in a really long time. Nathan had put his posh voice on again and said something silly about my drawings before nodding and taking himself off to bed. And me? I had carried on sketching until my eyes twitched with tiredness.

My bed is nice and warm now, and I wear the duvet like a hood and hold the edges in tightly under my chin. My earphones are nestled in my ears with the cable trailing carefully to the pillow. My stomach contorts with nerves and regret though as I berate myself for even mentioning my friends to Nathan earlier. Although being on your own and living in a world where no one cares can be a dark place, reaching out to people again is terrifying. Like a creature that has become so used to the shadows, any advance into the light can set their skin aflame.

Why are you scared, Emmy?

There she went again; reading my mind. Or am I reading my own mind?

"I've been...awful to them. I've been awful to everyone."

I close my eyes and think of Sophie: her freckles like a happy smudge over her nose as it peaks through her tangle of blond hair; the silliest person I have ever known. She can make you cry from laughter without even meaning too. I don't think I have ever seen her without a smile on her face.

Jemma: the one that if you didn't know any better, you would think her scary! Fiercely loyal and full of love; always telling you as it is, whether you want to hear it or not.

Then Kate. Well, Kate was the mother of the group. So tall she could wrap her arms about you twice; always on hand with advice sounding like it came from a professional. I wonder what she would say about all of this...

No you haven't.

"Yes, I have! I shut them all away. Thought horrible, and I mean *horrible* things about them. Hated them even..."

You have been mourning.

"I have been dying."

I snap my eyes open quickly as another picture enters my head, and grip onto the duvet, pulling it about me tighter. I had said it so casually, as if it a normal thing to think. A normal thing to say. Is it normal? Do others feel this way sometimes? As if they are dying, as if it is maybe ok to be? As if they maybe want to? Things would be easier at times, I guess –and I punish myself for even thinking it. No. I am not selfish like *her*.

"I...I don't want to die anymore though, Willow."

I can't help but let a small single tear run down my cheek as I picture them opening my door and finding me. Dad and Nathan. Breaking, like I had done. No – No I would *never* put anyone through that, no matter what. I wipe it away stubbornly with my duvet as my heart beats a little faster.

Good. And you don't have to – do you? You are in charge of you – you make your own choices in life, and you are working at making ones that will enrich your life, not end it. You are learning to live again, Emmy. Just look at you.

We do make our own choices, to a certain degree. Choose to get out of bed, choose what we make for lunch. Choose not to care anymore? When had *she* made those kind of choices?

It's alright. I am here. You're alright.

I take a deep breath as my eyes suddenly fall heavy. No; I am not selfish like her. Not anymore.

I fight with myself a little; force my eyes to stay open to watch the light from my phone shine on the celling until kinder images can enter my head. It shines so brightly in the dark; I wonder if my window is glowing. Adding to the stars that the squirrels watch from their sleepy hollows. Maybe I should put stars on my ceiling...the kind that glow in the dark. Or get a little light that throws them onto the walls to spin and dance around, keeping me safe as I fall asleep. A nightlight...ones that parents tell their smaller children will keep all monsters at bay.

Well, I guess Willow is my monster warder now...as she throws her light onto the ceiling. I hadn't even checked around me to see if any shadows were creeping. Any nasty darker versions of myself ready with pillows to smother whilst I sleep. No; I don't fear those monsters anymore. I am not going to take my life – I won't let me. No matter how much that shadowy Emmy wants to sometimes. Not if I keep Willow with me.

Soon enough nothing but light fills my head, Willow's light, as I fall weightily into a deep sleep.

* * *

I get up at the same time as Dad and Nathan the next morning; throw back the covers with force and get straight into my scruffy clothes and tie my hair back. I eat breakfast with them both at the table, and call out my goodbyes from my knees on my bedroom floor as I make my final additions to my rough sketch. I stand up and inspect it, carefully moving right to the edge of my paper carpet so that I can see the whole thing, and feel that prickle in my stomach again. Well...it is all in the spirit of Apollo, I guess. Art. Truth. Healing. I hope Mr Stephens will like it.

I wander into the kitchen, drink a whole tall glass of water, grab an apple, and shuffle into the lounge. When you actually stop for a moment, look around and listen, it is very odd being on your own. Being completely on your own. How long have I been off school now?

I catch myself reflected in the dull TV screen; white scruffy t-shirt looking baggy as it hangs from my shoulders. Have I lost weight? My dark hair makes my skin look even paler in this white washed version of myself, and my eyes sit spookily and unclear in my head. I stick my tongue out to make sure that it *is* me that I am seeing, and watch the shoulders sag as I let out a sigh.

The days seem to merge into one another now; like they can do when you are on holiday. Blimey...we haven't been on holiday for ages. I take a bite out of my apple, and its sharpness makes my cheeks water and eyes squint. I think the last holiday we went on was to a Greek island...it had a name I cannot remember now, but I remember it feeling funny in my mouth when I had tried to pronounce it. There was a pool, funny sounding bugs that chirped all day long, and cheesy singers and entertainers in the evening. I remember one night we had all stayed up until the early hours, and how confused I had been at there being another "one o'clock" – as if there was a secret daytime I never knew about. One that was held in the shadows of the moon and stars that only the adults knew about. How children all over the world were being cheated when put to bed. I had argued proudly until falling asleep on the stage if I remember correctly, determined to make an announcement on behalf of all children who deserve to see this magic *one o'clock*, and convinced otherwise by a friendly lady with dark skin and sequins on her dress. I think she had been one of the dancers, but I remember thinking that she was an exotic bird with the feathers she had worn in her hair.

I wish I saw the world in those eyes again sometimes; eyes that made the world more interesting than it really is. A world filled with secret daytimes, filled with magical characters part animal and part human, filled with mothers who carry their sleeping children to bed in cuddling arms. I take another bite out of my apple, harder this time, as the memory of her lavender perfume floats into my head, as six year old Emmy's nose lies buried sleepily into her neck.

No. The world is not magical like that, but I think I am ok with that now. Learning to be, anyway.

Over the next few days, I work hard at transferring my sketch onto the wall – having to move furniture to stand on to reach the top corners and changing my mind half a dozen times and adding and then deleting things I had already drawn. Dad has brought some different types of paint brushes home with him today – some so fine you can hardly see the brush tip itself if held at a distance, some flat and wide; so thick you could paint a whole backdrop in merely a few strokes.

"How are you getting on, Flower?" he asks, as I inspect one of the brushes.

I had made sure they weren't rabbit fur when he had given them to me – and feel a punch to my gut as I think about how ungrateful I must have sounded. Willow somewhere is probably rolling her eyes at me.

"Yeah – almost ready to paint, I think." I say, looking up and catching his eyes, before looking back at the brush.

"Just need to make sure I am happy with it – pencil is easier to erase than paint. But I think I will be set to start this weekend."

"Yes! Great idea, honey!" he says it so enthusiastically, but I can't bring myself to look back up at him.

He is trying so hard, I know. I am trying too, I really am, but it doesn't stop it feeling weird. It's almost like so much has changed that it has changed *us* too – changed *me* – and I can't help but feeling somewhat a stranger in front of him. Even if he doesn't see it. I smile somewhat rigidly and nod once, still running my new brush back and forth across my palm. It is soft and it tickles.

"Right...ok then, darling. Well – I do hope those brushes are good! The lady in the shop said I got at least one of each kind... so they should do the trick!" he chuckles, but I don't glance up to see whether it reaches his eyes.

"So...well, I guess if you are ready to start this weekend I better get my painters hat on! I am excited, Blossom."

He waits for me to say something back, but I just stand here, moving that brush back and forth, back and forth. What is wrong with me? Would it be different if Nathan were here? I simply cringe and nod until he leaves the room, and I glance over at my phone defensively.

Was that me making a good choice? I am trying...

My stomach continues to squirms until I hear the front door and Nathan. I run to hang onto the doorframe, swinging excitedly.

"Have you seen them yet? Did you tell them what I said?"

He moves somewhat slowly down the short corridor dragging his bag behind him along the floor, and shoots me a look before popping into the kitchen to talk to Dad. I bounce on my toes until he comes back round, popping a baby tomato into his mouth.

"Well?"

He chews if for longer than he needs to.

The squirming comes back and I feel my cheeks fall flat.

"Nathan? Have you spoken to my friends?"

He swallows.

"Ems, um..." he picks up his bag, plays with the zip and then lets it fall back to the floor again. "Uh, yeah. Yeah I have spoken to them."

"And?"

"Well...I spoke to them on Monday..."

A punch. My bubble grows, making my throat tight. I clench my teeth to stop the ache.

"But it's Thursday."

Nathan shifts. Is this how Dad feels when I won't look at him? Look at me, Nathan.

"Why didn't you tell me?"

Silence.

"Nathan! Why didn't you tell me!"

"Because I didn't want you to be disappointed – ok? You've been doing so well."

"Don't patronise me." I spit.

I can feel it again – that wall – can see myself with brick and trowel in my hands, ready to build it back up.

"Emmy..."

"What did they say then?"

"Emmy..."

"No, come on."

Yes – I can feel myself getting harsh – closing myself off. See, this is why it is better to be alone. Right? To not feel...not talk, not try...

"Come on, what did they say?"

I knew I should have discussed this with Willow. I knew I shouldn't open up this fast, make myself this vulnerable. Trick myself into thinking that things could go back to normal – be *better* than it was before. That letter though...were they tricking me? Did they mean it? No – no, I don't care. My throat burns more and I dig my fingers into my palms.

He lifts them then; his eyes. Looks at me deeply and I cannot help but to feel everything.

"They didn't say anything."

I don't even have the strength to place that first brick, as all tools fall from my hands. No wall. Not even barbed wire. Nothing around me to keep me safe - nothing but me. Alone, small and open, naked; like a target. Pale and thin, like the paper on my floor. Delicate, and tearing into pieces right beneath all of their feet.

Purple flowers

To make good choices – to choose to be happy. Remember? I am here, Emmy.

What use is it Willow being here? Really? Some voice I have most probably fabricated in my mind to talk me through my grief. To get *me* to talk, when I couldn't talk to anyone else. A faceless voice, whispering in my ear and filling my brain with happiness and light. Seriously – what kind of madness is that anyway? What is actually happening to me, on a health level? Am I mad? Sick? No wonder my friends don't want to talk to me now, despite my effort to reach out to them. Wait, what am I saying? My *effort*? Not like I haven't spoken to them for weeks – is it? Ignored them. Given them filthy looks full of hate. Hated them, just a little. This is my own fault. All of it probably is.

I go to bed early tonight. Eat a dinner I can hardly taste, nod and grunt back at dinner table conversations I can barely understand, and get straight into my bed and turn off the light. My curtains start growing dark a few hours later, and as soon as I lose sight of the details in my room, my phone begins shining. It lights the ceiling and burns my eyes with its brightness; like needles into the front of my brain. I bring the duvet up and over my head and ignore it, shutting my eyes tightly and bringing my knees into my chest. I don't know if it kept glowing – if Willow tried numerous times to get my attention. I just stay under the duvet, curled up like a sleeping mouse, until there is a quiet knock on my door the following morning.

"We are off now, Sweet-pea." Dad says through the wood.

I stay under the covers.

"Do you need any more brushes or paint?"

I say nothing, pulling my knees in closer.

"Emmy?"

A pause. I can almost feel him pressing his ear against the door, and I consciously hold my breath. No – would that make him panic? I quickly cough instead. There. No need for him to come in and check now.

A shuffle.

"Ok, darling. We shall see you later. Love you so much –"

I clench my mouth stubbornly to stop myself responding.

Another shuffle, and then footsteps and the front door.

Maybe I can hold my breath now? Maybe I should? Fill that bubble so full with air till it strains, pops, burst and shatters – taking me with it.

I must have fallen back asleep, as it is my rumbling stomach that wakes me. Like sharp claws pawing at the inside of my torso, as if an angry cat is trapped within me. I listlessly pull on my leggings and chuck on my white t-shirt – yes, it definitely is baggier on me – and stand looking at my wall for a bit. Faint, but all there; pencil lines depicting my journey to learning to walk again. Or at least, an honest depiction of how I want to. Will it be more effective once colour is added? As if I am painting a new life? Maybe I should just get naked and take the paint brushes to myself? Paint a brand new me? A happier version; with brighter colours and darker lines. Or erase the old me by pouring the paint down my throat...

A noise by the front door makes me jump, like a little snap of wood and metal. It wouldn't have been the handle, surely - someone trying to come in? What time is it anyway? My curtains hold an orange hue of near midday; surely a little late for the regular post? It's a nice colour though... maybe I could try and create it for my picture? I jump again as I realise I am holding a small tin of paint in my hands, my fingers already grasped around the lid ready to peel away. My stomach claws in a new way, and I place it down slowly and back out of my room. I am not selfish like her.

It was Dad's little makeshift postal box that had made the noise; its small latch all in disarray, and I quickly step out in my bare feet to look down the spiral staircase. No, I can't see anyone. I fold my arms across my chest as a slight chill moves me, and drop down to lift the lid. He has done a good job, Dad, at making this. The wood is smooth in my hands, the metal encasing it cold. I don't see it at first and start to close the lid again, till I spot it lying at the bottom, half hidden in shadow. A small, purple flower – the same as the ones in the hotel garden. I pick it up carefully and goose bumps flood my arms.

Mrs Locklea?

Her crooked smile floats into mind and I cannot help but lift my cheeks in return, as well as feel a stir in my chest. Does she forgive me? It *must* be from her – I should thank her... thank her properly. How funny that I would grow to care for the strange old lady. As I picture her holding her gnarled hand to her heart and doing that knowing nod, I feel a strong urge to take her hand in mine and squeeze. To say a million things to her with just one glance, and for her to somehow know it all. I hope she had been ok getting up the stairs.

I sprint back to the railings and lean right over, teetering right on the tip of my toes. No. I can't see her. She must be faster than she looks! I twirl the flower gently in my fingers, place it behind my ear and nod once to myself, running back into the house, the box lid slamming shut at my speed.

I pull out my old art books from my school stuff and sit cross legged on the floor, flipping through the pages. I used to sketch so much; before music became my escape. I guess drawing is more about expressing self...putting a part of yourself on a page for all to see, for all to judge. Listening to music through earphones is a private affair; something you do alone, as if you share a secret with the song that no one else is allowed to listen in on. Had I started closing myself off before it had even happened..? There! The drawing I am looking for. I think of Mrs Locklea as soon as I see it. An autumnal branch with three song birds sat upon it, the golden and red leaves matching their warm and woody features. She does like birds after all. I picture her face as that robin had landed in my hands. I carefully tear it from my book and turn it over, reaching for the pencil I had left on my paper floor beside the foot of my bed.

Dear Mrs Locklea,

Thank you for the flower. Thank you for everything –
Emmy x

Yes – that will do. It will be the thought that counts for her anyway; she isn't the biggest for words. I pull my fluffy socks on, grab my fleece and wrap it around my shoulders, pick up my drawing again, and leave the apartment.

Great – it is that same plain woman as before behind the reception desk. She recognises me immediately, and frowns quite openly at the fact that I wear no shoes and have a fleece like cape. I wave over exaggeratedly at her and start skipping, sending the fleece billowing out behind me.

"Ah. It's you, Miss. What can I help you with today? Your father hasn't left anything this time."

I must look a picture. Baggy shirt, flopping about as if it were still on a hanger, flower behind my ear. I readjust it to make sure it is still there; folding my hair carefully away so that it is in view. I haven't actually looked in a mirror since waking up. I can't remember the last time I have, actually. Probably that day at school. I am probably picturing a completely different person when I take a guess at what I must look like.

"No – I know," I say, with the biggest fake smile I can muster. "I am looking for Mrs Locklea."

I glance at the clock hanging on the wall behind her. Its 12:34. No wonder my stomach is growling so much.

"Sorry?"

Despite the bright coloured top she is wearing today and the tacky matching eyeshadow, the 'boring' just over powers her. I wonder if she has looked in a mirror either.

"Uh...Mrs Locklea? The elderly lady that works here? Well, I say works – I don't actually know what she does. Maybe something to do with the grounds? Or the gardens at least?" I touch my flower.

"Sorry, I don't know a *Mrs Lock-lee.*"

She says the name as if it is foreign in her mouth.

"Oh come on – the old lady! Missing teeth, doesn't talk. She is quiet, yeah, but not a character you'd soon forget."

She frowns: through confusion, thought, or constipation. I sigh, and grit my teeth within my smile. My voice comes out almost as a warning growl.

"Come on...I know it must have been in your job description to be as unhelpful as possible, but I really need to speak to her. It's important."

She bites her lip.

"Perhaps you're mistaken? Maybe she is a guest. I don't know of any elderly ladies on the staff, I am afraid. Not any that I have seen anyway. I can always call the manager?"

"No! – No, don't call him."

Idiot woman. I feel my own frown as I too play with my lip.

"Fine. Well, if you see an elderly lady who doesn't say *hello* back when you so warmly greet her –"

Wow. My own sarcasm even makes me cringe awkwardly. The reception lady shifts noticeably in her little office seat.

"– then can you please tell her that *Emmy* is looking for her. She knows who I am."

I wait for her to nod, double check that she has my name right, and flourish my cape as I turn dramatically.

My feet take me towards the mauve front door instead of back up the stairs, despite my stomach screaming at me, and I force myself to come to a stop. I guess Mrs Locklea's name badge could be from somewhere else...I hadn't really thought about it before to be honest. Maybe she volunteers nearby? I guess she couldn't tell me any different. I don't trust that reception lady to pass on my message though; even as I turn to look back she is already looking at her phone, absentmindedly twirling a strand of hair round a finger, a dumb expression on her bland face. Maybe Mrs Locklea is just outside? Waiting for me; as she always seems to be, when I need her the most.

Seriously, who could not know who Mrs Locklea is?

She catches my eye then, the reception lady, and takes a piece of hair out of her mouth. Was she chewing on it? Gross. No, this can't wait; I really want to find the old lady. Something in my gut says that this is what I should be doing.

"Hey!" I shout, and she drops her phone with a clatter to the desk. "If you *do* see her – I am outside, ok? In the gardens." and I let my feet take me over the threshold.

I have to step quite slowly and precariously over the gravelled front as my socks act as no kind of barrier against the ground, and I waddle around the side of the house. Really? Am I really just going to wander about outside? Stomach grumbling and cold feet aching? I guess my stubbornness is something that hasn't changed at least. Something other than the growling in my stomach says that I should be out here though, and the pull is stronger than that of my hunger. Maybe I should have grabbed an apple before I came downstairs?

My arms stick out awkwardly to the side, as if I walk a tightrope. I must look like a penguin. Or some strange circus performer what with my getup; all I need to do is paint my face. The act doesn't stop the stones pricking me nastily in the softest parts of my feet though.

Past our trough. Past the purple flowers. Is autumn really coming in so fast? The flowers are starting to die; crumpling at the edges of their petals and drooping their heads sadly, purple turning to a dull grey. My chest stirs and I come to a standstill for a bit. All life, even that of a small purple flower, ends. Resides in the world for what seems like a short moment, before it suddenly just isn't there anymore. I feel a stronger need to find Mrs Locklea then; to tell her how I feel, how thankful I am for her being a friend, and totter around the side of the house again, leaving the flowers turning to ash.

They are different though I guess, the flowers, as I force myself to think positively. Leave at summers end, retreat back into the safety of the dark, only to burst through their graves to bathe the world in colour again as the sun of a New Year thaws their faces. Everything else stays cold and still in the dirt. Where they belong.

The grass, despite being slightly damp with dew, is a welcome relief to my feet as I step off the small path and walk through the grounds. No, she isn't here either. The benches lie bare aside from the odd squirrel; not even one little song bird. I pull my fleece tighter around my shoulders and check my drawing. It has creased slightly in the corner, but it will still do. Maybe I should invite her up to have dinner with us too, if I find her? Show her the drawing on my wall? I am sure she would love to see what good use I will be putting those paints to.

I think to the shed, and make a beeline towards it. Some of the tree's leaves are already starting to turn slightly yellow, and they tremble at the slight chill in the breeze beneath a bright blue sky. No, she isn't here either. The shed lies alone too. I wish Willow was here... Someone to talk to. Maybe I should have brought her down with me? I open the door and pop the picture up against some tools, the little note on the back facing forward. I readjust it a few times till I am satisfied that it will be the first thing she notices upon opening the door, even taking a step out and back in to make sure it catches my own eye. I do hope she comes here; it is odd that the reception lady seemed to think she wasn't part of their staff. How else would she have known about this shed? About the paints? The wind prickles me, and I pull the fleece flush up against my neck as I am met with a heavy sadness in the pit of my stomach. The hunger pains are gone now; given away to simple emptiness, and the hollowness creeps up to fill my chest too. I do hope she finds it. As my throat starts to ache, I close the door carefully behind me, leaving the picture alone in the dark.

I lie on one of the benches for a time, watching the wispy light clouds glide across the sky. They move quickly and smoothly, as if skimming along still water or glass. Effortlessly; with the tide of the moving earth. I am flat on my back, my arms up and folded under my neck as my fleece covers me, turning me into my own fluffy white cloud. I wonder if they are just as soft. I know they are only made of water; cold water, hanging impossibly in the air, but what if they *were* soft? Solid enough to gather up in your arms and squeeze – like a giant pillow of cotton wool. Bouncy and sprung like an old mattress; flinging you higher into the air with every jump. Throwing you so far that you burst through the roof of the world, scattering blue fragments into the atmosphere and bathing in a new colour; a colour we couldn't fathom.

Maybe I could reach the stars that way? Hold their fire in my hands and fill myself with light. Crack them open like a walnut. Crush them to glitter and sprinkle them down on to the world; down onto the girl lying alone on that wooden bench. The girl who doesn't believe in goodness or magic anymore. Who is empty apart from the bubbles that consume her. The girl who loves her brother and father...but *can't* love them. The girl who lost her mother. Who found her...and who now cannot find herself.

"Uh – Miss Emmy?"

I jump violently. All clouds are gone now, and my own slips off my body and onto the floor. It takes a moment for my heart to beat normally again, and I turn to greet the voice, wiping my face with the back of my hand.

"What?"

It's the reception lady. She has put a floral coat on just to step outside, despite the sandals she wears. She shifts at my tone, and I swallow before starting again.

"Yes – sorry. Have you found her? Mrs Locklea?"

She takes a step towards me, pushing her hands into her pockets.

"Um – I am not sure, but there *is* someone asking for you."

That must be her. My heart grows lighter and I swing myself off the bench, landing lightly on the floor. The grass is still wet, and my damp socks are re-sodden.

"Is she round the front –" I start, picking up my fleece, but I stop dead in my tracks as my throat closes up. My chest suddenly feels like it is going to burst with the new bubble that grows; so fast that I have to put both hands to my chest to stop from exploding. It isn't Mrs Locklea.

They appear only slightly at first, peering around the side of the house. Three girls. Three faces masked in both relief, fear, and sadness – and as they meet my eyes one of them screams out. A scream, but not from fear, and she starts to run. Run to me. Arms out. Tears cascading down her face. I hear myself start to wail, and she catches me before I hit the ground.

Red sky at night

I am trembling on the bench, my fleece wrapped around my shoulders whilst cool hands touch my face, stroke my hair, squeeze my shoulders. Everything is hazy and slower, as if I have my head held under water; muffling all sound, blurring all vision. I am aware of my breath though as it heaves and hiccups in my chest, as well as the icy breeze chilling my wet cheeks.

I can't believe it. Is this really happening – have they come here? To see me? I hiccup again and notice a small bunch of flowers that has been laid down on the bench table top. My favourite flowers. Chrysanthemums; in an array of colours.

"– I know, I am a right mess too!" a muffled voice giggles from behind me, as I feel another squeeze to my shoulders.

"Do you think we should have called first? Before we surprised her in this way?"

"I tried, but her phone doesn't seem to be working. Besides, I couldn't wait to see her any longer..."

"No, nor me."

A deep smooth then to my hair, lifting some strands off of my forehead. It settles me, almost instantly, and I draw in my first deep breath.

"I know they say to give space...but it's been killing me –"

"– Yeah, me too."

"How long has it been? You know, since?"

"Shhh..."

A long pause. A tighter squeeze on my shoulder.

"I am not sure now...time has passed super strangely since the summer. It was early summer, right?"

"Yeah."

Another pause. A chorus of sighs.

"Do you think she is ok? Now, I mean. She seems a bit spooked..."

"Ems? You ok? Sorry if we shocked you. Can you hear me? Yeah?"

A face blurs into my vision then, as she crouches down in front of me, placing her hands on top of my knees. Sophie; her freckles magnified by some of the tears she still holds on her cheeks. She smiles anxiously, and rubs her hands back and forth over my legs. Her honey eyes crinkle.

"We didn't mean to scare you...I *do* hope you are happy to see us..."

"Of course she is!" Jemma's voice comes loudly and near my ears, as she bends herself round my shoulders and kisses me roughly on the cheek. I can see now that it is her hands that grip my shoulders so tightly. Her dark short hair tickles my nose as I turn my face to hers and she laughs as we lock eyes, her mouth falling wide and sarcastic.

"Ah-ha! There she is!" she roughs my hair and leaps to join Sophie crouched on the floor.

"You alright now? Hear us alrigh'?" she mocks and knocks into Sophie's elbow, nearly causing her to topple onto her bum. She squeals and punches her softly on the arm. I splutter.

"Oh Jem, be nice." Kate comes into view now and Jemma rolls her eyes dramatically, knocking into Sophie again with a laugh. She does fall this time.

"Hey...Ems, how have things been going? Well...not how have they been *going*, that's a stupid question. What I mean is..." she sighs loudly and puts her cool hand against my cheek. Her mousy hair is shorter than when I last saw her; it had stretched down near to her hips before. She must have had it cut. What other things have changed? I close my eyes and breathe in her smell. "What I *mean* is, we have missed you."

The silliness goes now – whether put there through fear or awkwardness – and I am met with just their faces; holding everything in each line that we weren't saying to each other. Everything that we hadn't said. My voice croaks as I try to speak.

"I've missed you guys so much."

They envelop me then, all of them, and I feel it all. Everything. And welcome it.

We all sit on top of the bench for hours; arms linked and cuddling into each other's shoulders, feet resting on the seat below and knees knocking. We spread the fleece to lie across all of our legs, joking about being like little old women and guessing what we will all be like when our hair goes wiry and white. Who would keep all of their real teeth? Who would have been married the most? Who would be the one dancing in the rain and throwing cocktail parties? No one mentions mortality, of course, and we speak as if life is ever lasting; like the flowers. We will all still be best friends though, that part of the future was sure. Even if we were all as toothless as Mrs Locklea.

For the first time since it had happened, my chest is lively, warm, full. Not full of painful bubbles; creeping about my rib cage and plaguing my heart. No, it is full of *them* – full of life, light and happiness. Full of stardust. If someone cracked me open, I would surely be glowing.

"...so yeah, we have been seeing each other for three weeks now."

"AND she is marking every day on the calendar, the soppy thing!"

"Aww, leave her alone. My Mum and Dad met in school! This could be it!"

"Gross!"

"Haha - what? That's what it's all about, isn't it? Finding love – finding your soul mate...

"What, with *Brian Fisher*?"

It is so wonderful, being surrounded with their laughter. Hearing my own. Not feeling quite so guilty about it. Forgetting, for a moment.

"Right...so *Sophie Fisher*, hey?" I sing – pulling her in closer as her freckles blur by the pink flushing her cheeks. She laughs and turns her eyes away embarrassed.

"What! He smells nice..." she wines, and Jemma on her other side pulls her back from me to tousle her hair and I grip my stomach from laughing.

We talk about school, about boys, and about girls. We talk about sleepovers, stories, and about dreams. Sometimes we just hold each other's hands in silence. Sometimes we dare to talk about life as it is now. Well, Kate is the one brave enough to start. I am fine staying in the bubble that we have been building around the four of us since they got here; shielding us from the ghosts of my past. Or is it shielding us from the ghosts that my past has created? They stand just on the edge looking in now, ready to shatter the new reality we are playing with. A reality that doesn't consist of the faces hidden beneath their hoods. We are safe in here; and I am relieved that my friends are happy to sit supposedly ignorantly in here with me. Where I can just be Emmy; Ems. Before it had all changed. Before I had changed.

"So...this does seem like a nice place, Emmy." Kate starts, leaning back to look at the old house. "Are you lot alright living here? Got a big bedroom?"

I feel her tense, as well as Sophie on the other side of me, and feel my own stomach prickle as the walls of the bubble around us tremble. They don't know this new life of mine...this life made out of circumstance. So what will happen once the illusion is over? Once it pops, exposing this new life; this new me – can we get back to this point? Get back to how we had been?

I put what I think is a neutral smile on my face.

Will they like this new me? Do I want them to know her? Do I even know what version of myself I am right now? The one that will be revealed in the long term. The Emmy sheathed in shadows with tear stained eyes, or the one walking towards the light, again. Towards Willow's light – towards theirs. I can kid myself and fool them, I suppose – thinking that things haven't changed or that they don't have to. But like Willow said...to move on we need to learn to live in a new way. Can I live this new way and keep some of the old, though? Can I keep them?

The sky is starting to bruise as the sun gets lower.

"Uh...yeah." I finally reply. "Yeah, Dad's made a real effort."

I swallow and consciously move my neck, attempting to shake off ghostly fingers before they wrap themselves around my windpipe.

"We have the old apartment on the very top floor. Dad's tried to make it feel as homely as he can..."

I trail off then, not sure how to finish or what else to say. Another ripple of tension.

"That's good then!" Kate sings, an edge held to the enthusiasm in her voice, and Sophie makes an odd squeaky noise before too breaking into a smile and nodding when I turn to look at her.

See – I don't want this! I want to stay *there*; stay in the pretend place we were creating under the setting sun. Where we didn't need to talk about what had happened. Before summer; when the sun and our smiles were warm on our faces. Before *she* ruined my life. Before she took my life. Even when I try to find it again, scrabble at it with my weak fingers as it fleas from me – like catching air or magic – my heavy reality presses down on me. Standing on my chest till I can't breathe, or at least until I open my fingers and hopelessly let go of anything that used to resemble my life. My friends being here now, and the way it is making me feel is the real illusion. A nasty trick as I watch my old life for a moment like a mirage; shimmering and disappearing as I try and get closer. I could run till I failed, crashing to the floor, and still it would be out of reach. It hits me hard, and I feel my breath go again as I dig my fingernails in to my palms. The three of them being here made it more real. That my life, as it had been, is over.

"Yeah. It's ok." I smile weakly.

Silence.

"Sorry...we don't have to talk about things like that, if you don't want to." Kate says, and Jemma and Sophie nod with smiles, darting glances to each other.

"No. Yeah. No, I get it. They are just normal questions,

right? Normal questions in a not so normal situation." I stutter, feeling a bit colder, and I break out of our linked arms to wrap my hands in the fleece. "I don't want to be weird. I don't want it to be weird – I'm sorry."

"Hey! Don't you dare apologise, ok?" Jemma says, learning around Sophie and gently punching me on my arm. "You have nothing to apologise for, alright?"

"I do though..." I whisper, thinking of all the nasty things I had thought about them. How they were here now. How they had always been here – just floating in the background, afraid to come too close. Just like Willow had said, the very first time we had spoken.

"I haven't been very nice...haven't thought very nice things –"

"– Hey! Don't you dare! You are free to think anything you want, ok..."

"– No! No, don't think that..."

"– Don't be so silly! You've been through so much! Don't worry about us..."

They all speak at once, each almost fighting with the other's outstretched hands in order to be the one who takes mine.

"I've been horrible though."

My insides are like jelly.

"Hey! Look at me, yeah?" Jemma's voice comes through now, and she grabs my hand roughly.

"You are amazing, right? You are here – you are standing, talking – blinking, breathing! Right?" she squeezes my hand hard, her eyes strong and fearless as they stare into mine.

"That is more than some people would be in this situation, yeah? Don't you think for one second about us, ok? Or feel bad about anything. All we care about is you – right? We are here for *you*. Whether that be for cuddles or verbal beatings, ok? Anything you need – and nothing right now matters apart from you and you knowing that you are not alone. Ok? Ok, Ems?"

I don't deserve them, I know that, but I can't stop the warm hot light that fills me up again, and I squeeze her hand quickly just as tightly and let out a little laugh. If any of them shot that fire arrow from Apollos bow, I know for a fact that I would glow as brightly as the sun. Our sun though, is turning red now; slowly sinking down through the sky like a bolder falling through ice. Their faces glow pink and their eyes sparkle. Maybe I don't need to break through the sky to find my stars? Perhaps if I hold them, my girls, just as tightly, I will glow too.

"I might not be able to stand for much longer if I don't get any food in me..." I sniff with a giggle. "Do...do you guys want to come up for dinner? I know Dad would love to see you..."

They all beam and laugh, wrapping all their arms about me like a tangle of love as we watch the sun drift sleepily behind the horizon. Time to learn to walk again for real, this time; as I lead them up the stairs and through the door of my new life. We hold hands the whole way.

Painting the new

Dad almost squeals when we come upstairs. His glasses definitely steam up as he hugs each of my friends in turn. Sophie even begins crying again, quickly melting into laughter as she sets Dad off too. I feel like I am frozen in a picture as I watch them all, wearing the largest smile I have in a long while that makes my cheeks sore and my lips strain. Nathan even does a slow applaud as he ambles in from his bedroom to see what all of the commotion is about, patting Dad on the shoulders as he passes him a tissue, giving me a big wink and an equally wide smile.

Is this real? Willow? Is this really happening to me? Is it ok, to feel this happy? I do though. I feel so happy, and it tingles within me in the same way lemonade fizzes in your nose. Being around them fills me with such sweetness that my cheeks ache and my stomach sings.

Dad orders a take away, and we all kneel on the floor around the small coffee table as we laugh, share, and eat until we can eat no longer. Each of the girls text their parents to say that they are staying over after Dad insists, having already brought in the spare duvet, an assortment of cushions, and many blankets into the lounge. He danced – literally danced – as he brought them in, huge bundles in his arms! He even grabbed Jemma and spun her around before tripping to land delicately on the sofa to a chorus of laughter. Nathan tries his best to roll his eyes at us now, but there is no mistaking the light behind them.

We set up tea light candles and leave the kitchen light on to shine subtly through the hatch, as we bundle ourselves up with each other. Dad announces that we "must have the lounge to ourselves", brandishing his new book that he is "*looking forward to reading in his room anyway*". Nathan simply wishes us a fun night with a smile before going to his bedroom.

I take them all in; fluffy human marshmallows buried under all of our blankets and take a deep breath.

"Oh my god, I have missed this so much!" Sophie beams, crunching on a spare prawn cracker left from dinner. "It is actually ridiculous how I cannot function properly without us all together. Oh Ems – your Dad is just the cutest!"

"Yeah, I almost cried!" sings Kate.

"*Almost* being the main word there, *Sophie!*" Jemma mocks, and Sophie blushes in the dark whilst popping another cracker into her mouth.

"Yeah, well! I couldn't help it..." She mumbles slightly defensively, and Jemma knocks into her playfully to show that she is only joking.

"Yeah...yeah I haven't seen him like that in a long while." I muse, and they all look to me; their faces shadowy and soft.

"I bet..." Kate whispers back.

"It's good though," I continue, "To see him like that. I've been...worried, I guess. About him and Nathan. Not worried enough though, I don't think."

No. I haven't been. I have been choosing to ignore their pain in favour of my own.

"But...It's hard to get out of your own head and actually notice those around you when...when things like this happen."

"Mate, you don't need to explain or justify anything to us, remember?" Jemma's voice comes from a fluffy pile as she lies nestled in the duvet.

"Can you remember, when I failed that test that Miss Parsons gave us? The one last year?"

"Yeah...?"

I think. Yes – yes, I do remember that. An English exam, looking at creative writing. Jemma had always been good at telling stories.

"Well, I was horrid! Wasn't I? I was so sure that I would smash it, that when I didn't I turned into a right little – well. You remember."

I do actually, now that she is saying it. She hadn't spoken to the three of us for a good week.

"Well...I know it is nowhere *near* the same...but all I could think about was myself, I didn't even bother asking you guys how you got on. I was just thinking about me. Me and my feelings. And you know what...what you've been though – wow, who could blame you for not getting lost in your own hurt for a while? For being human."

Nods from fellow fluffy cushions as I strain to see their expressions.

"They will forgive you." whispered Kate's voice.

"Of course they will." Came Sophie's. "But you've got to give yourself a break too, Ems."

I can't help but to float my mind to Willow then; closed away in my dark and empty bedroom, having to fend off any monsters I have left in there all by herself. It has been a battle, this constant one I am waging with myself. Feeling ok, feeling not ok to feel ok. It is exhausting; trying to push it deep down where it only ends up festering away and turning me rotten.

"Do you think they are ok though...?" I squeak.

The blankets all shift and move. Do *they* have their very own Willow that coaches them to fall asleep, Dad and Nathan? Who coaches them to make the choice to live rather than to fade away?

"They will be. Just like you will be. You all have just got to keep being there for each other. Keep talking...it will get better."

Maybe if they don't, don't have their own Willow to talk to like I do, maybe I can be that for them? Maybe I can be their Willow...maybe that should have been my purpose this whole time? My *real* project. To become Willow. To be Apollo. I should have been holding that bow and arrow this whole time. Catch a few stars and send it soaring into their hearts.

"Yeah...ok" I whisper, as I too nestle deep down into the blankets, feeling their warm bodies surround me as I close my eyes. The sound of breathing starts to get steadier and louder, twitching bodies falling still.

"...we will be ok." I whisper again through a smile. "I love you guys. I love you all so much..."

"...like sprinkles of stardust and lollies and such." I hear whispered back from Dad's room.

I think I smile the entire time I am asleep.

* * *

"I'm doing it, Willow. Learning to."

After the girls leave the following morning, all picked up by Sophie's mum in her big people carrier – calling and waving out of the window, blowing kisses and shouting obscenities, I shove on my scruffiest clothes straight away, take a dull knife to the rusty old paint lids and burst loudly into the lounge, throwing paintbrushes to Dad and Nathan.

"Paint monkeys – assemble!" I call, laughing fully and heartily.

"What...now?" mumbles Nathan, his floppy piece of toast half way to his mouth. The paintbrush lands fractions away from his steaming cup of tea and is spins on the coffee table.

"Yes, now!" I shout, holding my own paintbrush over my head and waving it like a flag.

He sighs sarcastically, folding the bread into his mouth till his cheeks swell, and pours some hot tea in there too just for good measure.

"Ooh! I'll just get into my old jumper." sings Dad, standing up energetically from the small dining table, mug of coffee in one hand, the paint brush in the other, and gives me some odd salute before disappearing into his bedroom. I would have cringed from embarrassment at any other time, a time from before perhaps, but I feel nothing but a skip to my heart to see him smile that way.

"Come on then, pig face!" I call to Nathan, as he struggles with his mouthful, tea creeping out of the creases in his lips as he tries not to smile at the pig face I am currently making at him now. It is disgusting, but brilliant. He chokes it down, makes his own face in return and pushes himself off the sofa with a feigned grown.

"Alright then. Put us to work, Captain."

Dad's jumper is probably as old as me; maybe even as old as

Nathan. It has holes in the elbows now so his bare skin peaks through, and he wears it proudly for our messy expedition as if a uniform for an important mission at hand. His hands are even on his hips. I do wonder why on earth he has kept it all these years though. He has plenty of other 'Dad jumpers' that could become his new 'scruffy jumper', yet he has kept this one. Dark green with small pinpricks of other colours dashed through the wool. Slightly scratchy when being cuddled, if I remember correctly. The type of scratches that you don't mind coming from the warm embrace of your Daddy.

Nathan is wearing an old long-sleeved band t-shirt that already has splashes of white paint on it, but surprisingly it looks like it is part of the shirts design. Well – scruffy is Nathan's natural ensemble. He wears it well.

"So!" Dad starts. The look on his face is just priceless. The three of us are cramped into my little bedroom; bed pushed right away and covered with an old sheet thrown over the top to protect it from any splashes. All odds and ends piled up on the other side of the room; my phone nestled carefully under my pillow, out of sight.

"What would you like us to do then? I see you have some lines on here already." He still grins although he frowns, nose so close it almost touches the wall. His glasses are on the tip of his nose. Nathan catches my eye and gives a little grin.

"You sure you can see, Dad? Do you need your magnifying glass?"

Dad chuckles shyly as he pushes his glasses back up his nose, and I feel a little guilty for laughing. Nathan winks kindly though and Dad gives him a warm pat on the arm.

"I can see just fine, thank you, son." He mutters, pretending to be cross and failing.

"So, Petal? We are here for you, so let us know what you want."

I want to start being here for *you*, I think. Like I should have been.

"Well...um...I think it probably best if we just cover it first. Um..."

I look to it, picturing the colour bursting forth and the images swirling into life.

"Leave the middle blank – this area here –" I point it out with my paint brush, "But actually...the rest we can wash with a mix of purples, blues and greens. They are going to be flowers, see. Like the flowers in the garden..."

I dare to glance at my window and think of Mrs Locklea.

"Sure thing, Blossom! Flowers, away!" Dad beams, shoving his paint brush into the air proudly and in turn making Nathan shake his head with an embarrassed smirk. I stutter a laugh.

We have never been this way, just the three of us. We had always been a party of four; and what a party it would be. It is all so weird, but I am doing it. I am *going* to do it. For them, if not for myself. To be that Emmy I imagined what seems like a lifetime ago. One with paint on her face. And actually, with us here now and after all that we have been put through...it doesn't feel like anyone is missing. Wow, that stings...

That's it – paint on our faces! We are on a mission after all. A personal one.

"But first!" I say, cracking open Dad's darkest blue tester pot and dipping my finger in. The paint is thick and cool, and makes a delicious squelch noise. "War paint."

I lift my hand which trembles ever so slightly, and draw lines on my cheeks. I squeal at the texture then quickly grin to them both, modelling the new me. Yes, the new me. I am trying,

Willow. Really trying.

"Uh...will that come off?" Nathan scoffs sceptically.

"I don't know. Shall we see?" I say casually, as I dip in my finger again and launch myself at him. He is taken fully by surprise and falls hard into the wall, the paint ending up over his eyebrow and on the tip of his nose, as he starts grappling with me – mouth open in a shocked laugh.

"Emmy! What are you doing!"

"Careful! Or it will go in your mouth!" I shout and he screams; a scream that's pitch is probably killing him from humiliation. I am even embarrassed for him – but I echo it, pulling faces of feigned distress as I fight against his hands as he holds my wrists.

"Yes, be careful, Nathan!" I hear Dad roar, as he too comes flying into my vision with paint *all* over his hands, and he smears it *all* over Nathan's forehead. We fall away panting and laughing, Dad ending the fight by putting his hand firmly over his own face, leaving behind a print worthy of any Braveheart battle.

"There!" he says proudly, putting his hands back on his hips. "This good enough for our *war* then, darling?"

I forget about it all then without even needing to try. It is just the three of us, surrounded by what will soon be a meadow of safe purple flowers. It's as if their prospective colour, without even having form or life yet, is keeping all monsters at bay. Banishing all shadows. Filling us all with a calm and a hope. Of a joy through our shared mourning.

"It's perfect, Dad." I smile.

I am riding my bubble now; standing atop of my wall and for the first time in a long time, looking clearly down at myself on the other side.

I *can* be an Emmy who runs and skips – who jumps and cartwheels.

An Emmy who doesn't force herself to be alone.

One with friends, with a light heart and no circles under her eyes.

An Emmy with paint on her face...as she laughs with her father and brother.

"Just perfect.

Nathan

"Good start, Munchkin face." Nathan says with a nod, arms crossed and looking at the wall.

The paint is cracking and peeling where it has dried on his face. He does look a mess, and I splutter to myself whilst looking at him now. He had protested about mine and Dad's ambush of course, saying that he was going to wash it off straight away; but pleas from Dad and I had made him give up. He had sighed a lot though. That and rubbed his face as if it itched. I am sure it didn't.

"Yeah...yeah, it is starting to look like something now." I sigh, looking at the smear of purples and blues across the landscape of my not so blank wall. It makes my eyes and head feel funny; the way that nature can do when you catch something particularly beautiful off guard, and I smile broadly.

We had ended up enjoying ourselves so much that we had carried on throughout the whole day – me giving them more tasks than just washing the wall with colour, and with some of the finer brushes they started tracing some of my lines to make the flowers stand out. It is looking really good actually, and a bubble of pride tickles my insides. I don't think I have stopped smiling actually.

"Well...technically if she was going to be a Munchkin, we would have been better off painting it red to be poppies..." Dad yawns loudly from my bed. He is lying across the sheet and it strains at the edges tightly. I think he got more paint on his jumper than he did the wall in the end. It's nice though, seeing him so colourful.

"What?" Nathan queries, looking over towards where he lies.

I can't even see his face from here; he really is sinking into those sheets. He does look comfy.

"You know..." he yawns again. "Like the ones from Oz that make Dorothy fall asleep..."

"Are you sure you haven't had any crushed into your coffee, Dad?" I say, and Nathan gives me a wink.

"Yes, very good." He tuts, and pushes himself up with a groan. His fringe is sticking almost on end and his glasses dangle dangerously close to the tip of his nose. Nathan coughs a laugh, but I just carry on smiling.

"Are there any leftovers from the take away last night? I don't really feel like cooking..."

"Are you kidding? Emmy and her piggy friends finished off every last morsel! I forgot how much you guys eat when all together!"

I could punch him for that remark, but all I can do is keep smiling. The starlight I have been dreaming of really feels like it's awakening within me now, and nothing can dull its glow. Well, I hope it can't. I will fight to keep the embers alight. My room feels safer already, just having had them in here with me today. There can't be any shadows if we all shine too brightly, right?

"Well...would it be bad if we perhaps ordered another one?"

I think Dad's asking himself more than he is us. "Oh – tell you what! The local supermarket does those pizzas that they cook at the counter for you to take straight home, don't they? Oh, yes! I'll take the car and do that. That's not *quite* a takeaway, so not as bad. Right?"

He doesn't wait for an answer before he determinedly pushes himself off from the bed and makes his way to my door muttering excitedly to himself. I can hear Nathan laughing too.

"Oh – by the way darling. Um..." He stutters and smooths down his hair, adjusting his glasses. His soft brown eyes look big and warm, and I hold their gaze in mine for the first time in a long while. It makes my stomach quiver, but I urge myself to keep looking.

"Thank you so much for thinking up today. For asking me and your brother to be involved. It...it really means a lot and I have had a really nice time...it looks brilliant. Well done." He nods once, his lips going thin in a shy smile. I look away then and feel my cheeks burn.

"Oh, and I think someone has text you or called you or something? I felt a buzzing coming from under the sheets."

Then I run cold.

"Right – see you both in a bit!" he calls, car keys already jingling as he disappears down the corridor. I dart to my bed and shove my hand under the pillow, grabbing my phone. It lies dead and cold now and my heart settles.

"Right...well I am going to *finally* wash my face." Nathan mutters.

To make good choices – I remember, and I bring my phone to my chest.

"Uh – Nathan?"

He turns, already scratching at his forehead.

"Do...do you want to go out and do something?" I cringe and close my eyes.

"Like?"

"Uh –" Ha! What am I doing? I could laugh at myself right now. That, or run away and hide. "Like...like we used to? I don't know...just like, *do* something, but together? Not just together...we could ask Paul and his sister too or something?"

I drum my fingers on the back of my phone. I can feel the rhythm in my chest. Come on Willow – look at how hard I am trying. No matter how weird it feels! To walk – to run – again.

"Um. Yeah? Can do?" he pauses by the door and starts to scratch at the new paint on his shirt.

I squirm.

"How about we go to the river? You know – the one we used to go to in the summer, with the rope swing? Its half term next week, we could go Monday if you like? I'll text Paul – maybe he could drive us."

I start.

"Yeah...Yeah?"

Outside? Somewhere away from the hotel? I haven't been out properly in so long, and the thought suddenly panics me. My heart picks up, but I keep my face smooth.

"Ok, yeah? The river then? Yeah, if you want."

Come on, stay calm. To make good choices. See, Willow. Look what I am doing.

"Uh...and Paul can drive now?"

Nathan smiles. "Yeah, he passed last month. Where have you been?" he rolls his eyes cheerily with a laugh.

I force a laugh back. It sounds more like a bark.

"Cool then – I'll text him and see what he thinks. It will be fun." He hesitates by the door and leans on the doorframe. "And Ems? Today really meant a great deal to Dad. Well done for...well. For just doing what you are doing." His mouth twitches into side smile before he disappears to the bathroom.

* * *

"Willow? Are you there?"

It's surprising how much faster the days go by when I don't spend them alone with my monsters. With myself. Even though I am still very aware that I am making the effort – that I am *working* at feeling this way and doing the things that I am doing, sometimes I find moments where they happen by themselves. As if being happy could come naturally, perhaps. Well, that's what I am striving for, I guess. That and finally putting Nathan and Dad before myself. Finally forgiving them.

I am always here, Emmy. Always.

Nathan has managed to get in touch with Paul, saying that we are going to go out after lunch on the Tuesday instead, and that Christa was going to be coming along too. Oh, and that she has blue hair now. Good – things are moving forward! I guess. I am taking another big positive step in the right direction. Doing things...fun things. For myself and for Nathan. *With* Nathan. Including myself, forcing myself to be involved and not just alone in my bedroom. Surrounding myself with people. Good. Right, Willow? Making good choices; right? I had found myself trying to calm down after he told me though; smiling at him, saying "Great, thanks.", and then closing my bedroom door in fear of having a panic attack. I certainly had found it hard to catch my breath.

Am I ready for this? I find myself second guessing my suggestion now. I mean, is it too much too soon? This is a *huge* step...this is much more than just painting in my bedroom. This is *outside* – out in the real world. This is...well, much, much scarier. Much closer to 'normal, real life' stuff.

"Am I doing the right thing? Is this too much?"

I hold my phone firmly in my hand – quickly grabbing a chance to talk to her before joining Dad and Nathan for dinner. I hadn't spoken to her for a while. My stomach squirms rapidly as I whisper to her, shooting quick glances over my shoulder to ensure we stay undisturbed.

Emmy, you have come so far and you are doing brilliantly. You know that, don't you?

"Yeah, I know – but is this too much? I just feel like..."

I swallow loudly, and jump as I hear the chairs moving in the lounge.

"...I just feel like I am running before I can walk."

I look desperately to the glow of my phone and bring her closer to my face.

Just know how you are not only walking for yourself now Emmy, but for others too. Just take a deep breath knowing that Nathan will be walking alongside you.

Yes, Nathan. Walking through the dark wouldn't be so scary with him by my side.

You are ready to walk, Emmy. To run. To fly. I know you can do it. I know you can.

I throw her gently onto the bed as Dad calls out to me.

* * *

I had done a bit more to my painting over Sunday and Monday, keeping myself busy but my mind blank enough not to come up with some excuse to cancel the whole thing. It is really coming along, and the three of us had even sat down to watch a cheesy film on Sunday night after the two of them had come in to look at the additions I had made. Dad's guitar had even appeared on its old stand in the corner of the living area, and he glanced at me a few times out of the corner of his eye after I noticed it with a little wry smile across his lips. The song he had mentioned a while back? To go alongside my God of art, truth, healing, and music? Hmm. I could almost feel Willow poking the side of my head, willing me to say something. To forcefully place the guitar into his hands and finally lose myself to music again as Dad erupts in colour. It certainly had been tempting. One step forward at a time, though. And this next shuddering step was with Nathan in tow.

Tonight I lie in bed with the glow from my laptop instead of that of my phone. Nathan had peeked his head in after dinner saying that he was being 'hassled' by my 'minions' online asking after me, and I had happily logged on to be bombarded by their group chat. Now, this alone is a little bit *too* normal for me! How am I going to handle tomorrow? We have been chatting for a good couple of hours now, and it has taken a good chunk of that time for me to stop picking up my phone and putting it back down. My stomach does still squirm nervously though, which picks up even more so when the topic moves onto half term.

E33y_bear: Well...

I start typing.

E33y_bear: Me and Nathan are going to the river past the gorge tomorrow actually. With Paul and his sister.

They all start typing simultaneously; the moving dots appearing at the bottom of the screen, and I play with my lip anxiously waiting for their responses.

JemJem56: That sounds good mate! Really good actually. Will be fun! Is that the place with the rope swing? And the big trees by the river? I love it there!

GopherSopher: Aww – Christa, is it? You haven't seen her in ages, have you? Since you were little? That will be nice.

Katie_Lou: Did you suggest that then? Going out? That is SO good, Ems! I bet Nathan was really chuffed!

My stomach swims and I look to my phone. Maybe I should be speaking to Willow instead? Planning my course of action for tomorrow? I itch a little inside.

E33y_bear: Yeah...

Is that it? My fingers hover over the keyboard to type more, but they don't, and I pop them back into my lap. A pause. Then I pick up my phone and quickly put it down again.

GopherSopher: Let us know how it goes! It will be good to get out and have some fun.

Katie_Lou: Yeah, have fun! Just...just talk and be yourself. And remember. It's just Nathan.

I start, and play with my lip again. Just Nathan? Yes. Right... It's just Nathan.

I lie awake for a while after logging off. My phone stays dark though, and I watch it until my lids get heavy.

* * *

There is a definite chill in my bedroom when I awake early with a writhing tummy and stiff shoulders. The first thing I do however is pick up my phone and hold it in my hands for a while, as if that will warm me or cure my ailments somehow. Well, cure the nerves that taunt me to the point of being sick.

What advice would Willow give, if I put my earphones in and crawl back beneath the covers? Tips? Ideas? Things I could say? How I should feel? It is like I need to go to this voice, this *ghost in my phone* to tell me – to remind me – how to be a sister to my brother. To get me to remember a time where I would never have felt nervous about spending a day with him. How he is *just Nathan.* Like Kate had said – he is 'just Nathan'. All I need to do is to 'talk' and 'be myself'. To talk. To talk to my brother.

I place the phone under my pillow now, keeping my hands there just in case vibrations come suddenly and urgently through the cloth, in case she tries to reach out to me through my own need to talk. '*Always here*', she had said, hadn't she? Here for when I need her – and wow, do I need her. I grab her again to bring her out, to stuff her deeply within the pocket of the jeans I am already wearing – to take her with me! She can come! Come with me! Help me, guide me! But I don't. I don't know what it is this time...but I feel like I need to try and do this on my own. To prove myself somehow – to her and to myself. To take that big leap like a baby bird does; see if I can truly fly on my own. Well, walking is one thing...would I learn to fly as well? If I haven't left it all too late.

No; come on. It's just Nathan.

I find myself already sat on the sofa at breakfast time; wellie boots placed and ready at the door whilst I sit bundled up in my coat and scarf.

"Um...you ok?" Nathan asks, giving me a sceptical look through the kitchen hatch whilst he butters his toast. I know my cheeks have flushed, whether from embarrassment or heat I am not sure, but I grin widely and nod until he walks off and back to his bedroom. I still feel sweaty now, even after having taken off all my layers and scrunching them up into my lap on nervous knees. They bounce up and down, and my stomach still wriggles; the idea of eating being enough to make me feel like I should be dashing to the bathroom. Do I feel ill? Have a fever? Enough to cancel the day and start again? Did Dad just say something? He is looking at me from the small dining table with what looks like the end of a question on his lips. I just smile and nod again, turning my face back to look at the blank TV screen. Only a few more hours to wait. I take a deep breath and let it shudder from my pursed lips.

Paul honks his horn almost the entire length of the stony drive when picking us up. He even attempts to do a skid thing – like they do with cars in films when they suddenly break; sending up dust impressively. He, however, ended up getting a gear stuck, making the most awful noise, and then stalling the car. I let Nathan do all of the laughing; I'm not sure how much Paul would appreciate it coming from me. It would have been hard to keep my face straight in any other time or place though, especially as Dad starts cheering from the door. I, in this time and this life however, am too busy working to stop my lips from trembling. Not one ounce of me wants to smile or laugh.

He has walked down to see us off, Dad, having the day off himself. I remember that he always used to try and take a few days off from work when we had half term, even if he did end up spending most of them on his own as the two of us made our own plans. Maybe we should do something with him – the three of us? Go to the zoo, or for a walk? Ask him what he would like. That alone makes my head spin, and I close my eyes quickly and clamp my already tight mouth together. Woah. One small step at a time. This one already feels like a step over a cliffs edge, and I shift my shoulders waiting for those baby wings to burst through my skin to aid me.

Paul waves at Dad now with a cynical smile, clearly still embarrassed as he tries to restart his car. Nathan starts to walk towards it and I follow. Wow, am I really doing this? My bedroom screams for me. As does my phone. Is it too late to speak to Willow? Should I say I need the toilet? Quickly dart back inside? Every part of me protests, all feeling is drained from my jelly legs, as I clamber into the back of the car. I am met by a cool nod from Paul in his rear view mirror, and my lips tremble in my forced smile. Is it hot in here? Is there air? Maybe I should get out.

Calm down, Emmy. Calm down.

My palms are sweating so much, and I shove them into the pockets of my big coat once I do up my seatbelt. I am glad Nathan warned me a little about Christa. She sits looking out of her window, fiddling with the zip on her black jacket and chewing gum quite casually. Although there is plenty of room, I feel myself trying to get smaller; pushing myself against the inside of my door till it hurts somewhat. I can't even remember who is the older, as I look at her now from the corner of my eye. She is so different to the little girl in the red cart. Back then we would be smooshed together; legs and arms all tangled in an embrace. She is like a complete stranger now. I am not sure I recognise one aspect of her. When Nathan had said *blue hair,* I thought perhaps he may have been exaggerating. No.

It is completely dyed; cut into a choppy style around her ears, shaved underneath near her neck. She turns slowly to look in my direction, and I fix my eyes onto my knees.

"Drive safely!" Dad calls as the engine starts. "See you when you're back!"

My heart picks up in a panic, vibrating in my chest enough to rival that of the cars chugging engine. Vibrating like my phone might be doing right now from beneath my pillow. Willow! Does she call me? I need her – I need to talk to her.

We start to pull away.

No! No, I am not ready for this! If I try to fly now, I will just go crashing to the ground! Get out! Run! Run and close my bedroom door to fall dramatically and exhaustedly into my bed. Stay there and unmoving until my legs simply waste away and I have no excuse to try and walk again! I really have to keep my fingers in check, as they start stretching towards the door handle as we begin driving, and I tuck them deeply into my pockets to prevent myself from tumbling out of the car. Come on. Nathan. I am doing this for Nathan. Willow? Are you sure this is the right decision? Am I doing the right thing? Will I be ok?

Christa pops her gum against her teeth and I recoil as if hearing a gunshot.

Forgotten stars

It is just as I remember it.

We pull up to a small dusty square of land full of potholes where people park their cars, several winding tracks leading away through long grass. We take the track on the right after glancing at the wonky sign; a map smattered with different coloured lines showing the many walks around the area. There are families pulling up too; baskets and carrier bags in hands, blankets thrown over shoulders as children hold onto bottoms of coats or trouser legs tightly with sticky fingers. There are dogs; jumping out of cars to go sprinting through the grass, or scowling in humiliation as they are towelled off by their owners. I watch one, as Nathan and Paul discuss the sign. Shaggy and brown, his long fur under his belly trailing near to the floor. He must have been in the river. His tail wags so fast it almost blurs, sending droplets of water into the air around him. He opens his mouth in what looks like a smile when he spots me; pink tongue lolling happily out of his mouth. It makes my stomach settle.

For a moment.

Our path has the wildest grass, but it looks to lead towards the river rather than walking away and back around. The boys seem most keen about finding that old rope swing by the water's edge, and they almost skip down it, their trousers getting damp already. I worry if I can even walk, let alone skip, and my own legs shake as if I have run for miles. My stomach hurts, as if I have been sneezing for days, and I wrap my arms around myself and wobble down the path carefully putting one foot in front of the other.

The car journey had just been awful; the three of them laughing and talking in what seemed like a language I couldn't understand. Or a language I hadn't learnt yet. They talk now too, amongst themselves – eyes thrown to me every now and again to include me – I think. I can't focus on them though, nor the things that they say, as I continue to focus on putting one foot in front of the other. This foot, then that foot. I know I am learning to *walk again* – but this is just ridiculous. How does he do it? Nathan? He almost spins as he talks – cantering forward for a moment before whirling on a foot to turn and talk to us all before hopping back again. He does it so effortlessly. All of it. As if none of it is frightening or unknown. As if he remembers completely how we lived before – as if he is living that way now. I cannot help but to feel a twinge of anger, of resentment, and sense it starting to settle on my face before I replace it with a smile as he turns to look at me.

Once through the wayward grass the path opens up into a large meadow. It stretches for what looks like miles, rising up to become hills to the left and petering out into a thick line of trees to our front. That's where we're headed. I can almost hear the water. It is so open out here – so big and vast – that after spending weeks looking at the four walls of my bedroom, I suddenly feel like a mouse in a realm of giants. A tadpole in the sea. When was the last time we had been here? The nostalgia starts to prickle within my chest; the kind of nostalgia that thumps at the walls around your heart and makes you feel a little sick. The kind that fills you with an anxiety, that makes you suddenly feel a lot younger, and I waver at the landscape before managing to get both feet securely on the ground. I think there had been blossoms in the grass the last time I had been here...when I had been an Emmy from another life. I cover my mouth as I swallow, seeing Christa glance at me from the corner of my eye. I pretend I don't notice, and shove my hand back into my pocket and force my face to look calm.

We press forward through the damp grass, and I am thankful for my wellies as I watch Paul's dark coloured trainers turn a new shade of brown as they become saturated, and Christa's skinny legs in nothing but torn black tights and shiny plastic boots. She towers over me, almost as tall as Nathan, and I feel myself shrink back into my coat again. I don't think I have ever felt this uncomfortable in my life. Like...I feel *so* out of place, that if they didn't keep glancing at me the way they do, I would think that I wasn't really here. Just a weird projection of some kind or made of smoke; following them like some stalking shadow. Not really here, but also trapped here – attached to a space and world that I can't really occupy. Even knowing that I am here, that I am *doing* this as part of my journey forward – even though I *know* I am trying, how I *have* been trying, I just feel wrong. I knew this would be my biggest step forward, my leap, but I am finding it harder than I could have imagined.

As the three of them talk I feel like I am almost on the verge of tears, and I have to keep blinking them back and showing my teeth in what I think is a smile whenever they turn to look at me. I feel very much trapped within my body's shell, but detached from it also, as if one version is holding on to another version of myself; one who floats above us watching the scene. With strings, like those of a kite. Two parts of me. Two lives I am trying to live.

What if I let go of myself; the Emmy who longs to be free? Will I drift on the wind to play amongst the clouds, finally rid of all pressing worries, fear, and pain that holds me to my mortal shell? To this nasty world? Or would it be like they say about dreams? How when in a dream we are connected to our bodies by a mere thread...two versions of ourselves living on two very different plains, perhaps even not aware of the other. But how if that thread breaks we too are lost, the one living in dream, to darkness and to death, never to find the other again. Never to be able to get back.

Well, at least I am aware of the two Emmy's living in conjunction with one another. How I can't really commit to either of them, as both scare me out of my wits. But I know both options are there, I guess. Waiting to be taken up when ready. To be rooted or to be free. To be here and present, or to simply leave and not look back. I look to Nathan again and feel weak. Can I be both? Is it worth the risk? I feel myself hold on tighter then, hold on tighter to myself. If I lose myself, who will be here for Nathan? He spots me now, and I put a smile on my face as he smiles warmly back. He seems calm; I can't see his hands or knees trembling.

Paul suddenly punches him playfully on his arm and sprints off, Nathan quick on his heels, and they dart towards the tree line. A dog barks somewhere in the distance, and a dark cluster of birds pour upward out of the trees, bend and twist, then melt back into the leaves like dust.

To be rooted or to be free? To save just myself – to leave it all behind? Or to try and save us both. Try and save all of us...

"You alrigh'?"

I jump as Christa touches my shoulder. She moves a bit of blue hair from off of her forehead, and crosses her arms, slouching to one side.

"Huh? Yeah. Yeah I am fine. Um...you?"

Christa frowns slightly and starts walking after the boys. I beg my legs to work and jog slightly to catch up.

"Well...you've been on a knife's edge ever since you got in the car. Haven't said two words."

Had it been that obvious that I don't want to be here? I do though – I do want to be here. Kind of. For Nathan. I hope he hadn't noticed...

"Um..."

Wow, can she hear my heartbeat like I can? It pounds so loudly in my ears that my voice sounds like an echo in my head.

"I mean...I'm not going to bite, you know." She looks to me and smiles gently with a shrug, her own hands going into her pockets.

Her eyes...Now that I look at them, I can almost recognise them; dark and heavy with make-up now but full of something that seems all too familiar. They carry that same slight sadness as Mrs Locklea's tend to do whenever she gives me that knowing look, though. Everyone's do now. I watch her, somewhat anxiously, till she runs her hands through that vibrant hair and shrugs away.

I wonder whether she recognises any part of me.

"It's weird - right? The four of us together." She scuffs the floor a little as she walks as if she has suddenly gone shy as well. "So much has happened since we were all like this. Time goes quickly, I guess. Quicker than you realise at the time, till suddenly it is lost."

She comes to a standstill, and looks out towards the tree line. "At least Paul and Nathan have stayed the same."

Her eyes are deep and thoughtful now, and I follow her gaze; two silly silhouettes running around like cartoon stick men between the trunks. Still I say nothing, but work on keeping my breath steady and quiet. Work at keeping my legs standing.

"He has gotten good at pretending."

I choke down my next breath.

"What?"

She looks to me again, bringing her hand up to play slightly with her lip. Is that a lip piercing she has?

"Nathan." She sighs and looks back at him, shrugging again. "I know him and Paul have spoken a little bit about..." a pause and a shuffle "...but I really think you should talk to him. About it all, if you can. I mean..." she swallows loud enough for me to hear and takes a deep breath. She continues to watch the boys with wide eyes. "...have you spoken to anyone about it yet? Has...has anyone helped you?"

A punch to my throat that makes me cough.

"Uh..."

It's like water is filling my ears and is pushing its way out of my eyes and my mouth. Like I am drowning.

"Me? Uh..."

Willow! I have Willow helping me! I think it almost defensively. I *scream* it almost defensively. I *do* have someone - someone to talk to if I want. Don't I?

"Nathan – what?"

No – look at him! How he runs, laughs – no one is that good at pretending! He is fine – I am sure he is fine –

"Uh..."

He *must* have moved on, he must have. How well he is doing – how this is all so natural to him. Right? Being here with him today proves that. Doesn't it? Why am I here, then? Why did I think up today, if I think he is fine...?

"Um..."

Not only my legs, but the whole of me now – like jelly – I shake so much. Ready to slowly crumble and dissolve into the ground below. Christa looks to me, only small lines etching the worry on her forehead, showing just how young she really is, but it consumes her dark eyes.

"Look...Emmy...I'm not going to talk about it, or make you talk about any of it. But...um..."

She takes my hand and I jolt a little as if shocked with static. Dark pools now, her eyes, as they fill steadily until a tear tumbles down her pale cheek. My knees quaver as my throat goes tight. I squeeze her fingers.

"...but...but I am so sorry we haven't stayed as close as our brothers have. And...and I am so sorry about what she did. "

The water in my ears gets louder until it is rushing, raging, roaring. I break away from her grip, close my eyes and bring my hands to my cheeks. They are hot and wet, and I bite onto their edges. No – No, I don't want to talk about it. There is *nothing* to talk about – it makes no difference – *no difference!* Why am I here? With this *girl* – this *Christa* I can only half remember from what feels like a memory from another life. No – it doesn't need to be talked about. I don't need anyone – not *anyone*!

Not even Willow.

Not Nathan, not my friends – not *Christa*.

What is she even playing at? This girl, this stranger? Why does she feel like I need to talk? What has she seen in Nathan that I haven't? What haven't I seen? Or what have a pretended not to see...?

I feel her hands on mine now, as she tries to pull them away from my face. To pull away my digging finger nails – can only half hear her shouts and cries as that water rushes, roars. Roars in my ears.

Christa...Chris-star? Star? Did I used to call her that? I can *almost* see her, see *us*, if I squint hard enough. A window to the past, almost played in black and white. Hiding under her stairs in our home made den, running away from the witch that comes with the flushing of a toilet. The two of us, sneaking away from spying on scary video games played by our brothers in a darkened bedroom, climbing up waterfalls on the stairs with skipping ropes and teddy bears. Was any of that real? In a life I barely remember through the pain of my current one?

Roaring, roaring in my ears.

Her hands cool on mine, wrapping her strong fingers and pulling them away, pulling them into her own chest.

Roaring, roaring...but not that of water, now that I listen. But roaring...rushing...like the small wheels of a wagon over a stony driveway. Roaring; paired with the squeals and laughter of two little girls sat cramped in a little red cart. Legs and arms wrapped about each other...as their mums have cups of tea on the garden furniture.

I open my eyes. Her face is almost to mine, her eyes so big I can see myself in them. See us, in them. Us. A new kind of nostalgia.

"I don't know what to do..." I allow myself to croak through a tear stained hiccup. My head feels like it could split open. My cheeks sting, and I test them with my tongue. Christa brings one hand to them and gently smooths.

"Well, you don't do *that*, ok?" she smiles gently, carefully touching my sore cheek with her fingers.

The nostalgia gets clearer now, and as it does so does she.

It's a strange sensation; the settled feeling you become aware of in your chest upon realising you know someone but don't recognise them to look at them. Like living in a world without mirrors; catching yourself years later in the surface of a pond and not quite knowing who it is that you see. She must think I am mad.

"I'm sorry –"

"No – no *I'm* sorry. I shouldn't have brought it up – and I don't mean to upset you, I really don't, but –" she looks out to the tree line again anxiously. "– but the longer you all leave it, the longer you keep pushing it under the rug, the more it is going to fester and go rotten – poisoning you all slowly and without warning."

I have had those thoughts already...the idea of turning rotten. Being filled with poison...with acid. But the longer we leave it? We have come this far...things *are* getting better. I have come *so* far. Willow can't help but to creep into my head though, as I think back to my promise. My promise to be there for *them* now – like she had been for me. To be their voice in the dark, to be there for Nathan. I hadn't given much thought on how to do that part, though. What does he need from me, other than this? Other than company on the sofa and someone who is learning to smile back once in a while? Does he need to talk? Talk? About it?

Her hand leaves my cheek as she cautiously raises both of her arms. She smiles but looks away, small pink circles playing on her cheeks.

"Is it ok if I give you a hug?"

I laugh unexpectedly then, an odd shape to my face after its contortion through tears, and she is taken aback, suddenly laughing herself once both of her feet land on the ground again.

"Sorry...I know it is weird –"

I almost knock the breath from her as I press myself roughly against her cool jacket and wrap my arms around her waist. I feel her sigh – her chest rising and falling – as her own arms wrap about my shoulders. She could probably rest her chin on top of my head, if she wanted.

"We were like sisters once, weren't we?" she muffles through my hair.

I link my fingers together at the base of her back. She smells the same as back then. Like rainfall mixed with honey.

"Do you think one day, we could get back to that? Maybe. I know...I know I would like that."

To be rooted or free? That's what I had asked myself. Leaving this mortal plain for pastures new. Like a kite, like the birds? Birds touch base though; they live in both worlds. They live amongst the clouds and amongst the dirt – to dream amongst the stars like I wish to, but to live on the ground. They could still fly though, couldn't they? They could have both. They needed both. Thinking about leaving people behind is the only thing stopping me from doing it. From leaving and not looking back. Besides, I am holding a Star right now with feet still firmly rooted.

"Yes...I would love that." I whisper into her chest, feeling my own filling with warm fire.

She pulls me back, taking me strongly by the shoulders. Yes... Christa – *Star* – I am starting to see her now. She too, as she stands in front of me, is a mixture of an old life, a very old life, with the new one I am now learning to live. A manifestation of how I picture it all, actually. My concerns of mixing the two – whether I can have the old with the new – whether they could live together in harmony. But here she is. My memory from my old life becoming something new in the one I am now living. It can be done. She is it.

"Just please...try talking to Nathan." A slight urgency on her face I can't quite place. "Without pretending...even if it is just listening, yeah? You need to do this for him. Take charge..."

"Hey!"

My stomach plummets to the floor as Nathan's voice calls over breathlessly as he sprints back towards us. I can feel my eyes go wide, but Star simply nods gently, quickly wiping her face before placing her hands strongly back on to my shoulders. She almost gets all of the makeup trails her tears have made, but she is still shadowy under her eyes.

"You guys alrigh'? What's taking so long?"

"Yeah!" Star calls back cheerily. "Ems just got a fly in her eye! We were just getting it out! It was *very* stubborn. We are coming now!"

She winks and sticks her tongue out, taking her nail polished hand to my cheek and softly wiping away any rouge tears. She frowns slightly at my cheeks and gently touches them before nodding.

"There," she whispers. "All sorted."

She gives one last squeeze to my shoulders, and starts walking towards Nathan who stands waiting for us, Paul calling rudely from the trees.

She looks like some sort of superhero, as the wind catches her blue hair. She looks strong, like a warrior. I can almost see arrows knocked in a golden quiver, slung over her shoulder – another Apollo standing before me. A solider in my battle.

Healing me – guiding me down the right path. She turns on a heel and grins, beckoning me over by reaching back her hand. I walk – no – skip forward, and grab it, suddenly feeling stronger.

To talk...to talk to Nathan. I know I will have to do it at some point, I know. But if I do play the part of Willow...perhaps we can talk without me doing so much of the talking. I don't need to talk, anyway.

"Oh, by the way." I say quickly, swinging her arm as I take a big leap forward towards Nathan. "I really like your hair."

The leap

Paul is up in a tree by the time we get there. Nathan cheers and runs over to join him, slipping on the first branch making my stomach jolt. Star starts shouting. She is still holding my hand.

"Don't you guys think for one second that me and Emmy will be carrying you back to the car if you break your necks! Although, I can give driving it a go if you want, Paul!" she winks at me playfully and squeezes my hand.

"Maybe you should be the one up here then, Christa! You are the ape of the family after all!"

She gasps in feigned shock, then sets her teeth and starts taking off her boots. They are long ones, and she has to unzip them and pull them off her leg like a sock. I almost miss her hand already, and clasp mine together in front of my stomach suddenly a little nervous again.

"Right." She gives me another little wink before she grins wickedly, tossing her boots to the ground and sprinting to the tree to leap up to the first branch effortlessly. "But if I catch you, I'm knocking you off!"

She is like a gymnast! Or a cat; a multi-coloured cat. Does she do gymnastics? I should ask her. I have *so* much to ask her. To tell her, if I can. Nathan first though. Talk to Nathan first.

Paul squeals and then coughs in a low voice as Nathan starts mimicking him, and I feel ok to laugh loudly at him this time.

"Hey! You can't comment if you aren't competing, little *Emmeline*!" Paul shouts down playfully, sitting awkwardly on the thick branch he balances on. He is very high; it makes my head tickle.

"Whoever is closest to the bottom is the loser, and gets thrown in the river!"

"That suits me, donkey boy!" Star sings, already half way up to him; taking a leap to a branch above and pulling herself up. I let out a little scream, and she waves at me in reassurance.

"What about you, *Nathanial*? You want me to fashion a rope and throw it down to help you up? Maybe made with Paul's manly facial hair? Oh that's right – he can't even grow a whisker!"

She dodges a spikey chestnut as it comes hurtling towards her, and sticks up a rude finger to her brother. Nathan shakily reaches up to his next branch. Is he really pretending? Has he been - this whole time?

"I'm getting there, I'm getting there..." he tuts with a laugh. "You two obviously come from another line of humans than me and Emmy. Maybe the missing link! I knew your jaw was too square to be full human, Paul."

"And me?" Star warns.

"Oh no – I'm not saying anything to you Chris. You are a better shot than your brother!"

"You coming, Ems? Your brother obviously needs a helping hand."

A double meaning, I know, despite her casual way in saying it. She has surpassed Paul now, and is teetering near the top where the branches start getting spindly.

"Come on! Us girls, leading the way! Taking charge!"

Learning to live again...to walk, run. To climb?

"Well, it may be you who ends up in the river then, Nathan!" I call out determinedly, as I run at the tree. My ears are filled with laughter and cheering; and it is my own voice that echoes the loudest.

No one had won in the end. We had all applauded Nathan as he managed to clamber to the topmost branch though, pulling him up somewhat unsteadily to join us in victory. His hands and knees were shaking now, that's for sure. Autumn really is rushing in now. Many of the leaves drift sleepily to the soft ground as we make our way carefully down, and the sun starts to hang lazily low in a greyish sky. It is surprisingly Star who sprints off towards the rope swing on the river's edge once all of our feet are back on solid ground. It's as if a part of her has remembered too, or travelled back – to the time where the four of us were like family. I hear her calling my name, but I resist running too by making sure I go back for her boots so that we don't lose them in the dark. I can spot her easily though, her blue hair contrasting the browns and oranges that dominate, as she swings back and forth on the old rope dangling from a knobbly arm of another chestnut tree. I can't help but smile.

When am I going to talk to Nathan? To 'take charge', as she had put it. To be his Willow. It doesn't seem like he is desperate to – to talk – as I glance back at him now. Laughing with Paul as they pat each other on the back, showing each other their battle scars on their hands. He seems ok. I guess I have locked away what I had seen in his bedroom; the sock aliens and ghostly photographs from a life lost. The anger that had surrounded their creases and tears. Pretended that I hadn't seen it almost, carried on with my own worries and forgotten about his. But I haven't locked it away, have I? As it comes back readily now just as easy. I have even mentioned it to Willow, kind of. So I *did* clock it...*did* see that it wasn't right. Did know that perhaps Nathan is struggling, even if he wasn't showing it as outwardly as I was. So why haven't I spoken to him about it?

I look to my own hands now. Mine are a little red too, I guess. That and dirty.

"Ah – great, thanks!" Star says breathlessly when I pass her boots. Her tights look absolutely sodden – her feet must be so cold! Mine certainly are...No! – I *am* going to talk to Nathan. Today.

"Right, my go!" Paul calls over as he comes sprinting determinedly, leaving Nathan in a flurry of brown leaves. Star darts out of the way as he launches himself to grab the rope in mid-air; spinning out of control as he goes soaring over the river. He goes so high! I almost think he is going to flip completely and fall crashing into the cold water. He doesn't though, and comes tearing back – cheering and shouting – punching a fist in to the air before wobbling and quickly grabbing back on to the rope. My stomach flips at his speed, and even more so when I feel Nathan approach to stand next to me. I dare a glance at him. His eyes are wide and bright as they follow Paul; up and down, up and down. They do look tight at the edges though...they have done for a while; as if he is quietly battling with a slight headache.

"You gunna do it then?" he says without looking at me.

A punch to my chest.

"What?"

"The rope swing? You going to have a go?"

Right...the swing. A test? Waiting for me to make the first

move? Just like Star said.

"Uh, yeah. Yeah, I will if you will." I test right back.

I watch him carefully. Yes; definitely as if he has a headache. He smiles but it doesn't quite reach his eyes. He nods, crossing his arms, not taking his eyes from Paul going back and forth, back and forth. Star starts pushing him now when he comes flying over the riverbank, and he is screaming at her as she laughs. He is spinning faster and faster now.

"I've got an idea." Nathan says, suddenly making his way towards the base of the tree and looking amongst the fallen leaves. "Hey Christa, I don't think he has gone high enough yet!"

Paul shouts back through shocked laughter, as she jumps into her next push – almost tumbling forward into the river – as Paul flies towards the branches. I laugh in both fear and exhilaration.

Am I ready to do it? Leap blindly and trust that Nathan will be right behind me; not leaving me to go crashing into icy water alone. The cold taking my breath, filling my wellies with icy rocks that drag me breathlessly under. What do I do if he says nothing?

My stomach is cramping quite terribly now. How come the thought of being trapped under ice with Mrs Locklea is a lot less terrifying than with my brother? I guess, the ice with her is still. Set and calm, encasing and protecting. But with Nathan? He is my brother. Life with him is fast, turbulent. Unpredictable and more exposing. To love and know someone so well can be dangerous territory to be in. As they are close enough to put those cold hands around your heart and squeeze till it bursts. Those closest to you hurt you the most, after all, and I don't know if my heart can bear another break. The thing is, it isn't necessarily the fear of him not saying anything...but about what he *might* say. Can I burden his pain along with mine?

What is he doing amongst those leaves?

Star grabs hold of Paul's feet on his next swing over the bank, and he shakily lets go of the rope, falling onto the muddy floor.

He swears loudly and breathlessly.

"I think I am going to be sick!" he is lying flat out on his back now, his hair going shiny with the mud. I squirm, and he must notice my scrunched up face.

"You not going to let the side down, are you Ems?"

"Nope." Nathan calls, coming back with a large broken branch in his hands. "We are going in to battle together, aren't we Emmy?"

He takes the rope and brings up the branch; lying it horizontally as he bounds the bottom of the rope around it.

"Together?" says Paul. I glance to Star and she is smiling.

Nathan fastens the rope tightly and steps away. He has made a large shelf. Wide enough for two pairs of feet...

"Yup! Come on then, Ems. Together, right?"

My stomach flips again, but in a different way. I can feel the pressure on my throat as I blink away teetering tears. Star is literally beaming at me, and I scrunch up my face at her and stick out my tongue.

Together.

I walk over to where he stands, holding the rope with one foot already up and ready on the new little shelve. Wow...did I ever say I hate him? I did, I know I did. What if I had said that just before something bad had happened to him? When words leave a lasting impact and echo through time, you cannot get them back, or the marks they leave.

"You ready?"

Nor can you get the kind words you may say. The ones that tingle when they leave your mouth, but almost choke you when shoved back down your throat.

Nathan wouldn't do that, though.

I take hold of the rope, rough in my hands, and step up onto the ledge. The water certainly looks cold. He bites his bottom lip anxiously, eyes full of excitement, and with a slight run, jumps his other foot onto the branch and we both go flying over the river. Together.

* * *

The sun is really sinking low now, and I pull my coat collar around me to stop the chill on my neck. Nathan is sat up on the bank underneath another tree with me, sitting on the large warm roots so as not to get cold and wet, as we watch Paul and Star have a go with the new improved rope swing. I am shivering. I need to talk to him. Come on. It's just Nathan.

"Do...um..."

I feel sick. What would Willow say?

"Do you think Dad's alright?"

There we go. A neutral topic to start me off. Well, kind of. I really wish Nathan would just say what we both need to say. Say what he needs to say. I pull my coat about me tighter.

"Yeah, I expect so. I bet he is cooking something extravagant for when we get home. He always likes to do that when he has days off by himself. My bet is on some pot roast or something. Or lasagna. He always throws the first one away when it's not perfect! Well, mushes it up and freezes it for his lunches. I tell him every time – it all gets mushed up in the end anyway! I don't know why he always wants it to look so perfect –"

Come on.

"– no. I mean...do you think he is ok? Like really ok?"

A pause. Am I really turning the subject to this? I look over to Star by the water's edge and she plays with her lip, giving me a little nod before turning her attention back to her own brother. Yes – I need to. Just like she had said...we shouldn't keep pretending anymore.

Willow? Is this the right thing to do?

Nathan's eyes have gone tight again and I hear a crack from his knuckles as he rubs his hands together. Everything around us goes dull, as if we sit miles away on our own.

"Um...what do you mean?"

"Come on..." it comes out harsher than I intend, and I rub my own hands together. I can't look at him, but I can feel his eyes on me.

"Can we just *try*...for a moment? Try and..." try and what? "...talk."

Nathan shifts. I take a deep breath. I need to do this. For both of us. I can feel them appearing again though; those shadowy monsters. Stalking amongst the trees. Preparing to shut me up by any means possible so that we all stay alone in pain suffering silently. I take my hand to my neck, afraid that my throat will split open at any minute. No, I am ok. I have my shining warrior Star on my defence now. Her bright hair as warding and as safe as any purple flower from my painting. Starlight defeats darkness.

Nathan sighs.

"Yeah. Yeah, alright."

Ok. This is my in. Is it? And I have no idea what to say.

We sit in silence for a while longer.

"Um...I don't really know where to start." I mutter with an awkward laugh. I look to him, and his knuckles are white.

"Yeah. Yeah, me neither."

Does he have his own monsters? Ones that threaten him into not talking? Surrounding him now, with warnings of fire? I feel Star's eyes on me again, and gain a little strength. My stomach is crawling, though.

"Um...well I guess I will start."

My voice sounds more solid than I expect it to. As if I have done this before. As if a leader, of some kind.

"Sorry that I have been so...well. Just spending a lot of time in my room. Being a cow, I think you said that one time..."

"No – no, you haven't. I'm sorry I said that –"

"No! No, I really have been, I know. And I am sorry – to both you and Dad. It's just..." come on. I've got this far. Be truthful and be yourself; that's all you need to do. *It's just Nathan.*

"...it's just that I have been really angry. Angry at you and Dad. Angry at me. Angry for us even being here...for having to deal with it at all. And I haven't been dealing with it very well. I haven't been dealing with it at all, really."

My heart is so rapid! I feel like I have just sprinted so fast and for so long that I could collapse in my own vomit as the harsh air catches in my raw throat. So fast. So fast I am sure you would be able to see it underneath my coat as it hammers against my chest. Stretching out of my skin – like a cartoon. I haven't talked like this. Not at all. Not like this.

Willow? Am I doing the right thing? Is this how I learn to walk again? I am trying so hard.

"Like...I thought you and Dad were just completely ok. Like... how you would sing when cooking dinner, how I haven't even seen either of you cry properly – how you would both laugh and go to work and school. And I just couldn't understand it! I *can't* understand it. It's like it hasn't even happened...for you, anyway."

Be truthful and be yourself. Air it all out.

"I mean... We haven't talked about it once. Have we? I mean... I haven't really wanted to – don't really want to but...but are you ok? Is it just me? Have you just forgotten and moved on already?"

Movement then, and for a moment I think he is getting up to end what I have started. I hadn't meant for my voice to sound so cross, to sound so accusatory. Yet...we hadn't had this out. We hadn't spoken like a brother and sister since it happened. We need this. Don't we? Please don't leave ...just talk – shout! Anything.

He settles again, runs his hand through his hair.

"I..." he laughs, but out of fear or awkwardness. "I just don't know, Ems. This whole thing, it..." he tries to find the words in his mouth, "it just feels like a film, or a dream."

He rubs his hands together again, shifts more in his seat.

"Like when you read a really good book...and you kind of think about it or see it projected onto the real world whilst you amble along. Like there are *two* versions of a reality. One which is yours and another that is how it should be...or a more interesting version from someone else's story. As if you are seeing double. But...the story – this *other* projected story – *was* our story. *Is*...but from before. And it's a better one to watch."

Two worlds...I get that, I know that feeling. Two Emmy's – two lives, I've said it this whole time. Who have I said it to, though?

He laughs awkwardly again, but his eyes shine.

"And...and maybe I have been living in *that* story sometimes.

Instead of this one. Because you are right – we *haven't* talked about it. Because I think talking about it brings *this* story to the forefront. *This* one becomes the main projection and the other – the story I want – fades to the back. Like a lost memory. And, I guess, I haven't been ready to stop reading from that other storybook and commit to this new one yet. Not yet. Does that make sense?"

How long has he needed to say this – to voice it – to construct it into intelligible words instead of just leaving it messy and trapped within his own head? Like me...how I first attempted to voice how I felt to Willow. Why hasn't he come to talk to me about it? Why haven't I asked?

"It does."

I shuffle. It really does make sense. Instead of an external voice to talk to when he closes his bedroom door, it sounds like he has a whole cinema screen. One he can step through, one that sends him back through time to another version of our lives he can live out instead. That doesn't sound any healthier than what I do when I close my door at night. How long can we both last, pretending it hasn't happened, before we can never get back? Is that why his room is the same – socks and band posters – is he trying *not* to come back?

I must be trembling more than I realise, as Nathan suddenly takes his coat off and wraps it around my shoulders. I don't feel cold...not really. But my body is shuddering quite violently. I almost can't stay still. I bring my other hand around my neck; taking my dark hair and covering any exposed flesh I feel might tempt any sharp fangs or claws.

Nathan sighs heavily, bringing his own hands up to rub his face and ruffle his hair. That headache is back it seems, and he closes his eyes as if exhausted. I feel tired too.

One of his long sleeves is rolled up awkwardly, his pale skin peeking out shyly from his grey jumper. But something catches my eye, as he runs his hands back and forth through his scruffy hair. Something not so pale – something raised and angry – and my blood runs cold.

"Wait - what are those?"

So cold; but my shaking stops completely.

Monster marks

Nathan's eyes go wide as he notices his arm, and he quickly rolls his sleeve back down with fumbling fingers.

"It's nothing –"

I grab him with stinging eyes, a burning throat. It *is* ripping open now – my throat – I can feel it. My hot blood and tears cascading down my neck and soaking into my coat. He struggles, only a little, as I yank his sleeve back to reveal his arm again.

Those scissors on his bedside table, the ones that could dull any existing constant pain, shoot into my vision and I fall away. Fall for what feels like miles in the crushing dark. His very own monster marks, trailing angrily up his arm like nasty scratches.

"What are those?!" I scream, although I know the answer.

I have managed to avoid my monsters teeth and claws...but he hasn't.

"Look, Emmy..." He grabs me suddenly, trying to pull me in. "It's ok – alright?"

"It's not ok!" I scream again.

He has me by my wrists, but I struggle and struggle. How could he!? How could he be so selfish? Like *she* had been. I only half notice Paul make a sudden nervous dash towards us, slipping from Star's outstretched fingers, and she shouts out at him to stay back.

"When?! When did you do this?!"

"Emmy –"

"When?!"

"Woah! – What's going on! Everyone ok?"

"– its fine." Nathan stutters, still fighting with me.

"It's not fine!" I shriek back.

It feels like all of my blood is in my head; so much so that it might start pouring from my eyes.

"Paul! Come on – *leave* them – they have to talk –" Star grabs Paul by his shoulders and forcefully pulls him away. She shoots me a glance though; one that I can't quite identify.

"– but what the hell is going on? Nath – are you ok?"

"No! No! He's not ok! Look! Look at what he has been doing!"

I can hardly take a breath my throat is so raw from screaming, as I brandish my brothers arms into the air. I am shaking so much internally I feel like I could be crumbling, but my grip on him is as strong as stone.

"Emmy...come on..."

"No! We are going to *talk* remember?! *Try and talk* – so come on!"

I can hardly see him, hardly see them. Maybe blood *is* pouring from my eyes. Something hot certainly is.

"So come on! Talk! Is this what you meant, Star? Did you know? Did *they* know, Nathan?!"

I want to hit him! Shake him! Hold him...squeeze and never let go.

"Paul, come on – they need to be alone –"

"No! Its fine – right? Like old times – yeah? All together!

Climbing trees and building rope swings –"

I picture him: alone with his door closed, stalked by his own nightmarish creatures, scissors in hand. They weren't used to fight them off though – not used for his protection – but in his punishment. The pain and fear he must feel...the amount of pain he would *need* to feel in order to dull the ones caused by those photographs on his chest of drawers.

"– I mean – where is your bike, *Paul*? Shouldn't we all ride around on that laughing? *Pretending*? We are *all* pretending, it seems – aren't we Star? All of us! The whole world – *lying* – making out that it is a *great place to be!* I can't believe I have been so stupid!"

I break away from him completely now although I don't think I have the strength to stand. I throw my arms into the air though; angle my head to stare up at the sky and laugh mockingly at my life through my tears.

"Oh, to be alive!!"

Paul's expression is one that I can only imagine being worn by someone getting ready to defend themselves; physically defend themselves from a monster. Maybe Nathan should give *him* his scissors!

"Ems...please, take a breath for a second – we can all get through this –"

"Oh right – cuz we are like family, right, Star!?"

Aren't my hands trembling? I feel like I am made from petrified air as I move my wet hair from my face and look at her. I can feel those spines growing up and out of my skin. Piercing through my coat – long claws sprouting from my fingertips. Acid coursing my veins.

"Cuz it's just like how it was before, isn't it! The four of us here together. Like sisters, aren't we, Star? That's what you said! Like a sister, aren't I? You must care about me *so* much. Funny how you're the kind of *sister* that only gets involved when everything else has fallen apart! Stars are supposed to make the world a better place – full of glitter and light – of hope! But all *you've* done since being back in my life – in just the *few hours* you've been back in my life, is brought me face to face with *pain!*"

The look on her face. Like the kind I have seen on Dad's so often. As if something within her is breaking.

"Why are you even here, *Christa*?! Huh?! Go! Go on! Go away! Piss off!"

"Hey – Emmy! That's enough! Calm down!" Nathan takes me by the shoulders and shakes me hard. Star quietly turns and walks away.

"No! I won't calm down! How is any of this happening?! What the hell is wrong with everyone?!"

I break free from him again and push my back right against the tree trunk.

"Why didn't you tell me, then?! Huh? *They* knew! Paul and Christa, didn't they? – So why didn't you tell me?!"

I know why. Because I haven't wanted to talk. Haven't wanted to listen. I have been hating them all. Not even joining them for dinner. Ignoring their attempts. Really, really hating them. I want to grab something right now – something sharp! Thrust it into my chest! Twist it, wriggle it till I am torn completely open! To be overcome with pain unimaginable. For them to all leave me – dying slowly in the cold autumnal dirt. Like I deserve. It's hard enough for me not to shove my fingers in to my temples right now. To hurt myself in some catastrophic way.

"I can't...I can't believe this is happening..."

My head spins. Fills; with every nasty image it has held over the past few months. Over my life. All revolving around *her.* I feel such a pressure in my chest – surely holding enough power to rip me open – rip through time and space itself – to confront her! *Show* her what she has made us all feel – show her what she has made us do! To stop her from doing it.

To do it myself.

"Paul – can you give us a moment?"

I don't even see him turn away. I can't see anything anymore. My sun has completely set, and we both sit in the pitch black alone and exposed. It is her fault...all her fault. I hate her. Willow? Help me, Willow! I wasn't expecting this. Was I? Was that why I hadn't wanted to talk?

"Look...I know you are upset and angry..."

"You have no idea how I feel."

"Ok – ok...I have no idea how you feel...but you need to just calm down and let me talk – alright? Talk – that's what you said, yeah? To talk?"

He reaches out to touch me but quickly retreats as I recoil away.

"So...no more pretending, ok? I'm going to talk. *We're* going to talk – ok?"

My heart beats so fast and hard in my chest; pumping that acid.

"When, then?" I say coldly.

A part of me shouts out in my head – the part that wants nothing but to fold into his arms and hold him until all pain goes away. But that Emmy is weak. She is probably the reason all of this is happening.

Nathan shuffles, rolling his sleeves down again and bringing his knees to his chest. Hugging them; probably to replace the hug he needs from me.

"Well...I guess you try and be ok, so that others think you are ok and that *they* will be ok..."

The sun is shining through the tree we sit against now, casting its shadows in an orange hue. His brown hair glows in gold as his face becomes dark and shadowy. The day is starting to end.

"But...but I haven't been ok. I've tried so hard, but I haven't... "

He takes a deep breath that trembles from him. All of him does actually – all of him trembles, and his face goes pink and crumpled.

"I...I loved her so much, Ems."

Something stirs within my monster's chest. I don't need a weapon; I hurt more than I ever have done, as he buries his face into his knees and shakes with crying.

"I mean...was it something we did? How - how can someone be that unhappy? We were happy, weren't we? The four of us?"

No. No, I won't talk about her. I won't! I can't! My stomach does nothing but churn for her. My hackles rising.

"I think about it all the time. Like...how someone can go that far and not look back. I mean..." I watch his damaged arm twitch around his legs. "No matter what I do or how I think...I could never – never go that far."

To hit him, slap him and shake him...to shed my own armour and cover him in it so that no one can ever hurt him again. So that *she* can't.

"She must not have seen any other way." He finishes.

I don't accept that for a moment.

"She was selfish and cruel." I growl.

No – No, I don't want to talk about her. I won't.

"No, no don't say that..." he quickly wipes at his face. "She just had problems. She must have done –"

I think of her then – can't help not to. Her eyes. Her effortless smile.

I quake in the coats I wear, despite how much I am starting to sweat. I hadn't seen any clues that she was struggling. Had I? Like I had with Nathan where I had just not said anything? No. No, I don't want to talk about her – to think about her. She doesn't deserve it, I see that now. This whole time punishing myself for being here whilst she wasn't – punishing *them*. The way Nathan had been punishing himself. No. No, that is not ok. How can *anyone* be that wicked? That selfish?

I wonder if she would have thought harder about her decision if she'd known that I would be the one to find her...

"No – No, sorry – I can't do this, Nathan –"

It's getting really dark now. Where have Paul and Star gone? Not like I care. No – no, I do care. Star? Star – I am sorry! I use the tree to help me to my feet. To talk. To talk to Nathan – *just Nathan*. But it isn't just Nathan, is it? It is *her*. I can't – I can't. Not her.

"Emmy – please, please just talk to me –"

"No. No, Nathan – not her, I can't."

"Emmy, come on – please, not like this. Come on –"

How do I put one foot in front of the other again? How do I take my next breath? How do I get her out of my head? The first star is peeking out of the dark blue of the sky. It twinkles weakly. Pathetically compared to the threatening night.

"Emmy, please –"

One foot in front of the other. That one, then that one. I stumble, hands out in front of me.

"Emmy! Come on, don't be stupid –"

He grabs me. I shake him off. One foot in front of the other. He grabs for me again.

"Seriously, get off of me, Nathan..."

This foot, then that foot.

"No, Emmy – come on. We need to talk. You were right! We need to do this – no more pretending – come on." He calls suddenly over to the other trees in the dark. "Hey guys! Can you help? Emmy – come on, we need to do this..."

Again – that one, then that one. This foot, then the next. I am surprised he doesn't cut his hands on my sharpness.

"You need to get off of me."

I can't. I can't do it. I thought I was stronger than this, Willow! I am meant to be here – be here for him, play your part! Can we just go back? Can painting in my room be enough? I can see that...see a glimpse of a life for the three of us through the purple of the flowers on my wall. Not here though – not now. Not whilst *she* lives on in him. I can't do it.

He grabs me harder, pulls me in – turns me round and into his chest. I push! Push away – like I would do when Dad tries to hold me. Push him hard, right in the ribs. He stumbles back but grabs for me again.

"Emmy! Please!"

He cries, hard.

I try and picture his monsters – the ones who did that to his arm – as I push him away. The pain he wears on his face now may even rival it, and it stabs me so hard in the chest that I almost lose all of my strength. The only monster I can see is her. Her, and myself.

I cry back. Hard. Push at him harder. Again! Shove him as hard as I can, and he falls over the tree root – crashes into the ground.

"Emmy - please!!"

One foot in front of the other.

Faster.

Star and Paul have gathered, helping him to his feet – shouting after me. Begging me – screaming my name. I fall myself; bringing dry leaves away with my hands as I push myself up again. My breath loud in my ears. His cries even louder.

This foot, then that foot.

It's dark. So dark now...

Faster - until I am running! Running faster than I have in my life. As if my life depends on it.

As if his does.

Faster! I can't see where my feet land as the sky turns indigo. Only one thin streak of light upon the horizon now. The only bit of light left in my life.

Willow? Willow, where are you? I need you! I've ruined it – I am ruining it all! I can't, I can't do it on my own! I can't even do it for Nathan, I can't!

"Emmy! Come back! Emmy!!"

Running. Running so fast that my legs blur in the black. Drifting – floating up out of my body, leaving my mortal shell.

"Emmy!!"

Like a kite...except the Emmy with her feet on the ground has let go of that string now, and I drift, I float, I soar. Leaving it all behind. Leaving them all.

I hear Nathan scream, and their voices follow. Desperate, frightened, angry. Heavy feet on ground, hard breaths in chests, then their voices, fading, as I run.

Running as if I can fly.

As if I am flying.

Flying away.

Alone at last

"Willow? Willow, I wish you could hear me. What have I done?"

The round bright moon and the stars are the only light. They cast everything in a strange blue hue, as if I have ink in my eyes. My breath as it billows is even blue. Blue smoke.

"Willow? Willow, I don't know what to do. I am lost now. Truly lost."

I had run until I could no longer hear their voices. Had run so hard, I think I had even been sick...but I can't really remember. Nathan's had lasted the longest; his pleas loud and hoarse, until they too fell to the wind as it raged in my ears with my hot blood.

"Willow? I was doing it. I was learning too. I was really trying... "

I had stumbled down to the river, at first. That blue, inky light from the moon, shining upon the water; pushing its way through balding trees to paint the clear water in dangerous black. I had gone right up to the edge. Knelt down in the leafy dirt. Seen my shadowed and dark reflection. Seen a monster wearing my skin. I had even thought about drowning it; drowning myself. Creeping up behind that Emmy – grabbing her by the back of her hair and shoving her face down into that water. Crawling up on to her back as she struggled. Pushing away her desperate arms – pushing her down, down – holding her head firmly under that cold, dark water. Holding her; until the monster, until I, stopped moving.

"...But I've ruined it all now, Willow. Haven't I? What do I do? How can I come back from this?"

I had felt calmed by the idea; the idea of dying. Thought, if someone had shoved my face into the water, I wouldn't have struggled or fought. I wouldn't have screamed or thrashed. I would have welcomed it; welcomed that cold, dark water. Breathed it deeply into my lungs with a smile. It didn't feel selfish, this time. Not selfish like her. It felt almost freeing. A way to let go – a way to move on. To end it all – to end mine and their suffering. To finally fade away; to break down until there is nothing left. To finally be free of myself.

"Do I want to though, Willow? Do I want to come back?"

Despite the moons paleness, some of the trees I huddle near now have given birth to strange silvery shadows. They streak across the inky ground like dark lightning; flipping the world upside down as I perch precariously amongst their branches of white fire. It is like I have fallen into a dream; one that blurs around the edges as if too bright, despite the darkness I sit in. I don't even know where the car park is from here. I don't even know where I am, or how long I have been sat here. All I know, is that I am alone. Completely and utterly alone. Like I had wanted to be from the start, right? No brother, no father...no friends, no Willow. No mother. That's what I have been trying to strive for, right? To be alone. To be left alone. Finally.

I tuck my nose right to my knees and blow out that hot blue smoke from my lips.

Maybe this is a dream? One I am now trapped in? Especially if I had let go of that thread that bound me, or if I let it snap. I think it may have been cut...cut by those sharp and shiny scissors in Nathan's bedroom.

"And Nathan, Willow. How do we get back from Nathan? From what he has been doing? I can't bear it..."

His coat must have fallen from my shoulders somewhere back along. I can't say that I noticed at the time, but I hurt from the cold now. Hurt; as if my blood slowly freezes. Really, really hurt. What was I thinking? Running away – leaving him when he probably needed me the most? When we were finally, *finally,* going to talk. Talk about it all. I blow into my legs again; feel it condense into little drops on my face almost immediately. Feel them freeze.

Perhaps I have been the weak link this whole time? Perhaps Dad and Nathan would be doing much better – be moving on already – if it wasn't for me holding us back. Am I really the one doing that? The one stopping us all?

I should have just left myself pruned and rotting in that dark river.

I take a deep breath and wince at the ice in my throat.

"I've – I've already said I am angry. H-Haven't I? W-What else is there t-t-to say?" I stammer aloud to the air through my convulsions.

I half expect to hear an echo, but my words too freeze on the air and fall like heavy stones. I speak louder.

"W-Why do I need to talk about her? H-Huh? Why d-do I have to talk about *you*? W-Why *should* I?"

I dare to look around me through the trees and out across the vast black land to where I think I have run from. It all looks the same now, and it is deathly silent.

"Ok – Ok, f-fine. If I am meant t-to talk, I'll talk!"

I shout it now.

"Yeah, Willow? I-Is this what you meant? How I *heal* – how I m-move on? To talk about her? About it all? F-Fine! Y-You want t-to hear it? H-Hear what I t-truly have to say?"

My eyes fill and turn to harsh crystals in the frigid air.

"Why d-did you to do it then, M-Mum? W-Why?"

My chest feels like it could rip open from how hard my heart punches at the inside of my ribcage at saying that word. At saying her name.

"C-Come on then! This is what you w-wanted, isn't it, Willow! Mrs Locklea? Dad – Nathan? For me to f-feel it, yeah? To r-really feel it!"

I stand up, shakily, my legs like stone. Scream at the sky.

"My pain isn't e-enough, is it? I h-have to go back? Go back and f-face it? Face her? Well I d-did face you, didn't I, Mum! I faced a-all of it – all of it."

The stars; so far away now as I look up to them desperately. The stars that I long for. The stars that I dream of.

"How c-could you do that t-to me, Mum? I...I thought you l-loved me."

The stars; like pinpricks in an otherwise hopeless dark. Like how the light catches someone's eyes and they sparkle with the same fire.

Stars...Funny how the ones I see up in the sky now are already dead.

"I-I loved you so much, Mum..."

On my own. Finally, on my own where there is nothing to hide behind. Nothing to distract me, as my own stars fall from my eyes.

I stumble breathlessly from laughing through the front door, my small shoulder bag already falling to the carpeted floor. Sophie had just walked straight into the lamppost outside of my house; bouncing off like she was made of rubber before toppling to the ground. Jemma laughed so much that she had given herself a nosebleed to match that of Sophie's, and I cough a laugh now as I picture the moment again. Just like a rubber ball! Kate has linked arms with her now, as Jemma taunts and teases as they all sway down the road. I love that we all live in walking distance of each other. That, and the longer warmer days.

"I swear if any of you have filmed that!" Sophie screeches through her own laugher, and she trips again just before being caught by Jemma, and the three of them fall about laughing again.

"I don't know – did you manage to catch anything, Ems?" calls Kate loudly. I can see the tears on her cheeks even from here.

I swing on the door, stomach aching.

"Well – it's burned into here for a lifetime, that's for sure!" I squeal back, tapping on my temples.

"It's fine – you'll look super distinguished with a black eye. Maybe a certain someone will think it sexy!" Jemma grabs Sophie in a headlock, the blood drying under her nose making her look like a sad clown.

"Oh my god – don't even! Shut up!" Sophie blushes through her freckles and Jemma ruffles her hair whilst Kate rolls her eyes,

trying to keep her own feet on the pavement.

"Right, call me later, ok?" I laugh back, wiping the tears from my own eyes.

I miss what else they shout out as I close the front door, jumping over the back of the sofa to land lightly on the cushions; grabbing my white fleece and wrapping it around me like a cape. I laugh again.

The sun shines strongly through the net curtains of our front room and shines so much on to the TV that all I can see is my own reflection once I turn it on. My cheeks are pink and eyes bright; full of summer warmth.

"Nath? You home yet?"

I kick my shoes off, leaving them under the coffee table, as I wander off to the kitchen, fleece still in tow.

"Nathan?"

I grab an apple from the floral fruit bowl and hold it in my mouth as I pour out a glass of water. The sun shines brightly here too, and I have to squint at the glass so as not to be blinded. The noisy kitchen clock says it is almost half past five, and I feel a hint of guilt at eating a snack so close to dinner time. Nathan is probably at his girlfriend's house, I have hardly seen him since the summer holidays started! Rather over at hers then them both here – they do like to hog the sofa with their loud kisses and baby voices. Dad at least should be home from work soon. Not long at all now actually; and I fill the kettle up and stick it on ready for his cup of tea.

"Mum? You home too, yeah? Do you want a cuppa?"

I grab out hers and Dad's mugs from the top shelf of the cupboard, having to climb up onto the surface in order to reach, and I jump down effortlessly. His has 'Dad of the year' *on it in big red writing, a silly cartoon man holding a golden trophy just beneath. It is his favourite, and he insists on having his teas in this one despite the ridiculous amount of mugs we have. Mum's has a sleeping grey bunny on hers; holding a purple flower as a parasol to protect its sleepy eyes from the sun. Nathan and I had got it for Mother's Day a few years ago, I think. I am not sure whether we got her anything this year, actually.*

"Mum?"

She has taken the day off of work today. She has taken a few off actually: said that she had a 'summer flu' of some kind, yet I hadn't seen any evidence in more tissues being used. I think she just wanted to take a break, to be honest. Skive off. Like how sometimes you say you are ill from school when you feel perfectly fine – when you just need to take some time out to do nothing. I guess adults feel like that too sometimes. A cup of tea will be a nice gesture anyway.

I get my bag from the front door, throw my fleece back on to the sofa, take up my apple again from the kitchen, and make my way upstairs. She is probably in bed watching TV. I have asked for a TV in my room countless times – Nathan has one! But they always say I can wait until I am older. That my generation spends 'too much time looking at screens anyway'.

I quickly check my phone, send Jemma a quick text back with another laugh, and throw my bag into my bedroom to land gently onto my bed.

Yes – I can hear sitcom voices coming from Mum and Dad's room. I wonder if she has bothered watching any of the DVD's I left out for her this morning. They aren't outside of her door anymore anyway. I take a big bite out of my apple and pop it ontop of the cabinet in the landing.

"Mum? How much junk have you watched today, then? I should have left you a pile of chocolate too!"

I push the door open with a giggle, apple juices at the side of my mouth. Her curtains are still drawn, and the sun pushes fiercely through the edges.

"Oh, Mum! How many times have you told me off for leaving the curtains closed? Let some fresh air in, yeah?" I fling them open, and push out one of the windows. The breeze is nice and sweet smelling on my face.

"I've put the kettle on, not sure if you want a –"

A pile under the thin duvet; her face almost completely covered as her hair spreads like a fairy over her pillow.

"Mum? Sorry, Mum, you asleep?" I whisper, as I walk over to her.

Her nose is peeking just above the covers, her eyes peacefully closed. I could be looking at myself, when our eyes are closed, we look that alike. So relaxed she is, that almost all lines have smoothed away from around her eyes. I smile and brush away some of her hair.

"Good evening, sleepy head!" I laugh. But then something heavy drops in my stomach, and I let my smile fade away.

"Mum?"

Too smooth, her face. Too still.

"Mum?"

I put my hands to her face. Cold.

I stutter within myself suddenly, déjà vu strongly tugging at my chest. No – No, I don't want to live this again. Don't want to remember. Are my hands numb? Why does my breath billow before me?

I pull the cover back, right back. Bring my trembling hands to her chest. Push her. Push again.

"Mum? Mum – come on, what you doing? Come on, wake up..."

I push her again. Again.

Pull the covers right back.

Bottles. Pills. Hidden amongst the folds.

Lead fills my stomach.

"Mum?"

The cold creeps in my chest, my bubble freezing within me, making it hard to breathe...

I grab her now. Shake her. Her head lolls dangerously. Enough to snap. Shake her! Shake her harder!

"Mum! Mum, come on!"

A sound downstairs. A door closing. My voice fails through its screams.

"Dad! Dad, quick! Dad!!"

Everything blurs around me. Time shifts, moves, and stutters. Stutters.

Just like my music.

"DAD!!"

His feet on the stairs, like panicked thunder.

It echoes within my hollow chest.

He runs through the door, turns to me first, and takes my face in his hands before he sees hers. Hers. Too still. Too calm.

He is holding her now. Holding her to his chest. His head bent back, screaming at the ceiling. I stumble back, unable to look away. Feel my back come hard against the wall.

Nathan's voice now, calling from downstairs. His heavy feet as he runs. How he stumbles and falls to the ground when he sees the scene. How I see his heart break. See it plain on his face, the moment it breaks in half. The moment mine did. How they all scream. How they keep screaming.

I fall hard to my knees and land back in the dark, the moonlit dark, on sodden ground.

It lasts forever...and it plays out for me now in slow motion. I can hardly breathe.

It plays again.

Again.

The thing I have been trying to forget – trying to bury.

The thing I had left buried the day we buried her.

New versions pressing in: if I had come home earlier. If I hadn't gone out at all. Versions of her shouting 'boo' from underneath the covers, of us curling up to finish watching a film. Versions of Dad and Nathan never coming home...of calling out for help forever and ever, being trapped in there with her for the rest of my days.

I try and thump my fist into the ground, but it barely grazes the frosty grass. Blue smoke steams between my clenched teeth. The pain overwhelming.

How Dad had slept curled up at the bottom of my bed.

How I hadn't slept at all.

How it took a whole day for the men to come and get her.

How they handled her roughly as they put her in the back of that ambulance.

How the neighbours had watched.

It all breaks out of the coffin in my mind, throwing shattered shards into the back of my eyes, and I bring my hands to my head and squeeze. Where is my music? Where is my painting – my Willow? It's only her now. Only her and me.

"See, M-Mum!"

I try to scream but it comes as a mere whisper. A whisper into my knees as I hunch down, curl right down, all strength lost. I can hardly form my frozen mouth around the words. Can hardly take a frigid breath through the sobs.

"See how you have r-ruined us! H-How you have ruined us all! I hate you f-for that! I hate you! I hate you! I hate you!"

A far away voice in the distance. Or is it an owl?

"What r-reasons did you have, Mum? Did you w-want to be f-free of us that much? You wanted to leave us? R-Ruin us completely?"

She should have done it somewhere we couldn't see...kept it her dirty little secret.

Like by the river in the woods? Alone in the dark?

My sobs catch in my throat. No – No, it's completely different. My situation is totally different. Why did I even think that? Willow?

Thinking they would all be better off without you? That their lives would be better without you in it? To end the pain?

She couldn't have been in pain though – she had no reason! No reason!

That you knew of.

I never would have done it, though. Not really. I wouldn't have.

But you wanted to. Like she must have wanted to. Once it's done, it can't be taken back.

Another noise – another voice out from the deep dark. I am so cold I feel like I am freezing into the ground. Has my shaking stopped? My breaths are definitely shallower.

"We wouldn't have b-been better off without you though, Mum! We aren't...I d-don't know why you didn't know that..."

Another noise. I manage to move my head to the side. See

lights. Bright yellow lights casting beams into the sky, moving along the ground. My starlight?

"If I d-didn't say it enough...i-if we didn't say it enough, Mum, I'm sorry...I'm s-so sorry..."

A loud voice then – as all beams point towards my direction. They start moving, furiously. Getting brighter. Getting louder.

"If you knew, M-Mum...I d-don't think you would have gone. If you k-knew...t-that we loved you..." my words fail. I can't even hear them in my own head as my starlight gets brighter. Loud voices I cannot understand.

"That we l-loved you more than a-anything. That w-we love you...I love you...please, c-come back..."

My eyes close as I feel warm hands wrap around me.

"Come back to me, Emmy."

The fifth stage

This really must be a dream, as I float above the ground guided by starlight. Six individual beams of warm starlight, leading me through the dark as I rest in strong arms.

There are flashing blue lights too; not ones cast in the moons hue, but bright harsh ones, and I float into the back of a large white box surrounded by bright yellow jackets that hurt my eyes.

"It's ok, Flower. It's ok, I'm here..."

Wrapped in tin foil like a turkey ready for the oven, but even my panic cannot move my limbs as I lie down on a harsh feeling bed. A bed? Why do I think that? Where am I?

It is not starlight that surrounds me now, and I scrunch my eyes tightly, ready to wake – to wake up – as the pain in the front of my head grows sharp. The lights – they are too bright! Too bright!

A hand takes mine, and its heat burns me.

"It's ok, Flower. It's ok baby – I am here..."

Lots of noise. People grabbing me, moving me – another set of bright lights as my white box opens. I now float – float really fast on my back above the ground, overhead lights flitting past: that one, then that one, then that one – hands again, the rustle of my cooking foil, then softness. A soft, pillowy, warm safe softness, and I fall into real dream immediately.

* * *

I'm not sure what time it is as we drive back to the apartment. I am bundled into the back of Dad's car, wrapped up in countless blankets with Nathan sat next to me; his regular place in the front passenger seat lying empty. I think that every blanket we own forms part of my cocoon. Even my favourite white fleece is playing a role, and I subtly try and move my nose into it and take in its smell.

Nathan holds my hand too, his eyes fixed straight out in front of him. His hair is a little damp, and his eyes tighter than ever before. Only a part of me stirs as I remember the look in his eyes as I had left him earlier this night, as well as the memory of his weight against my palms as I had pushed him. Only a stir though; the rest of me is sleeping.

We had only been at the hospital for a few of hours I think, but I can't really remember what had happened there. I know I had been very confused at first; confused by the rushing, the voices and the beeping, but also confused as to how I had got there. How Dad was there. And had it been Christa and Paul's mum and dad too? I may have made that up. But the four of them had definitely been there, I remember the blue of Christa's hair. Or had that been the blue of the lights?

Nathan squeezes my hand as I shuffle in my blankets.

The main thing I remember is being cold, and the strange tingling feeling of getting warm again. How it hurt a little; as if metal beads moved about through my veins and beneath my skin, using sharp tools to create new tunnels in the block of ice my body had become. How I had stung, as if a mini electrical storm were happening somewhere within me. I remember Dad hugging the doctor too, once they came in and said that they were happy with my temperature. That, and how Nathan hadn't looked at me once.

Now, Dad keeps his arms securely around me as we walk in darkness towards the mauve door lit by its little beacon, the stones crunching like snow beneath our heavy feet. A part of me stirs again, this time with the memory of our first night here, and I move my eyes carefully in my head looking for the old woman's smile and tap to her nose as we enter the bright hallway. Her trembling hands as she held that paint from the shed waiting for me to come back down the stairs. The songbirds and her bag of crumbs. The wind playing on her hair as she closed her eyes. All of this, paired with an ache as I realise the hallway is empty, and my legs grow heavier as Dad helps me up the stairs. Nathan carries the trailing blankets in his arms behind us.

Dad sits me down straight away onto the sofa and brings me the largest mug of hot chocolate, simply saying "doctor's orders". The two of them sit with me in silence until I finish drinking.

I have so much to say now. So much I couldn't say to Nathan before – things I haven't said to Dad this whole time. It's like a part of my brain has lit up after spending so long in the dark, shining a warm light onto all the parts of me that have been lost these past months. But it's also as if my brain is working slower than usual; it fights groggily with itself unable to remember how words or sounds are formed - as if waking up from being turned off for a long time. As if it is resetting.

Nathan still hasn't said a word either, and quickly kisses me on the forehead without looking at me before disappearing to his room and the ache comes back tenfold. He must know I didn't mean for this to happen...right? That it wasn't meant to happen like this at all. That it wasn't planned - that I didn't want it to go the way that it did.

I try desperately to put form to the words moving too fast to see in my head, but instead lift my mug tentatively to my lips where its final dregs are tasteless in my mouth.

Dad makes me another large mug, heated up orange squash this time, grabs an old hot water bottle with a fluffy cover from his room, and helps me to my feet to guide me to my bedroom. My little bedside lamp is already on, providing a much gentler light for my tired eyes than the one in my head, and he waits outside of the door as I get dressed into my pyjamas. He is straight in when he hears the creak of my bed and helps me with the covers, piling a few of the blankets on top for good measure. I can even start to feel beads of sweat blossoming in the pit of my back.

Dad? Were you the one who found me? The one who carried me through dark starlight? The one with strong arms.

I look at him, but still cannot say a word.

Once snuggled down into my pillow, he sits down next to me, smoothing my hair with his hand. It trembles slightly, as does his breath; his eyes big and steaming up his glasses. He opens and closes his mouth a few times, before he finds his own words.

"I love you so very much. You know that, right baby?" his voice catches as a large tear rolls down his cheek. He wipes it away quickly, attempting to put a huge smile onto his lips. "More than you could ever imagine."

He looks around my room, blowing puffs of air out between quivering lips, wiping underneath his glasses again, and comes to settle on my half painted wall. His lips turn downward dramatically and he takes a deep steadying breath, wiping at his eyes again.

"More than all the stars in the sky. More than every flower."

He brings his hand to his face now and hides himself away as his sobs take him.

"And...and if there has ever been a time that I haven't told you enough...or that you didn't know just how much, I'm sorry, baby...I am so sorry."

My stomach tightens as I see his other hand begging to be taken as it rests on his lap. I bite my lip as my own tears roll down my cheeks, my own words to my mother echoing in my head. My silence holds and his hand remains desperately alone.

"I couldn't bare for you to think that you weren't loved, Emmy. To not know how important you are to me and your brother – how much we love you. If I don't say it enough...if we don't say it enough, baby, I'm sorry...I'm s-so sorry..."

He turns to me again, his face pink and broken, brings his shaking lips to my forehead, and quickly leaves.

My Dad. My strong and happy Dad...does he whisper those words to Mum, too? Has he been battling not only with the loss, but with the unrelenting guilt as well? Did I bring that all back to him tonight – on a night where I could have left him asking those same questions over me?

I pull myself into a tight ball beneath my covers despite the sweat that now takes hold, and my white fleece comes against my nose. As I breathe it in, I crumble, and take it in my hands and push it into my face as pain buries into the very pit of my stomach. I realise now that I don't love it so much because it smells like home, but because it smells like her. It smells like Mum.

I cry harder than I ever have done, until my shakes for the second time this night, fall still.

* * *

I guess it must be really early, according to the steely grey of the sky; it shines ever so slightly through the bottom of my curtains. I had a very broken sleep in the end: turning off the lamp on my bedside table sometime around two in the morning, chucking off my blankets in a sudden flush some other time, and then feeling guilty and putting them back onto my bed a third. Now, I lie on my back with just my white fleece across my chest, running my thumb along it back and forth, back and forth. I won't be falling asleep again this time.

It's a strange sensation; being awake at a time you can imagine everyone else sleeping. Even stranger in a hotel: I can almost feel the walls around me snoring gently in a combined peaceful dream. Almost sense them. When the world is this quiet and this still, I wonder how it can even coexist in the same space as the one that is so loud, bright, and chaotic. How can we, at one moment be blurring so fast – making noise, making mess – scream, shout, laugh, cry and feel – suddenly be so still? So completely still and silent as the world around us sleeps. It's almost like a practice for death, isn't it? Spending so many hours of our day on pause. For the world keeps on turning. It is only we who freeze momentarily in these moments, as others somewhere else are awakening to carry on living again.

Yes. A strange sensation. I wonder if people dream once

dead.

I didn't dream last night, but I thought about Nathan a lot. Probably why I couldn't sleep much actually, and my stomach continues to swim nervously as he floats about in my head. Both him and Dad, really. About all the things I need to say. That I know is time to say. I even start to whisper words aloud to myself in the dark to check if my brain has remembered how to send them to my mouth. They start of simple and slightly pointless: words like "rug", "book" or "windowsill", but slowly start to take true form. Forms such as, "I'm sorry" or "I've been selfish". "I'm ready to talk about Mum" or "I thought about killing myself last night."

The last one shakes me somewhat, but I brave it at a whisper. It doesn't even echo in my room. I say it again, a little louder. A little louder, then push myself to sit up before my chest feels too heavy. Nathan has been much braver than me this whole time, hasn't he? Trying to talk to me about something he knew would be difficult. He had told others before me, yes, but that's because he was trying to protect me, wasn't it? Well, that and how I haven't even been around for him to do so. At least he had talked to someone. I start to play with my lip, my legs getting fidgety. If I had been *willing* to talk in the first place, and in turn to listen, Nathan may have told me from the beginning, mightn't he? Told me even before he made the choice to do it.

My heart flutters up my throat as I hear a creak of a door, and I get ready to cowardly throw myself under my covers all bravery gone.

It may be hard to do so; say the things we only half admit to ourselves out loud to others, but what happens when you never say anything? I bring my white fleece back into my lap and smooth it with my hand. We know what happens when you don't talk, though. We all thought Mum was fine.

It isn't my door that creaked, so I hold my breath in my mouth, ignoring the snoring walls, to see if I can pinpoint where it came from within the apartment. Are those footsteps too? Their owner must be tip-toeing or cushioned by air somehow they are so light, and I lose them almost as quickly as I found them. I listen, almost perched on the edge of my bed now; a map of the apartment filling my head as I start to track where the noise had come from and where it had ended. Another sense; different to how sounds find you when your eyes are taken, and it prickles at me in the dark sending fingers up into the base of my neck. Nathan comes tumbling back into my thoughts, and I grab my fleece quickly with trembling hands, a busy stomach and a suddenly empty head, and float to my bedroom door.

The whole apartment is covered in an anti-light, all colour drained from the walls and floor as I creep. It's like I am suspended in a black nothingness, and I almost expect to fall down into it with each impending step. I even imagine myself on a type of tightrope – and wobble down the dark corridor with arms out to both sides. I'm not sure I have even taken a breath yet when I notice a dark figure sitting on the inky sofa. A shadow cut from pitch black. A sense must have prickled them too though, for they turn to face my silence.

"I couldn't sleep." Croaks Nathan's voice.

I think we hold each other's eyes for a moment; a dark shadow looking upon another, till Nathan's slumps in its seat. The sense I felt before builds in my stomach, and my fleece falls to the floor as I rush to him, wrapping my arms tightly around him – something I should have done this whole time – and he cries weakly into my neck, soaking my hair. He squeezes me back tightly, and I realise just how much I have been aching for it.

"I'm sorry," I squeak, my practiced words tumbling from me as I hold him even tighter. "I didn't mean to go yesterday – I'm so sorry I left you like that, I'm so sorry, Nathan. I want to talk – I do. I've just been so selfish –"

"No, I'm sorry –" He mumbles through his tears. "I should have been there for you more. I've been a crap brother –"

"No! No, I was pushing you away! I've been pushing everyone away – this is on me, not you! You have nothing to be sorry for!"

To finally talk. To say what we think and what we feel, even though it may be frightening.

I take his shoulders and pull out of the hug, the pain on his face only momentary, but it still cuts at me like a razor as it mirrors his one from yesterday. I hold him strongly, finding his eyes in the dark and lock them into mine. I blink away my tears and his soft edges go sharp.

"We have to be here for each other, and I know I haven't been – I know I haven't. But I don't want to end up like Mum, Nath – I don't – I can't do that to you or Dad."

I shake him slightly till he looks into my eyes again.

"But you can't do that to us either, do you hear me? You can't Nathan, I can't bear it."

I run my hands down his arms, his damaged arms, and he takes my hands strongly in his.

"I know. I know, I won't. I promise –"

"No – no, don't promise. *She* may have said that to us once if we had asked –"

But we didn't ask, did we?

"– and I don't want you to lie just not to hurt me, or to end up breaking a promise you can't keep. Just –"

I take a deep breath and take notice of the irony of the words; wonder how many times they have been said to me.

"Just...talk, ok? Tell me, tell Dad – Paul, Star, anyone – if you are not feeling ok. Right?"

Is it getting lighter? Or am I just starting to find light in the darkness.

"Ok? And – and I will too. Starting now. I will – Ok?"

Am I lying now? Just not to hurt him?

His eyes, their hazel specks breaking through the blueness of the dark, crease slightly as he nods.

"OK. To talk. We can do that."

I nod back, the tightness in my chest easing slightly, and I let go of his warm hands to run my own through my hair, expelling the spare breath held in my lungs.

"What do *you* mean though?" he says, "That you don't want to end up like Mum? You haven't –?!" I snag my hair as he grabs my arm suddenly, desperately trying to roll up my sleeve.

"No! No, I haven't done anything." I reassure, as I sense the panic rising in his chest. He runs his hands through his own hair with relief, and I squirm thinking about my own advice.

When he starts to smile, his teeth breaking through the heavy light, I find that I can't quite look at him. Feel myself looking over my shoulder back to my room, even. My room – Willow! I hadn't even thought about speaking to her! I haven't given her one thought since coming home! What would she have to say about all of this? About what I did last night? About this now.

She's been telling me to talk to Nathan this whole time.

"But," I bring my eyes down to my knees as they start to tremble. My eyes fill quickly, and I blink away falling stars to drip onto my black pyjama bottoms.

"Um," there aren't any bubbles left in my chest, they have all popped. They are popping now – like fireworks in my rib cage.

"But,"

It's scary: how decisions we make in haste out of anger or pain, can ripple through the rest of our lives and disrupt everything we have. Disrupt everyone we have. Change it forever. Could I have ever done that? To Nathan, to Dad? Looking back on it now, I can't believe I had ever sat upon that river bed and dreamed for it. That I almost did it. It doesn't even seem like me – it must have been a different Emmy – the dark one I thought of sometimes. I could *never* do that to them! Could I? It terrifies me that anyone could actually make that choice. It absolutely terrifies me.

I put my hands over my face and cry. I can't look at him – I can't say it and look at him.

"But I nearly did last night, Nath. When I left you. When I ran away. I wanted to die – I wanted to kill myself."

I am terrified even saying it now. Had Mum been this scared before? How I wish she could be in the position to look back at it with hindsight – oh my God how I miss her. It's not fair! I start to shake, and feel Nathan's arms around my shoulders. I can't look at him.

"I have never *hurt* so much, Nathan. Never been in so much pain as I have these past few months. It's been like my chest is full..."

I search for the words. The words I haven't been saying.

"Full of...painful bubbles. And...and they've been pushing against my heart and my lungs – making me feel like I can't fully catch my breath or as if I am breaking apart from the inside. And - and I just didn't want to hurt anymore. I didn't want to have to miss her anymore! I just thought it would be easier – and it wouldn't be, I'm so, so sorry! I can't even imagine, thinking of you and Dad finding me –"

I see it – I can see it all. It plays out for me like when we found her.

"I just – I just miss her, Nathan. I miss Mum so much I can't even stand it. Why did she do it?"

I bring my hands away from my face, exhausted, and sit there panting. I wait for him to explode. For a strike across my face. For swear words and anger. I flinch at my trembling hands – or are those his that tremble? They are suddenly holding mine, and he brings me round to face him. To finally face him, and to face our mother. To face myself.

It is definitely starting to get a little lighter; his sugary brown hair looks just that now, and his fringe hangs slightly into his eyes which aren't angry at all. Red from crying, but anything but angry. What time is it? Is that Dad I can hear starting to stir? Has he got another day off of work? Oh, Dad! – I hadn't even thought about him yet! What am I going to say to him? What have I started? I start to panic, but Nathan's sudden calm is catching. He nods, a rogue tear falling down his cheek, and sets his face.

"Ok. Let's talk about it, Ems. Let's talk about everything."

The girl beneath the willow

It's the first time I have been into Nathan's bedroom since the alien socks and crumpled photographs. I even find the courage to tell him, now that we are working at laying everything out in the open: tell him that I had snooped around and found things that had made me anxious for him. He in turn admits that he has been into my room too – probably looking for the kind of things you might hide in plain sight such as the scissors on his bedside table. He hadn't found anything though; my weapons I had carried about with me in secret.

Why hadn't we both just *said* all of this? Back when it could have influenced or changed some of the events that went on to take place? Approached each other – demanded explanations? We muse about it for a while – about how long it has taken for us to come together in our grief. Or at least start to. How horrible it is that we have both had to do it on our own and for so long. How we really don't want to anymore.

His little bedside light is on, despite the sky being a brighter grey through his window now, and it's nice not having to battle with my eyes in order to find proper shapes and micro movements in his face. I even find myself wondering for a moment what I must look like after noticing the dark bags beneath his tired eyes. That and how his lamp looks so much more *boy* like then mine, despite being its twin. How the shade is crooked, and stained as if it has been smoking.

We talk about what happened after I left him from both perspectives. How it had been Star that had called our Dad as Nathan couldn't think straight. How Paul had sprinted back to the small car park and asked everyone he could find if they had seen me. How he had driven up and down the road in case I had done something stupid.

We talk about that day...about Mum.

We cry. We sit in silence.

It is probably around 8 o'clock now, and we break from our most recent silence when we hear a sudden panicked shuffle outside of Nathan's door, along with what sounds like a stifled cry. Nathan runs straight out after shooting me a worried look to find Dad outside. I figure he must have panicked upon looking into my room and finding it empty. They talk for a little, Nathan's low tone more obvious than Dads, until the situation seems calmer and Dad pops his head in just to make sure. I smile anxiously with my white fleece wrapped around my shoulders, giving him an awkward wave, and his eyes brighten when he sees me. He nods, says something to Nathan on the other side of the door and Nathan comes back in with a smile and a plate with some toast on it. Peanut butter and honey, of course, and my heart swells.

Dad. He has been brave enough for the both of us – he really is some kind of superhero. Thinking about it now, after finally talking about it with Nathan, after truly admitting what I feel about the whole situation – I can't quite believe just how strong he has been. One of us fell apart, stopped going to school and became a prisoner in their own bedroom; the other used physical force on themselves in secret whilst smiling in public. But Dad? He carried on going to work. He found us a new place to live. He cooked, he cleaned. He kept us both alive, really. I watch the door as I eat the sugary bread in silence and know what to do for him immediately. He needs a gesture. A proper gesture from me – one that will mean a lot to him and speak in his language. To try and get across what these last couple of months have been like. To try and get across what I have faced, what I am facing now, and that I am sorry. That I am so sorry that I have focused on my own grief, my guilt, and forsaken his. That I love him...and most importantly: that I don't blame him for what happened to Mum.

Nathan only hesitates for a moment when I suggest it to him shyly – and when we hear the shower turn on, he creeps out and comes back with Dad's guitar.

"Do you think he will like it though?" I cringe, sucking my cheeks at the sweetness of the honey.

"Oh – he will love it."

When finishing my toast and realising that the plate he had put it on was my childhood favourite one: the one with the faded bear Alfred on the bottom, I burst into tired tears; finally saying aloud just how upset I am for how I have treated our father. How I hope he can forgive me. How horrible I have been to him.

After popping his somewhat wet head in again saying that he has some errands to run in town, and after checking numerous times that I was warm enough and that we were both ok, we hear the front door go and set to work. Nathan throws me a notebook and pen that I catch in mid-air, and, as an anxious smile lifts my cheeks, I start to write as he tunes the guitar.

I am itching by the time we hear Dad come back home. He clangs about in the kitchen for a while, puts the kettle on I think, and now he must be sat in the lounge reading a book or the paper or something as everything has gone quiet. I am literally bouncing on my toes – teetering somewhere between being desperate for the toilet and the moment before you enter the exam hall at school. Nathan squeezes my shoulders and whispers, "Are you ready?" into my ear. I nod, and when I turn to him for reassurance, he smiles and winks as he too stands ready with guitar in hand. I have to really settle my chest before I burst into tears – in both a strange happiness and in fear. I breathe in, and take the cold door handle in my grasp.

We start to walk, Nathan playing the gentle chords to accompany us and immediately my eyes fill dramatically. How am I going to be able to sing if I can't even catch my breath? I'm not even a very good singer.

I had never even appreciated why music was so important to me. It's one of those things that you just take for granted when you're a teenager. Even when your life is normal – as normal as you allow it to be when this young – you take all those little things for granted. How you love music because your Dad would play an old Queen tape cassette for you when you were tiny. How certain attitudes or passions you have towards things aren't your own, but are encouraged and grown by others. How everything we have, everything we are, actually – everything – is because of the people around us who love us. And we should never take that, or them, for granted. I will never take it for granted again.

Dad's sat on the sofa, and looks up in surprise when we pass the kitchen and enter the room. He is holding something in his hands that I can't quite make out, and he places it carefully on the small coffee table. I keep my shaking steps going, coming to a stand just by the small dining table, Nathan stopping to stand beside me. I look to him again, and he nods and smiles, his eyes shining and lips trembling. He moves into the bridge, and I part my lips.

"When the stars rain down from darkened skies, the world can seem so grey.

You grab the fire with both your hands and prey the light will stay.

But sometimes in the deep, deep dark, you find you stumble and fall,

And the world that was once your home and heart has no room left for you at all.

Please stay, please stay, please stay a while with me –
I know that I've been hiding,
But I'm here on bended knee.
Please Dad, please stay – please stay a while with me –
I am sorry that I blamed you,
But I've finally set Mum free."

I wipe my eyes, and take another deep breath.

"You think you're alone and beg to be – so you can't harm those around you.

Who wants you in their life anyway, you're poison through and through.

Filled with anger, filled with hate, before your eyes you transform,

Into a monster – a wicked thing – and you wished you'd never been born.

Please stay, please stay, please stay a while with me –
The person that I changed to,
Was not your girl, Emmy.
Please stay, please stay – please stay a while with me –
Forgive the things I said and did,
I love you so much, Daddy.
I know now that you're hurting, working at being so strong,
Both for me and Nathan, you've carried us for far too long.
But it's time that we took some of the load, for all the love you've shown,
And I am sorry that I wasn't there, how I left you on your own...
Please stay, please stay, please stay a while with me –
The blame held in my heart,
Was not for you, you see.
Please stay, please Dad, please stay a while with me –
I'm here now, here, forever,
Your flower, your star, your baby."

Nathan ends on a long chord, and slowly turns to leave the room as I burst into tears, Dad running and wrapping his arms around me. We stumble and almost fall down, and I grip him so hard that my fingers ache.

"Dad, I am so sorry –" I barely recognise my voice as I scream into his chest through my sobs. I can hardly stay on my feet.

"Oh, my baby girl." He croaks, bringing one of his hands to his face as he kisses into my hair. "I've missed you so much."

We sway for a bit in each other's arms. He smells so warm; his familiar dark blue cardigan scratching ever so slightly at my face as I nuzzle hard into his chest, now damp beneath my wet eyes.

This whole time I knew that if I had even just given him one hug, if I had asked how *he* was feeling instead of concentrating on ignoring how *I* was, that maybe I would have helped him. But I have been selfish and spiteful. I have turned my back on him, ignored the pain behind his eyes and pushed him away. Sometimes physically pushed him away. The time in which we probably needed each other more than we ever would...I was too busy making sure that we were all alone. My song hums in my head, and I squeeze him even tighter. I hope he knows what I am trying to say. I hope that he can forgive me.

He leads me to the sofa and sits me down, my eyes still closed. I'm not sure if I can even open them yet, and I let him lead me blind; feeling completely safe in his arms. Completely vulnerable and happy to be; for the first time in a long time. I am seven again and have scraped my knee. I am nine and have had a bad dream; the ones that leave you sat upright under the sheets screaming till someone comes in to save you. Comes in to tuck you in and tell you that everything is alright. I lean back into him and snuggle under his arm as he wraps it about me again, swaying me back and forward softly, humming along to the melody Nathan had played so wonderfully on the guitar. He must have wanted me and Dad to have this time – to have this moment together – and I will be forever indebted to him for that.

He moves then, light hitting my closed eyelids with an orange eruption of colour, and I peel them open. I really don't think I have ever felt this exhausted. He reaches for something on the coffee table, the same thing he had been holding when Nathan and I had started our song.

"Thank you for your song, darling." He sniffs, then takes a deep and tortured sigh as he picks it up. "It means so much to me that you have finally let me in – it has broken my heart that I haven't been able to be there for you like I've wanted to be."

It's a photograph, and my throat closes up. He wipes his nose quickly as he sits back into the folds of the sofa, holding it on his lap and looking to me carefully and searchingly. My heart starts pounding so hard that I can feel it in my head, tapping beneath my skull and echoing in my ears. It's the photograph from the frame. The one I had broken our first night here.

"There is only so long that we can keep on living like this. Only so long that we can keep hurting so." He whispers, his words shaking. "And I don't want to anymore."

He smooths at the edges, the ones that had been ruined by the broken glass, and wipes away a tear from under his glasses. Mum's face still shines through though...her hair, dark and wavy like mine, her eyes deep and thoughtful. Her smile genuine, warm, and truthful.

He places his thumb gently against her cheek and I feel him tense. I grip onto his arm, nuzzling my cheek in to his shoulder.

"She loved you and your brother so much..." he whispers, his voice catching in his throat as a rouge tear falls heavily from his cheek onto the photograph below. "She did. And she would want you to know that. You – you should have seen her face the day we brought you home..."

A small laugh through his tears.

"...she was so nervous that your brother wouldn't like you, or that he would think we loved him less now that we had you – so she made me buy him a present. One that we said was from you! Now, what *she* didn't know, is that your brother - even though he was still so young himself - had asked me to do the same thing in his own special way. He had asked me to help him colour in a picture for you and for your Mum on coming home!"

Another laugh, as my own tears start silently pouring down my face.

"So, your Mum...in the car kept going on about making sure that the present was ready for when we got home, had a big shock when the first thing Nathan did was run up and give *you* his little picture. I don't think I have ever seen her look so happy. She absolutely adored the two of you..."

He pauses in his memory as if suddenly seeing the room before us again.

"I know that she never would have –" his voice catches again, "n – never would have wanted you to think that she didn't love you enough. I sometimes worry that maybe I didn't love *her* enough."

He breaks then, bringing the photograph to his steamed glasses as he sobs, and I wrap my arms around his shoulders, burying my face into his neck. His shoulders heave, and he brings his hand around my back and holds me tightly, putting his own face into my hair as we cry together.

"It's not your fault, Dad. I love you so much..."

My own sobs ache in my stomach and rub my throat raw. How could I have punished him for so long? What the hell has been wrong with me? I *hate* the Emmy I had become. I am so glad I left her to die at that rivers edge instead of me.

"I love you so much too, my little flower." He bring his other hand to wrap around the base of my back as he holds me closer. I can feel the photograph through my shirt, and I sob a little harder imagining my mother's arms there too.

"You are so much like her, Ems. So much. But don't lose yourself along the way. Your mother lost her way and in turn lost herself – and I cannot bear to lose you too." He kisses me on the cheek and brings my tear stained face to look him in the eye. His glasses are so crooked and dappled as if he has been out in the rain, the purple flecks he has held so often these past few weeks smattered under his eyes like sad bruises. I wipe my nose with the back of my hand as I try to catch my breath, my own eyes feeling tired and swollen. My whole chest aches looking at him. Seeing him. For the first time in a long time. I *have* been so lost.

He takes another deep breath and blows out hard between his lips, forcing a watery smile.

"Did I ever tell you about the time I first met her?"

I shake my head stiffly, still trying to settle my breathing. Come on, I can do this now. This is what I have been preparing for – this is what I can do now. Not just to talk, but to listen. I am terrified...but Dad's eyes lighten as soon as he brings that photo round for us to look at again. She is blurred now as I struggle to see anything clearly.

He needs to talk. Just like Nathan did – and I am not going to make the same selfish mistake again. That Emmy is gone. I smile at him, and his face relaxes.

"We had both been so young. Your mum was simply beautiful. Well, she always was. Her hair was all the way down to her waist back then! As wild and as untameable as her personality. I cannot believe how much you look like her now..." he beams at me momentarily before moving his eyes back down to the picture. "I was out playing football with some of my friends up on the common near one of their houses. It was up the hill – a large open area that backed onto a gentle and wide river. We would go wading there in the summer. A gorgeous place...surrounded by low sweeping trees where the sun would make patterns on the still water through the branches. It almost looked magical. I should take you and your brother there sometime."

His eyes look like magnifying glasses as he smiles such a wide and reminiscent smile. His tears swell over his lashes and I can't help but feel my heart lift slightly knowing that he can see her now. See her for how she was. He takes my hand.

"This one particular time...Seth Anderson kicked the ball too hard, and it went tumbling through the trees and toward the river. So I went to get it..." A small laugh as the tears breach and fall onto Mums own smiling face held carefully in his hand below. He is moving his thumb gently as if stroking her hair the same time he moves his other thumb over my knuckles.

"...and as I ducked under the sweeping branches and was plunged into cool shadow, there she was. This particular tree grew out of a small mounded bit of earth, its sloping trunk leaning away from the river's edge as its branches reached high above before sweeping down and towards...some even trailing their fingertips into the cool water. Like a feathery fan or parasol. She was sat, leaning against the trunk reading a book. I'll never forget how she looked then, and how I loved her in that moment."

He squeezes my hand.

"The long skirt she was wearing brushed against her bare feet as she sat spread out without a single care in the world...that long main of dark hair tumbling scruffily over her shoulders with catkins tangled in its strands. Gosh, she looked like a fairy."

I can see her myself now. A version of me, sat happily with a book, not a phone...and a light head on her happy shoulders instead of one weighted like stone. I don't think much of myself...but the girl under this sweeping tree looks beautiful.

"Well. This fairy looked upon me as I stumbled clumsily into the water like a fool, creating a ripple that pushed the football further away. You should have seen my cheeks, Blossom. I could see them glowing red from the dull reflection in the water! Well...your Mum came sweeping down, her bare feet dusty and grubby, and waded right into the middle of the river. The water went all the way up to her waist! Her skirt billowing out around her like a...well, like fairies wings. She gave me the ball, pulled a catkin out of her hair and put it through my button hole, then glided back up to sit beneath the willow and to her book. And that was it. Your mother –"

"Wait, what?" I jolt then, my heart suddenly coming into action again and my legs aching as I already stand on shaking knees. "Sat beneath a what?"

Dad frowns puzzlingly, his day dream shattered, and I feel a pang of guilt, but short lived. My hands are trembling and my lips start rising.

"A willow...they surrounded the river. It was nicknamed the '*Weeping River*'. Why, what's wrong?" but I am already sprinting back to my bedroom on jelly legs.

Walking again

I laugh whilst racing, falling through my open door and landing on my knees hard in front of my bed.

"Mum! Mum?" I search manically, seeing my phone sleepily on the windowsill and leap for it, grab it in desperate hands, pressing my earphones shakily into the port.

"Mum! Is it you? *Willow*! Talk to me!" I laugh again through my tears. I can't even feel my body – it's like I am the bubble this time, my head filling and floating up off of my neck. Could it have been? This whole time? Not my own madness coaching me – guiding me – but *her*? My very own ghost in my phone – my mum! Her voice in my head! Being there for me – teaching me how to move past her! How to live again!

"Baby? Everything ok?" Dad is standing in my doorway, the picture still in his hand, his glasses still steamed.

"Yes! Oh Dad – you won't believe it! This whole time – it was her this WHOLE time!"

"Flower, slow down..."

"Mum! She's been helping me – talking to me through my phone! I know – I know, that sounds ridiculous!" I turn to face him fully, brandishing my phone, brandishing Willow, waving her joyfully in the air. Laughing through my tears, my heart soaring. "But she has! Since we've been here – since I've been shutting myself away – she's been helping me! Getting me to make right decisions – getting me to learn to move on, to be happy, to forgive!"

I turn back to my phone, shake it in my hands, hit it hard against my palm. I hear Nathan's bedroom door open, hear him whisper something to Dad, but it doesn't matter. I can prove it! Come on, come on – light up! Speak to me, Willow. Speak to me!

"Emmy?"

I feel Nathan's hands on my shoulders as he kneels down next to me. I don't take my eyes from my phone. Come on – come on – light up!

"Nathan, it's amazing! I should have told you about it earlier – but I thought it sounded silly! But this whole time, Nath! This whole time!" I hit it against my hand again. Again. Again. My smile wavers but I hold on to it. Hold on to the feeling in my chest – push down the other feeling creeping in.

"Come on...I'm sorry I didn't speak to you when I got home, but come on – I need you now. I need to talk to you, Mum! Dad and Nathan are here too – come on – come on please, light up! Say something!"

Maybe I should have spoken to her sooner. What was the last thing I had even said to her? I feel Nathan shift next to me, and Dad approach my other side. He too kneels down next to me.

"Sweetheart..."

"No – listen, Dad. You'll see! In a minute – oh maybe you can talk to her too! Oh, Dad – this whole time, I can't believe it! Come on...come on, light up. What's going on?"

I press down on the on button; press so hard my thumb feels sore. Come on! Where are you? Why aren't you lighting up? A vibration! Yes! I squeal out – tears falling down my cheeks as I laugh. Any moment now! Willow! Willow, this whole time? I can't believe it!

The screen shines brightly – my stomach clenches! – But –

'Welcome.'

The welcome screen for my phones network comes on, shows the word in pixilated black letters against a white screen, and then fades – my home screen dancing onto the glass: a photograph, of me and my friends pulling faces.

"What? No, no..."

I hit the phone against my hand again. My heart quivers up my throat.

"No! Willow? Mum? Come on!"

I hold the off button again. Hold it hard. My lips sting against my teeth. Nathan's grip on my shoulders tighten.

'Welcome.'

"No! No – it's broken! Mum! Mum! Willow! Come on!"

"Baby, its ok...its ok..." Dad gently puts his hand onto mine, tries to slowly lower my phone to my bed.

"No – but, Dad! No – honestly! I am not mad!"

I fight him off. Bring my phone to my chest – to my heart. Hold her there.

"She – she's been talking to me! It must be! She called herself Willow – like when you met her, Dad! The willow tree! It all makes sense now!"

He glances to Nathan who is already crying, but I shake my head, force a smile.

"No! No, guys! Look! This is a good thing – an amazing thing! This whole time! She – she got me to talk to you Nath, about my school project! The painting – my wall! Even to go outside – to make friends! All these things were her ideas.

Helping me reach out again! To talk! To listen!"

"Emmy, don't..."

"Nath! No - no don't cry – don't! I'm fine! I knew you wouldn't believe me! I just..."

I look to my phone again. Kate, Sophie, and Jemma smiling back at me.

"...I just need to get my phone to work. Find the place where she can reach me..."

"Baby..." Dad sniffs, taking my hand in his again. "She's gone, baby."

I fight a little – looking to the screen. Begging with every fibre for that white screen to show again.

"No! But she –"

"She's gone, sweetheart. She's gone, darling..."

I let him take the phone from my hands...a part of myself... away and place it on the bedside cabinet. Nathan sobs next to me. My heart crumbles all over again.

Willow? Don't leave me now. Mum? No – I've only just forgiven you – I have so much I want to say! So much I want to share with you – to share my life with you!

A long smooth to my hair. Another sniff from Nathan. A sniff from Dad.

"But...but I'm not ready..." I squeak, and Dad pulls me in – pulls me and Nathan in – and their arms surround me. "I'm not ready, though! I'm not ready for her to be gone..."

I collapse weightily in their arms. Hear my own cries in the strange echo of theirs.

Willow? Please...I'm not ready yet. *Please*, Willow. I'm not ready yet...

* * *

It's my first day back at school tomorrow. I have been having email conversations with Mr Stephens; told him all about my project and he is really happy for me to come back. He even said that the Pompeii project has just finished and that I will be in time for the next one which will be going towards our year grade. He almost made it sound like it would be as if I had never left...which was kind of nice, I suppose. Settled the nerves I had initially felt when reaching out to him. Settled the nerves of eyes looking at me and girls whispering in the toilets. At least now I know that I will say something back. Not something filled with anger or nastiness, though. If they have questions...that's ok, and I am ok to answer them now. I don't want anyone to feel uncomfortable with me being there. People need to learn to talk. That it is ok to – that it is kind of important to; even if the topic isn't a particularly nice one. We all need to talk.

Mr Stephens had also said he was very excited to see my painting, and that I could do a small write up to accompany it if I wished. I think I will do that...I think it will be good to get some closure. Oh - and that he and his wife were off to Canada over Christmas to try and catch a glimpse of some whales. I had smiled when I had read that, and looked up some pictures of them on the internet.

I look to it now, my painting, finished in its entirety, and my lips lift in a delicate smile. It had turned out a lot different to how I had initially imagined it would look like, thinking back to when I was sketching on my floor in a baggy t-shirt and fluffy socks. I must remember to take a photograph of it to print off and take in. Maybe with Nathan's? I think his camera phone is better than mine. Maybe if I print it off big, or take a copy in so that school can blow it up...maybe I could ask to put it somewhere? For a short while, anyway. A tribute, perhaps. A warning, and a piece of advice. To learn to live...

Nathan and I have been talking a lot since that night, too. The three of us do, actually. A type of 'check in system', if you like – usually around the dinner table. But it is more than that too. We have finally learnt just to *be* with each other now. To be honest; to be a new family. To be silly. To be careful. I had even sat down with Nathan when he told Dad about what he had been doing in secret. It was hard to start with...Dad was very upset, but it was needed – and the two of them are closer than ever before. They sing even louder now to the kitchen radio whilst cooking, if you can believe, and with no fear of annoying our downstairs neighbours despite one complaint brought forward by the manager. I even join in sometimes...

He has also started to wear short sleeved t-shirts around the house now too; his monster marks turning a pale purple instead of their original angry red. Although it grips my stomach to see them, flashing that night and nastier images into my head before I can take a hold of myself, I revel in their slow fade and feel lighter as they get so. His girlfriend really isn't that bad either, I suppose. She makes him lighter too...and she gently rubs his arms with her soft hands whilst we all watch our Saturday night films together. I have her number on my phone now, in case I ever need to talk to her.

My phone vibrates on my pillow now, and I lift it and send a text back to Star with a small giggle, before placing it back down. We are going to meet up next weekend; she has invited me round to their house, and I am really looking forward to it.

I wonder if there is still space underneath their stairs to make an old makeshift den. I wouldn't mind doing something like that...and I am sure she would love to go back in time too. I am *really* looking forward to seeing her, actually. And Paul, I guess. Maybe Nathan could come round too? That would be nice.

"Dinners ready, Sweet-pea." Dad smiles round my door with a wink, and I stick my thumbs up proudly as he disappears. I swing back on my mattress, ready to take a playful leap, but hesitate for a moment before throwing my legs into the air. I know that there is still a way for us to go, as we walk down our long and darkened tunnel of grief together, but this one we tread now has a glass roof so that we can see the stars. They are always visible now, even more so when I look to my father and my brother as they keep the lights flickering even in our darker moments. I have even found that as of late that my cheeks ache from smiling or laughing instead of crying. That I actually feel...*happy* sometimes. How I smile when I think of our little family. How I am always thinking of them, actually. And how I always think of her.

I do swing now, covering some ground as I fling myself from the bed and land swiftly on my feet, and give myself a little cheer. A leap...just like in my painting, I guess.

I pull on my slippers and grab my white fleece, wrapping it around my shoulders, and look to my painting again. Yes. I am really happy with how it turned out. How my project turned out...how I could only finish it with them, really. Maybe I could show it to Mrs Locklea, too? My drawing left in the small shed had gone when I had ambled down last week, so she must be around here somewhere. Waiting for when I need her again, I guess. Like Willow...

I quickly grab a thick black felt tip pen from my small shelf and make one last addition to my painting, when I hear another little knock on the door.

"Oi, chicken legs. Dinners up!"

Nathan grins when I turn around, placing the lid onto the pen with a small click. I smile back, pushing my dark hair behind my ears.

"You alrigh'?" he frowns.

I look back to my painting one last time and feel warmth erupt within me. A fire in my calm and happy heart. A light that keeps all shadows at bay. Or at least, one that works hard to. And that's ok. That's all I need. Just a little light that is always there. A little flame I breathe in to. I pull my fleece around me tighter and sigh, fuelling that flame – setting it ablaze.

"Yeah." I laugh.

A blazing comet. A shooting star. I am starlight now. I know I am. I can feel myself shining. Shining for them. Shining for me.

I laugh again, and throw the pen to land gently on my bed.

"Yeah, I'm alrigh'."

I chase him out of the room as he pulls a face, and turn my light off before letting my door swing slowly closed. Our voices trail into the lounge area, coupled with Dad's as he sings about the dinner on our plates. We laugh, and we love in the light, as my phone sits alone, unneeded, in the dark.

Printed in Great Britain
by Amazon

61588371R00156